AWAY FROM KEYBOARD COLLECTION

TRUSTING HIS INSTINCTS

PATRICIA D. EDDY

Copyright © 2023 by Patricia D. Eddy

All rights reserved.

No part of this book may be reproduced in any form or by any electronic or mechanical means, including information storage and retrieval systems, without written permission from the author, except for the use of brief quotations in a book review.

Cover Design: Deranged Doctor Design

Cover Photo: CJC Photography

Proofreading: Book Dweller Proofreading

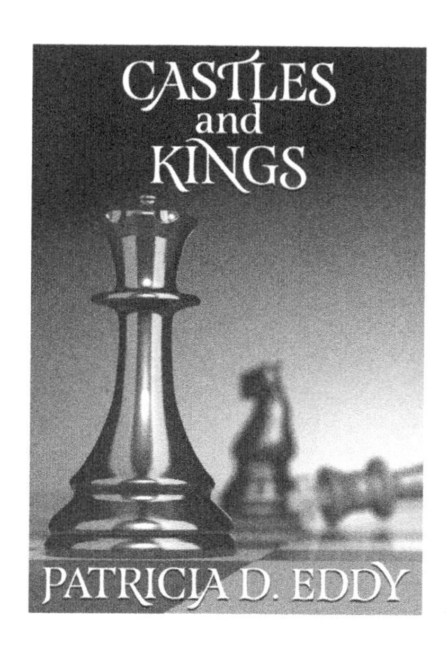

If you love steamy romantic suspense, I'd love to send you an exclusive short story set in Dublin, Ireland. Castles & Kings is ONLY available for my newsletter subscribers. Visit my website and let me know where to send your free short story! http://patriciadeddy.com.

For Sue...who with one amazing comment, reminded me what a joy it is to discover a new character's story.

PROLOGUE

Twenty Years Ago

Nash

SOMETHING THUDS IN THE HALL. Rolling my eyes, I throw back the blankets. My little sister can't go more than a few hours without a nightmare. Not since our parents moved us to this old house in the middle of Minnesota, told us we couldn't be Nathan and Mae anymore, and started calling us Ned and Melissa.

Mae swears the house is haunted. I wish she'd grow up. You don't believe in ghosts when you're fourteen. But she's only eight, and Mom told me I wasn't allowed to make fun of her anymore. Not about this.

I grab the flashlight from my nightstand. She'll want me to check under her bed and in the closet before she'll go back to sleep.

My foot lands on something soft, and the door opens. I skid as two quiet pops break the silence. Something hits my head. Pain—worse than anything I've ever felt—

overwhelms me. I can't see. Or move. Heavy footsteps come closer. I should care. Find Mae. Or Mom and Dad. But all I can do is lie on the floor until the world fades away.

WITH MAE'S stuffed sloth clutched in my hands, I stare out the hospital room window.

"Nash?" Duncan—my parents' handler with the U.S. Marshals—taps me on the shoulder. "You have to get used to the new name, son."

"I don't *want* a new name. I want to go home. Back to Chicago." Tears make the room shimmer, but I won't let them fall. When I woke up three days ago and found out my parents and Mae were dead, I cried for so long, the doctor had to sedate me.

"You know that's not possible." Duncan scoots his chair closer, glances over his shoulder at the door, and rests his elbows on his knees. "I don't know how they found your family, Nash."

"My name isn't Nash!" I throw the sloth across the room, then instantly regret it. It's all I have left of Mae. Of my entire family. But when I try to get out of bed, the room starts to spin.

"Whoa." The marshal presses down on my shoulders and eases me back against the pillows. "You were shot in the head. You're not supposed to get up on your own."

"I need it...back..." I manage.

Duncan scoops the sloth off the floor and returns it to me. The stupid thing saved my life. Dad was shot in the back. Mom and Mae in the head. But I slipped on the stuffed animal, and the two bullets meant for me lodged themselves between my skull and my brain. I'm lucky—according to the doctor. A miracle. But I don't care. All I want is to be with my family again.

"Nash..."

I turn onto my side, my gaze pinned to the trees swaying gently on the other side of the window. "You said we'd be safe." Nine months ago, he showed up at our house in Chicago, told me and Mae to call him Uncle Duncan, and promised to protect us. "You lied."

"No one knows how they found you. But Ned Vasco was buried along with Melissa, Nathalie, and Owen Vasco in a little cemetery outside of Rochester. Nash Grace is just a kid from Minneapolis who was injured in a drive-by shooting. No one—not even my boss—knows you survived. As long as you don't take anything from your old life when we move you this time, no one will have any reason to come after you. I'm sending you with my old partner, Frank. He'll be here in a few hours so you can meet him. He'll protect you."

"Like I'd believe anything you say."

"Son—"

"I'm not your son!" After a beat, I close my eyes. "Go away, *Uncle* Duncan. I want to be alone."

One Month Later

"GET A MOVE ON!" Frank strides out to the car, keys in hand, checking up and down the street constantly. "You're gonna be late."

"I don't care." The first day of class at my new high school is the last place I want to be. But I don't have a choice. Grabbing my backpack, I take a long moment to stare up at the sloth on the shelf above my bed.

Duncan had it cleaned, and there's only a small spot of

reddish brown left on one of the paws. My blood. I've taken it everywhere with me since I woke up in the hospital. I even thought about stuffing it into my backpack today. But if anyone at school saw it, Frank would probably find me beaten to a pulp behind the gym this afternoon.

"Nash! Get your butt in the car. Now!" he yells.

"Coming. *Pops*." I cringe, and my throat feels...weird. It's hard to swallow. I didn't want Frank—one of Duncan's oldest friends—to legally adopt me. But they swore it was safer that way. Safer to move to Denver. Safer to start over with my third name in as many years. Safer to take nothing with me except Mae's stuffed animal. They tried to get me to leave it behind, but I wouldn't. Couldn't.

The sun's brighter here. It's the altitude, Frank says. The air is thinner too. If I could still run track, I'd be slower. But that's not allowed either. I was *good* back in Chicago. Really good. Junior State Championship good. College scholarship good, my coach said. Now, it's football or nothing.

I hate football.

"Seat belt," Frank says, his brown eyes only landing on me for a split second before he starts the car. "Remember. You see anything strange—"

"Hide in the bathroom and call you. I know." I pat my backpack. Frank sewed a hidden pocket on the inside to hide my cell phone. *Before*...only my parents had one. And Frank spent hours the other night telling me how much it cost, how hard it would be to replace, and how important it was that I never let the battery die.

We don't say another word to each other until he pulls up in front of Larimer High. "It's going to be okay, Nash."

His quiet words don't reassure me. Nothing will ever be okay again. Not really. But even though I hate it here, he and Duncan are the only "family" I have left. So I nod. "Yeah. Maybe."

I shut the door, sling my backpack over my shoulder, and stare up at the single-story building that takes up an entire city block. Nash Grace's first day of school. Nash Grace's first day of...anything.

Kids wander up the steps in twos and threes, and I start to follow, but then turn and offer Frank a little wave. "Bye. Uh... Pops. See you later."

He doesn't smile. He knows better than that. "Have a good day. Nash. And remember."

Be careful.

Yeah. I'll remember. I'll always remember.

Four Years Ago

Raelynn

LIGHTNING ARCS across the gray-black sky. I call out to Brooks, but the heavy rumble of thunder steals the sound.

Rain falls in thick, blinding sheets, plastering my clothes to my skin. The Stetson keeps the water out of my eyes—barely—but the rest of me is soaked through.

My horse rears up, and I tighten my hold on the reins. "Whoa, Gracie. Settle. *Settle!*"

She does, though if I'm not careful, she'll toss me ass over tea kettle and I'll break my damn neck.

At the far end of the pasture, Brooks kneels next to one of the fences, running razor wire between two freshly reinforced posts. The storm blew in early this morning, and we found a dozen cows wandering toward the road after dinner. I coaxed two of the injured back to the barn, then started rounding up the herd while Brooks worked on the repairs.

We've been out here for hours. All the cows are penned in

the upper pasture, and if we're lucky, we'll both be back in the house, warm and dry, before the storm gets any worse.

"Brooks! Wrap it up. We need to get inside, *now!*" I urge Gracie faster down the hill, but my husband's horse, Buddy, spooks at the next thunderclap and bolts toward the stables.

For a long moment, Brooks holds my gaze. I nod. Twenty-two years together—even if I *did* spend ten of them in the Air Force—and we don't need words. He's almost done and needs me to get to Buddy.

I urge Gracie around and dig my heels into her sides. "Come on, girl. Get a move on."

It takes forever to catch the brown and white gelding, and even longer to get him to follow me back to the edge of the property.

Brooks isn't where I left him. His bag sits next to one of the posts, but razor wire flaps in the wind, untethered.

"Brooks! Where'd you get off to?" I holler into the wind. I'm still five hundred feet away up the hill. If he went over—or under—the fence, I wouldn't be able to see him.

Buddy whines, pulling his reins free from my grip. But he doesn't bolt this time. Just starts trotting down the hill. I point Gracie after him and squeeze my heels around her massive barrel.

She follows, but it's so muddy, we start to slip. If she breaks her leg, that's it for her, so I pull back on the reins.

Buddy stops, and I squint into the deluge. Until my heart seizes in my chest.

His black Stetson tumbles toward me, mud staining the brim. In a shallow ditch, my husband lies on his back staring up at the angry sky.

"Brooks?" I jump off the horse, slipping and sliding in the thick muck until I fall to my knees at his side. "Baby, talk to me."

Cupping his cheek, I pray he'll look at me. Blink. Say

something. Anything. Even in the rain, I can smell the ozone. Patting him down, ripping at his shirt, I find the wound. "Oh, God. No."

A spiderweb of reddish scars spreads over his chest. The black scorch mark at his shoulder from the lightning strike would still be smoking if it weren't for the rain.

I bite down on my glove and yank it off with my teeth. Pressing my fingers to his carotid artery, I hold my breath. One beat. Two. He's still alive.

"Brooks, open your eyes, you damn fool. Right now!" Another bolt of lightning hits the fence a few hundred feet away, and in the glow, I see his lids flutter. "That's it. Come back to me."

"Rae..." I don't hear his voice so much as see his lips move. The clap of thunder makes my ears ring. His eyes open, bloodshot, unfocused, and his breath stutters in his chest. "Love...you..."

"Shut up! You ain't dyin' on me. Stay awake." I slap his cheeks, then slant my lips over his. For a second, he returns the kiss, and I know everything's going to be okay. Until his mouth goes slack.

"No, baby. Fight!" I check his pulse again. I can't find it. Pulling off my other glove, I start CPR. The Bee Gees' "Stayin' Alive" runs through my head—the song happens to be the perfect speed to time compressions—but by the time I finish the first verse, I want to damn every member of the band straight to hell. It's not working.

My cell phone is back at the house, and even if it weren't, there's no reception out here. My husband hasn't stirred, and after the refrain, I check for a pulse one last time before I let loose with a string of curses that would make even the most seasoned pirate blush.

"Baby," I say quietly, pulling him into my lap and cradling him close. "You're my everythin'. I've loved you since we were seventeen. Don't leave me alone. Not like this."

But he's already gone. Brooks would never stop kissing me. Not unless he had no choice.

BY THE TIME I drag his body into the house, I have no more tears left to cry. I never should have left him. The herd was safe. He didn't *need* to fix the fence in the middle of the storm.

"It's not that bad out, darlin'. I'll be done in an hour." He cups the back of my neck and pulls me in for a swift, hard kiss. "If I wait 'til tomorrow, the field'll be flooded so bad, it'll take me all day. Plus, I can't leave my tools down there."

"I don't like the look of those clouds, baby." All day, I've been nervous for no reason, and I wish we hadn't put off hiring a couple of additional ranch hands.

Another kiss, and he slaps my ass just hard enough to sting. "Get the rest of the herd penned in, and I'll be done in two shakes. Then we'll hunker down in front of the fire with that bottle of bourbon I picked up last week."

"Just...hurry." I slap his ass back, which earns me a wicked grin as he mounts his horse.

"Love you, Rae. I won't be long."

I should have said the words back to him. But he took off so fast, I didn't get a chance. Now, I never will.

Laying his body in front of the wood stove, I brush his damp blond curls away from his face. "Stay here, baby. As soon as I call the sheriff, I'm gettin' that bottle of bourbon."

I hold Brooks close for as long as I can, until the sheriff walks in and I have to face the fact that my husband is truly gone, and I wasn't there to save him.

CHAPTER ONE

Raelynn

"Catch up, probie!"

I glare at Hidden Agenda's tactical genius, retired SEAL West Sampson. He stands at the edge of the indoor track, holding a stopwatch. Graham, Tank, Inara, and I run two laps around the warehouse—after slogging through a sadistic obstacle course *and* a stint on the climbing wall.

West's drills are only getting harder now that the leader of the Kidnap & Ransom firm, Ryker McCabe, is about to be a father.

"I ain't your damn probie," I pant, pushing myself even harder.

"Until Wyatt starts joining us for workouts, the honor's still yours." West calls out Graham's time—eleven minutes and thirty-two seconds—then Inara's, then Tank's. I'm almost a lap behind them.

Ryker—who, despite his size, beat everyone else by a full minute—cracks the seal on a bottle of water and stares me down. It's meant to be intimidating, but he can't get inside my head. No one can. Not anymore.

I plaster on a sweet smile as I skid to a stop in front of West and brace my hands on my thighs.

"Damn, probie." He whistles, and if looks could kill, I'd have just murdered him.

"Don't you give me any shit, y'hear? I made it through the climbin' wall without usin' my right arm. As instructed. And Inara *still* only beat me by two minutes."

"I was about to say, 'I'm impressed.'"

"Oh." Snagging my towel from the bench, I mop my forehead. "I'm fixin' to knock on Wyatt's door and drag his sorry ass here for the next workout so y'all have someone else to gang up on."

Ryker snorts. "I'd like to see you try."

"Watch me." I drop onto one of the mats in the corner to stretch. Despite my bravado, there ain't no way I'll give Wyatt shit for sticking close to home. Not after his girl—Hope—almost died tryin' to escape her psycho ex last month. If I had someone warm and willing, I wouldn't be here either.

"How's the shoulder?" A few feet away, Ryker groans as he lowers himself down and crosses one leg over the other to stretch his back.

Every inch of his exposed skin is covered in scars—except the left side of his face. The Taliban tortured him for fifteen months, leaving him in near constant pain, but he rarely lets it show. Not even when his spine lets loose with a series of pops that sound like they're excruciating.

Grabbing my right arm with my left hand, I pull it gently across my chest. I'm about to tell him I'm fine when he narrows his multi-hued eyes at me. "Think twice before you answer."

Damn Special Forces training. The man is a human lie

detector. "Fair to middlin'. Only hurts first thing in the mornin'."

He nods, apparently satisfied with my answer. "When do you see Doc Reynolds again?"

A spark of pain skates down my back, and I let my arm drop, flexing my fingers. "End of the week. I'm doin' my PT every day. Give it a rest."

A single brow arches, the other bisected by a thick scar. "You want to try that again?"

"Nope." I switch to the other arm, turning my back on the big man to see Graham and Inara with their heads bent over their cell phones. Shit. I need a distraction. Or an intervention.

Ry lumbers to his feet. He's close to seven feet tall and built like a tank. I have to crane my neck to look up at him. "You want to stay on this team, Raelynn, you'll knock that chip off your shoulder before it crushes you."

Dammit. I stare at his massive back as he strides over to the kitchen in the corner of the warehouse. Ryker gave me a chance when I was so mired in my grief, I didn't know which way was up. I have to fix this.

By the time I finish stretching—and beating myself up over my attitude—Inara and Graham are facing off across the foosball table. Tank—clad only in a white towel—heads for the showers. And Ry's on his phone. From the look on his face, he's talking to his wife, Wren. She's due in a month, and though he's all business when we're on mission, he's been increasingly distracted during workouts.

Stop stalling and fix your damn mess.

"Good job today," West calls from the lockers. "Don't forget. Wednesday at six, we're running simulations with the new drones."

I jog over to him, clearing my throat as he pulls off his running shoes. "Got a minute?"

He snags the towel draped over the bench and nods. "Sure. Have a seat."

That's the last thing I want to do. But I don't have much choice. "I need this gig."

Surprise registers in his blue eyes for a single blink. "Money troubles? Ry can spot you—"

"I fucked up in Salt Lake City."

His cool stare bores into me. I don't look away, but the urge to squirm almost does me in.

"Wyatt was hell-bent on gettin' to Hope. I was ready to follow him down into that basement, but one of the hostiles got the drop on me. It knocked me off my game, and before I got a handle on shit, I was starin' up at the ceiling with a partially dislocated shoulder. It won't happen again."

You're gonna talk yourself right into being shit-canned if you don't shut your trap.

West arches his brows. "You done?"

"No," I say, lowering my gaze to my clasped hands. "If you're gonna fire me, get it over with before I sink ten grand into a new heater. My house is a goddamned money pit."

With a heavy sigh, West shakes his head. "Raelynn, Hidden Agenda and Second Sight are a family. We don't fire probies for a single mistake."

"You've never fired *anyone* from what Graham says." If I were smart, I'd shut up. But I ain't built that way.

His hand moves to his side, and he chuckles. "He's right. Though Ryker should have kicked Coop's ass to the curb before my first mission. Maybe then I wouldn't have ended up almost bleeding out in a veterinarian's office in Bogota."

"So, you're not gonna bench me...?"

"Not unless you insist on keeping that stick firmly planted up your ass. Stop seeing the rest of us as...'the rest of us' and get it through your head that we're a team. When Ryker wants to know how you're doing, tell him. And for fuck's sake, stop thinking you can handle everything on your own."

I give him a quick nod and push to my feet. "I'll try."

West narrows his eyes, unconvinced. "I mean it, Raelynn. Hidden Agenda works because we've all learned *not* to keep secrets. You want to go it alone? That's your call. But you can't do it here. So get your head on straight or I *will* bench you. Indefinitely."

Nash

Wallet in hand, I stare into my backpack. Inside a special, waterproof pocket, my little sister's ratty old sloth peers up at me. Twenty years, and I've carried it everywhere. Always safe. Always close.

In Cheyenne, Wyoming, it had its own shelf above my bed. In Durango, Texas, I kept it in my nightstand drawer. Lodi, California? The stuffed animal perched on top of an old wine barrel I used as a coffee table.

Here, in this tiny studio apartment over a coffee shop in Seattle, the sloth spends its nights watching me from a bookcase across the room. But whenever I leave, it comes with me.

Every day, I lose more of my memories of Mae. All I have left now are flashes. Big green eyes, red hair, freckles. Her small fingers wrapped around mine when she'd crawl into my bed at night and ask me to tell her a story.

"You doing all right in there, Bandit?" The matted ball of brown and white fluff won't answer me, but I feel closer to Mae whenever I see him. "Good talk. Thanks."

With the backpack slung over my shoulder, I thud down the back stairs. The rich scent of coffee tickles my nose, and my mouth waters.

Since I moved in to this studio perched over one of the best coffee shops in Seattle, my caffeine habit has gotten out of control. In less than two months, I've gone from the occasional latte or drip to a double espresso every day. I should switch to decaf before I'm truly addicted.

Yeah, right.

"Nash!" Adam, Broadcast Coffee's owner, waves at me from behind the counter. His eyes light up—or maybe that's all the caffeine he's had today—as he works the lever on the fancy espresso machine. Whenever the man sees me, he insists on making me *something*. Usually with at least two shots. "Have a seat!"

"I was just on my way out..." My protest fades as he slides a small cup across the bar, his wide grin infectious. So what if I'm vibrating by the time I get to Georgetown? It'll keep me warm. The weather report said it was supposed to rain all day.

I set my backpack on the stool next to me and take a sip. "Peruvian?"

"Hot damn. You're getting good at this. Watch out tomorrow. I'm going to throw you a curve ball." He slams the filter full of compressed grounds down over the in-counter trash bin with a dull *thud*.

"Bring it." The coffee tastes of citrus and vanilla, and I finish the cup quickly—too quickly—because Adam offers to make me another. "Can't today. The upholstery for the new chairs is supposed to be delivered in a couple of hours. Shaking hands don't make for straight stitches."

He chuckles. "Everything you've built for the shop has been amazing, Nash. The stools, the shelving unit for the storeroom, and hell...you fixed that bad outlet in the studio less than a week after you moved in."

"I needed to charge my phone. That was the closest plug

to the bed." I shrug off the work like it was nothing, even though it took me two full days to find the fault in the wiring.

"Don't be memorable. Stay under the radar. Everyone you meet needs to forget you as soon as you're gone."

Pops—Frank—would give me hell if he could see me now. I'm doing a fucking terrible job of staying incognito.

"Earth to Nash..."

With a hard blink, I lift my gaze. "I gotta go if I want to be there when the courier shows up. I might be able to finish all four chairs by Monday."

"Already?" He toasts me with his own espresso. "You're a machine."

I force a smile as I haul to my feet. "The cabinets upstairs will take me another couple of weeks. After that, you'll be able to list the place for twice what you were getting before."

"You're not moving out, are you?" Adam looks me over with earnest eyes, a crease forming between his brows. "The studio's yours for as long as you want it."

"Uh...yeah." One shoulder lifts in a half shrug. "I thought I'd move on soon. Maybe check out Idaho for a while."

Leaning against the back counter, defeat darkens his gaze. "Sure I can't convince you to stick around for a while?"

Shit. I can't tell him *why* I need to keep moving. Why I never stay in one place for more than six months. Not even a place I love, like Seattle.

"Sorry, Adam. I've been on the run since I was fourteen. I have no idea if anyone's still after me, but I don't want to find out."

He'd either ask endless questions or write me off as delusional. Probably both.

"Nash," he says, breaking the awkward silence. "You've done great work. And you're any landlord's dream—even without paying a dime in rent. Selfishly, I was hoping you'd stay long term. I'm opening a new location in Green Lake this summer and I could really use your talent. Say...for a custom coffee bar? Among other things."

"Seriously?" The idea of a gig that large sends my mind racing. Bamboo? No. Teak. Unless I have to keep the costs down. Then maple. Or oak.

Say something, dumbass.

"I could hang until June. Maybe July, if you have that much work for me. Handyman work doesn't pay the bills like the custom jobs do." I lean a little closer. "Not when everything is..."

"Off the books?" Adam holds my gaze. One afternoon, not long after I got to town, I stopped into Broadcast and found a craft beer tasting. I had a few too many, then helped Adam clean up. We got to talking, and I told him a hell of a lot more than I intended. Including my lack of a current driver's license and *missing* social security card. "I got you, man. I can buy all the materials and square it with my accountant."

My phone dings, and I check the time. "Shit. Gotta run or I'll miss the delivery guy. But...you've got a deal. I'll stay until the new shop opens. Whatever you need."

His wide smile returns. "I'll text you the address for the space. Maybe you can meet me there tomorrow morning?"

I feel lighter when I sling my tool bag over my shoulder. I always do when I'm about to start a new project. Even if Frank is still in my head telling me to move on.

"Name the time, and I'll be there."

CHAPTER TWO

Nash

BEYONCÉ'S latest single blares through the small Bluetooth speaker on the window sill as I stretch the hand-dyed cotton over the cushion.

I finished sanding the wooden arms of the chairs an hour ago, and my muscles are still burning. I should stop for the day. I'm more than a week ahead of schedule.

But once I return to my small studio, I'll have nothing to do but binge Netflix on my ancient laptop—courtesy of Adam's password—or re-read one of the half-dozen paperbacks I bought at the used bookstore when I got to town.

On nights like this—when the rain and wind are at their worst—being alone with my own thoughts can lead to the darkest of nightmares.

Blood. Shots. Pain. Mom's scream. Dad begging for our lives. Memories I've repressed for years. But lately, they've come back, fighting their way to the surface all too often.

I spent the morning taking measurements for the custom

coffee bar at Adam's new shop. It'll be a challenge, and I've had precious few of those recently.

When *was* the last time I had something to look forward to?

Taylor Swift takes over from Queen B with "it's time to go."

Fuck. I need to scrub that song from my playlist. I drape the dyed cotton over the arm of the chair, strip off my gloves, and head to the door for some air.

Leaning a hip against the jamb, I watch the rain. It was a day just like this when Frank passed away. Maybe it's a sign. One I don't want to listen to.

"Promise me, Nash," Frank says as the hospice nurse hovers a few feet away. "Leave no trace."

"It's been fifteen years," I whisper. Bedridden for a month now, he can barely squeeze my fingers when I take his hand. "No one's coming after me."

"Because I kept you safe!" He grabs my shirt, pulling himself half way to sitting before a coughing fit takes over. I slide my arm behind his back and ease him down to the pillows. "You're too soft, son. I should have trained you...better."

"You did. I know what to do. How to hide. I'll be safe. I promise." His eyes close, and I rest my hands on his shoulders. "Frank? Pops?"

The nurse inches closer, but I don't need her to tell me the man who adopted me at fourteen, who's been my surrogate father ever since, can't hear me anymore.

I only shed a single tear. The rest I cried the day he told me about the cancer. Stage 4. Metastasized from his colon to his bones and his brain. At least I got to spend the last two months with him.

A flash of lightning arcs across the sky, and I wonder if Frank's looking down on me.

Pulling my lucky penny from the pocket of my jeans, I flip it from one finger to the next. After seven trips back and forth, I spin it in my palm, rest it on the first knuckle of my thumb, and close my eyes.

"Heads, I stay. Tails, I go." The coin sails into the air. Seattle feels more like home than anywhere else I've lived. Frank loved it here. So much so, he put off leaving for almost two years. Longest we ever spent in one place.

And then we moved to Reno. Or...Frank did. I only lasted three months before the heat got to be too much and I tried San Francisco for a while.

The penny's metallic clank against concrete brings me back to the present, and I swallow hard. I found it my first day of school back in Denver. It had been run over so many times, it was half flattened, most of the detail worn clean off the front, but that just made it perfect.

No matter how many times we moved or how often we had to start over, I never failed to bring Mae's stuffed sloth and this penny with me.

I don't want to look. But I have to.

Tails.

Fuck.

It's never steered you wrong. Not once. Stay long enough to help Adam open the new location, then get gone. Somewhere new.

I've never been to Montana. Or Tennessee. Or Utah.

I can come back. Eventually. Four or five years on the road and I'll do another stint in Seattle. Or hell—just visit once in a while.

More than anything, I wish I could stop running. Or get so tired, I just won't care.

Raelynn

At five on the dot, I wheel a fresh cart of towels out from the back room. The Tuesday night Intro to Krav Maga class is just starting, and West leads the group of eight men and women through a warmup exercise.

Damn if I don't want to be out there with them.

Only a few more days, and Doc Reynolds will clear me so I can get back to my life. Until then, I'm trapped on the sidelines.

I hate the sidelines.

"Krav Maga teaches you how to defend yourself—no matter your fitness level, weight, height, or physical limitations," West says from the front of the room. "Rule number one: Everyone in this class deserves to be here. Rule number two: If something hurts, speak up immediately. Rule number three: Some of what you're going to learn tonight might scare you. If you need a minute, take it. Water cooler is in the corner. Any questions?"

No one says a word, and I move to one of the heavy bags. As West teaches the class how to break a chokehold, I start off with some light jabs and crosses. I'd lose to an eighty-year-old with how little power I'm putting behind my blows, but at least I'm doing *something*.

I run through all the moves West has shown me over the past six months—modified for the still-healing injury.

Doc Reynolds would rat me out to Ryker if he knew I was pushing myself like this, but being at the dojo is part of my cover. I *have* to work out. At least that's what I tell myself.

Every member of Hidden Agenda needs a "day job." A fake identity—and a way to make a few extra bucks between missions. When I showed up, one of West's junior instructors had just quit, so I took his place. The former SEAL doesn't trust me to teach classes on my own yet, but I assisted more than once before I went and fucked up my shoulder.

Half an hour later, the class is almost over and my legs are shaking. The few times I met West's gaze in the mirror, I could feel his disapproval. I'll catch hell for overdoing it.

Unless I get out of here first. Maybe he'll forget by tomorrow night when he's supposed to train us on the new drones Ryker spent a fortune on.

Just one more round.

A glare blinds me through the windows on my second jab. The heavy bag swings wildly, my punch glancing off the side. I lose track of it—until it hip-checks me and sends me stumbling.

I expect to go down, but instead, hit a wall that smells like fresh cut wood and spice.

"I've got you," a smooth voice rumbles in my ear. Strong arms tighten around my waist. He's solid. And warm. Steady.

For one—almost perfect—moment, I don't breathe. No one's held me in four years. But then West calls a halt to the class.

Wriggling free, I take a step back and give the man who saved me from landing on my ass a once over.

"Are you all right?" he asks, shoving his hands into the pockets of his black sweatpants.

"Sweeter than stolen honey," I say with a smile.

What the hell?

Two seconds with Mr. Strong and Smells Good and I'm flirting?

"Fucking idiots," West mutters, stalking over to me and peering across the street at the sun reflecting off the windows of his biggest competitor. "Cross Your Fit put up some new tinting last week and it's only a matter of time before someone gets seriously hurt from that glare. Sanchez?

Handle the cooldown. I'm going to go have...*words* with them."

Sanchez shakes his head while he watches West storm across the street. The kid looks like an MMA fighter, but his baby face says he's no older than thirty. "Back to the mat, Nash," he says. "You don't stretch, you're going to be in a world of hurt."

The man who caught me—Nash—shrugs. "Gotta go. Sanchez could kick my ass without breaking a sweat. Nice... uh...catching you."

I'm drawn to his smile. How his lips curve. To the light brown stubble covering his cheeks and jaw. He's built. Bulkier than West. At least in the arms. Softer too. Real.

My gaze follows him, lingering on his ass for too long when he bends to snag his towel from the floor. I need to get the hell out of here before I do something stupid. Like introduce myself to the handsome, strong, and fast-on-his-feet Nash.

I rush back to the locker room, use my teeth to loosen the hand wraps, and toss them in the laundry bin. Staring at my bare fingers, I can still see the wedding ring I took off when I left Texas. Still remember how it felt to be touched. To be...loved.

I'm happy alone. I am. But I'm still human. Still a woman. And that man? He sent me spinning out of control.

CHAPTER THREE

Raelynn

"SHEEE-IT!" A wall of water blinds me, and I lose control of the bike. Skidding off the road, I land in a foot of icy runoff rushing through the ditch. Pain races from my good shoulder down my arm. "Fuckin' asshole!" I scream.

The massive SUV roars away without bothering to stop or even slow down.

The storm rolled in a little after noon, and it's a toad strangler. Fat, frigid drops pelt my face as I stare up at the dark sky. My hip and back ache, but I ignore the pain and climb to my feet. Nothing's broken. Other than any semblance of dignity I had left.

Why didn't I take West up on his offer to drive me home after tonight's training session?

Because he wanted to talk about your "sunshine attitude." Again.

I handled those drones better than anyone except Ryker. But West still rode my ass the whole damn night.

If I were braver, I'd be warm and dry right now.

Pulling my bike from the flooded ditch, I curse under my breath. The front rim is bent. "Well, ain't that just grand."

Thank God for the best saddle bag on the market. There's enough water running through the culvert to drown a small animal. But my cell phone and wallet should still be dry.

I'm gonna have to call a Lyft and pray they'll pick me up on this deserted stretch of Industrial Way.

Thunder rumbles in the distance, and suddenly, I'm as yellow as mustard without the bite. Until another car hydroplanes past me on the flooded road. Water slaps me in the face hard enough to sting. "Goddammit!"

The old sedan fishtails for a second before the driver regains control. Another asshole who won't give two cents about the woman he or she just drenched.

I drop to one knee and start digging for my phone. But headlights cut through the deluge, forcing me to shield my eyes.

My fingers tremble until I clench them into a fist. Shit. I'm alone out here, and though I'm nowhere *near* a damsel in distress, I'm soaked to the skin, freezing, and shaken up enough to doubt my ability to fight.

The car rolls to a stop twenty feet away. I fumble for the phone, but it slips from my hand as a man opens the driver's side door, stands, and calls out, "You need some help?"

The voice is familiar. Deep. Warm. Or maybe that's the flush creeping up my cheeks as I remember his arms around me.

"Nash?"

He jerks, his shoulders hiking up to his ears. "Do I know you?"

I take a single step closer. "Yesterday? At Lakeview Krav Maga? You saved me from landin' on my ass. Blond hair, red tank top? I work with West."

Nash still hasn't moved from behind the car door. I'm

actively shaking now. My adrenaline's crashing—hard—and I can't feel my fingers.

He runs a hand over his chin, then slams the door. "Blue eyes."

"That's me." I cast a quick glance at my poor, mangled bike. "If you're still offerin' to help..."

Jogging over, he scans me from head to toe, concern furrowing his brows. "What happened?"

"Big-ass puddle in the middle of the damn road. Bigger-ass SUV. Bike meet ditch." My teeth start to chatter in earnest. Leaning on my handlebars is all that's keeping me upright. "I ain't tryin' to be ungrateful, but do you mind if we finish this conversation *inside* your car? I'm as cold as a frosted frog."

"A what?" Despite his obvious confusion, he picks up my bike and sets the crossbar on his shoulder.

"Sorry. Texans have our own language. Just means I'm freezin'." My hip screams in pain with each step, but I grit my teeth and follow him to the car.

"Where can I take you?" he asks as he wrangles the bike into the back. "And...shit. I don't even know your name."

"I live off Beacon Ave. On South Rose Street." The passenger seat has seen better days. Springs creak as I sink down. But the heater is on full blast, and I hold my hands up to the vents. Everything hurts. Except my fingers. They're completely numb.

Nash checks his mirrors and flips on the blinker. "Am I supposed to call you 'West's blond friend'? Or 'West's cycling friend'?" He cuts his gaze to mine for a second, a hint of amusement in his eyes. "'West's hot friend'?"

Hot?

"I'm Raelynn. But 'West's hot friend' sounds a hell of a lot nicer. How long you been takin' classes at the dojo? I don't remember seein' you before yesterday."

Shivering, I pull off my bike helmet to find a glob of mud

the size of my thumb stuck to my temple. Great. It's probably all through my hair, too.

Lightning arcs through the sky, almost blinding me. *Shit.* The storm is barreling toward us, hell-bent for leather. I huddle lower in the seat, as if the headrest and old vinyl can save me from my memories.

"Raelynn? Did you hear me?" Nash reaches over and touches my shoulder.

My cheeks catch fire—at least they're finally warm—and I stare down at my knees. "Sorry. You said somethin' about... hell. I don't even know. Coffee?"

"I didn't think the story was *that* boring." Nash tries for a laugh, but the sound dies in his throat, and he returns his attention to the road. I should apologize, but the storm's too close, and all I can do is dig my fingers into my palms until my hands shake.

After another few minutes of awkward silence, Nash slows and turns onto my street. "Which house?"

The next lightning strike is even brighter, and a deafening *boom* follows on its heels.

Too close.

The harsh scent of manure stings my nose. Then ozone. Burnt flesh. Brooks's cologne.

No. Not here. Not now.

"Raelynn? What's wrong?"

The voice isn't the one I want to hear. The hand covering mine is rough and strong, but bigger than I expect. With a hard blink, I pull myself out of my memories and peer over at him. We're stopped, the wipers swishing across the windshield at hyper speed.

Orange flashes illuminate Nash's forehead. His wet hair. A thick scar above his eyebrow. Hazard lights.

"I called your name three times. Where'd you go?"

My lips...I can't feel them. Another peal of thunder

shakes the car. "S-sorry. Must be the c-cold. Ain't thinkin' clearly."

He knows that's total bullshit, but just when I think he's gonna call me on it, he shakes his head. "Which house is yours? We need to get you inside and warm." The concern in his tone makes my eyes burn. No one's tried to take care of me in so long, I forgot what it feels like. But I don't let anyone see this side of me.

Hell, Nash is a complete stranger. I shouldn't let him see *any* side of me.

"I can get myself warm." Glancing out the window at the raging storm, I gesture to the end of the block. "Four-sixty-two. That's me."

He casts his gaze between me and the house, then sighs. "Fine." Less than a minute later, he pulls into my driveway and stares up at the hundred-and-thirty-year-old Craftsman with its wide-open porch and big picture windows.

I'm out of the car before he can say a word, my saddle bag slung over my shoulder. I have to get inside. Hunker down and find some way to ignore everything happening outside.

But when I reach the door, I freeze. The bag slips to the ground, and I'm so close to losing my shit, I can't form a coherent thought.

The lock swims in and out of focus. Why can't I make my hands move?

Bag. Keys. Inside.

Nash's warmth at my back shocks me enough to blink up at the wreath that's been hanging on my door for months. I should take the damn thing down, but...Graham and Q gave it to me when they invited me to Christmas dinner. An invitation I politely refused so I could spend the day alone drinking too much bourbon.

"You're shaking. Where are your keys?"

I glance down at the saddlebag, then watch, unable to move, as he drops to one knee and rummages around inside.

I should care that he's pawing through my things, but when he rises, keys in hand, nothing else matters.

Another flash illuminates the porch. My vision goes white, my heart racing. A strong arm wraps around my waist.

"Easy now," he murmurs. "I've got you."

I've got you.

Like yesterday. Was it only yesterday?

The door swings open, and I catch the lingering scent of the candle I burned last night—citrus and sage—from my living room. It helps center me enough to lean into him, to let him take control.

"Careful." His deep voice is like spun sugar. Sweet and rich and oh so dangerous. But I don't protest when he guides me over the threshold, flipping on the lights before he shuts the door behind us.

He's in my house. Holding me.

Hell, no.

I twist out of his arms—I don't like to be touched, let alone held—but before I can tell him to leave, blinding light flashes in every window, thunder explodes overhead, and the old house shudders.

I can't think. My lungs won't work. It's like all the air in the room is suddenly...gone.

I'm back in Texas, mud soaking into my Wranglers as I sob over my husband's body with the storm raging around me.

My ass hits the floor. A voice in my ear urges me to breathe.

"You didn't listen. Why didn't you listen?" I whisper.

"Listen to what?" Gentle fingers skim my cheek. "Raelynn, look at me."

Even if I wanted to, I can't. All I see is Brooks gasping for air, his life fading away in front of me.

"Raelynn!"

Nash. He's still here, his arms tight around me, his breath warming my neck. I swallow a sob, and instead of miles and miles of pasture, over his shoulder, I see the pale, painted bricks surrounding my fireplace.

Grief—as fresh as the day Brooks died—flares ice cold. For a moment, it's like I lost him only hours ago. Until the ache in my shoulder grounds me in the present.

"I'm...okay," I rasp when my chest no longer feels like someone's prized heifer is taking a nap on it. "You can let go."

"Take a deep breath for me and I'll consider it."

I should protest. I don't let anyone *handle* me. But in his arms, my panic starts to fade. Maybe...being held isn't as terrible as I thought. So I stay put. Drop my head onto his shoulder and inhale his scent. Coffee. Fresh cut wood. Leather.

I was right about him being strong. And he's so very warm, even now that my wet clothes have soaked his sweatshirt.

"That's better," he says. His fingers skim down my arms, coming to rest on my wrists. "But now you're shivering. Where's your bedroom?"

Reality hits me, hard. I jerk away, painfully aware of the loss of his touch. "I appreciate you comin' to my rescue, but I don't know you at all. You ain't goin' anywhere *near* my bedroom."

Nash straightens his shoulders and stares me down. "You're about two seconds away from hypothermia, Raelynn. I wasn't trying to get you into bed. Just into some dry clothes."

Oh.

"I can dress myself." The retort dies on my lips when I get to my feet. Dark spots float in front of my eyes. "Shit."

For the third—fourth?—time tonight, he's at my side, steadying me when I sway. Thank the stars it's just with a hand to my waist. I've had about enough coddling.

So why do I lean closer?

"Stood up too fast. Shoulda' known better. I'm all right."

"*This* is why I asked where your bedroom was," he mutters with a little shake of his head. "You had a panic attack. One of the worst I've seen in a long time. Clearly, you don't want me here, but I'm not leaving while your lips are still blue."

I touch my fingers to my mouth and sigh. "Fine. Light a fire, will ya'? My heater's on the fritz."

The idea of this man alone in my living room should be about as welcome as an outhouse breeze, yet as I head for the stairs, I'm relieved he's here. Rain pelts the windows, though the thunder is no more than a dull rumble in the distance now. I pause, looking back at him.

Nash runs his hands over the painted bricks like he's caressing his lover, before plucking the book of matches from the mantle.

Damn. I want to be masonry right now.

He starts to whistle as he stacks wood in the hearth, and I trudge upstairs. When I'm alone, I strip off my jacket, sports bra, and leggings. My bed beckons, begging me to crawl under the covers and sleep for a week. But I hear Nash moving around, and the comforting scent of wood smoke wafts up from the living room.

For years, I told myself I hated being touched. But maybe...I only *wanted* to hate it. Because I miss Nash's arms around me.

Dammit. In the space of ten minutes, he's shattered my entire belief system.

And I have no idea how I feel about that.

CHAPTER FOUR

Nash

THE LOGS CRACKLE in the hearth, dispelling a fraction of the chill in the room. Raelynn's footsteps make the old wood floors creak above me. It was pure, dumb luck I found myself on Industrial Way tonight. The same luck that let me catch her during yesterday's Krav Maga class.

Frank's words echo in my ears.

"You're the luckiest kid I've ever met."

I was. Once. Even if I didn't believe it at the time. I can still feel the blood running into my eyes. And hear Mae's whimper before two quiet pops silenced her forever.

I tug at my sweatshirt. The wet fleece sticks to my chest. Even standing in front of the fire, I'm starting to shiver. Is it only the cold? Or my memories too?

I should have grabbed my jacket before getting out of the car, but Raelynn looked so unsteady on the side of the road leaning on her mangled bike. I didn't know who she was when I pulled over, but no one deserves to be stranded and alone in the middle of a storm.

Water drips from my hair, sliding down the back of my neck. As soon as I know she's okay, I'll leave. The thunder has faded, though rain still pelts the windows in wind-driven waves.

I want to ask her what caused the panic attack. Texas storms are much worse than anything Seattle has to offer. Hell, when Frank and I lived here a decade ago, I can't remember even *one* thunderstorm. And we had an apartment in Renton for two years.

She comes down the stairs almost silently. Only a single whining step gives her away. Some of the color has returned to her cheeks, and her lips are a healthy shade of pink again. Like yesterday.

The bulky green sweater dwarfs her slim frame, but it turns her eyes a darker blue. Thick socks, fleece pants. Good. She should be fine now.

"I...uh..." Raelynn holds out a heavy flannel shirt. "This should fit you."

For a beat, I stare at the gray and red pattern. "I don't need—"

"A drownin' rat is drier than you are right now, Nash. Take it. It's the least I can do." With a sound that's equal parts sigh and huff, she thrusts it at me. "That and offer you some tea before you go."

We stand in silence for long enough, Raelynn takes two steps closer and presses the shirt into my hands. Her fingers are still half-frozen when they brush mine.

"Tea would be great. Thanks." I hate the stuff unless it's dark as sin and twice as bitter, but up close, Raelynn smells like orange blossoms, and the memory of her curves—of how good she felt in my arms—makes my jeans tight as fuck. Turning away quickly, I strip off my wet sweatshirt and hang it from a hook next to the front door. Her footsteps fade away, and water starts to run in another room.

The flannel is warm, and once I do up the buttons, I head for the kitchen.

Raelynn stands at the sink, staring out the window into the darkness with the tap on full blast.

"Fits just fine," I say. Her shoulders jerk, and she blows out a breath. Is she still panicky? Or did I actually startle her? She hasn't made a move to turn around. Or fill the kettle she's holding.

"Let me take care of that." I ease the red enamel pot from her hands. "You should sit down. You've had a hell of a night."

"This is *my* house," she protests weakly.

"Yes, but you're exhausted. Sit."

She slinks off to the built-in breakfast nook in the corner of the kitchen and almost collapses onto the cushioned bench. When I caught her at the dojo, her eyes drew me in. Clear blue, with so much fire they burned. But now, all that heat is gone.

Before I say something that'll get me thrown out on my ass, I return my focus to making tea. The ancient gas stove reminds me of home. Of the house I grew up in—before my family was taken from me.

"I haven't seen an O'Keefe and Merit in years." Running my fingers along the old clock above the burners, I grin. "My mom cursed ours every time she had to bake, but when it finally gave out, she cried a little. Dad never could find another one for sale. He looked everywhere for years."

"West told me not to buy a house this old. I should have listened," Raelynn says. "The electrical is buzzard bait. Just like the heater. I spent a fortune replacing the windows last month, and it was *snowing* when I had it done. Couldn't get the downstairs over sixty degrees for three days."

The burner catches, and I set the kettle over the flame. "Please tell me your upstairs isn't this cold."

She cracks a weary smile. "Baseboard heaters up there.

Pretty sure the second floor was added twenty or thirty years ago. I live up there most of the time."

Leaning back against the counter, I study her. Yesterday, she was the textbook definition of strong, powerful...even intimidating. The way she went after the heavy bag distracted me from class more than once. Even if she *was* favoring her right shoulder. West kept giving me the side-eye because I couldn't stop staring. But now, she has her knees drawn up to her chest, practically curled in on herself.

God. I'd do anything to see that other Raelynn again. To bring her back from wherever she's hiding, still afraid of the storm.

But I have no idea how.

"What's wrong with your heater?" I should stop with the questions. Finish making her tea and get the hell out of here. But I think she needs someone in her corner tonight—even if she hates it.

She shrugs, and small lines of pain bracket her lips. "The damn thing won't turn on. It's so ancient, no one in town will work on it. I'm gonna have to get a whole new system, and that's a good ten grand. If not more."

"Can I take a look?" The water starts to boil, and I turn off the burner. "After you tell me where your tea bags are."

Raelynn's gaze flicks to one of her cabinets, then back to me. She's skittish, rubbing her shoulder gently. "Up there. I'll...uh...get the mugs." Slowly, she pushes to her feet and retrieves two mismatched cups hanging from a shelf in the nook.

Unlike her living room, which was mostly devoid of personal touches, her kitchen looks lived in. A small painting hangs below the shelf—a cup of coffee with steam wafting from the dark brew. Plants line the window, all healthy and lush, despite the cold. One of them even has a handful of bright red flowers.

I find four tins of tea in the cabinet, each with a handwritten label, but don't recognize any of the names. "Which one do you want?"

"The Vera's Tea. It's chamomile with apple pieces and lemon peel."

Opening the black tin, I fish out two bags and drop one into each cup. She moves closer. I can almost feel her warmth as I pour the water.

"Thank you, Nash," she says softly. "If you hadn't shown up when you did...and stayed..."

She won't look at me, so I reach for her hand. Or try to since I can't force my gaze from her lips. My fingers curl around her wrist, and I'm shocked when she doesn't pull away. "My sister used to get panic attacks. Loud noises, darkness, and ambulances were her biggest triggers, but storms got to her too."

She backs up until she hits the sink. Her cheeks flush a darker shade, and she stares down at her feet. "I haven't had an attack in over a year. Thought maybe...I was over them. This storm...I didn't expect..."

"Hey." In two steps, I'm in front of her again. This time, I link our fingers, squeezing gently. "Panic isn't rational. You know that."

"Knowin' and acceptin' are two different things." After a beat, she sidesteps me, pulls a spoon from a drawer, and scoops out the tea bags. "Come on, if you're serious about wantin' to see my heater, I'll show you where it is."

I cup my mug, letting the warmth seep into my fingers as I follow her to a door half hidden behind her coat rack. The narrow stairway leads to a large, unfinished space. A fluorescent shop light hangs from an exposed beam running across the ceiling.

"Holy shit. My entire apartment would fit down here."

She chuckles, the husky sound making it hard to

remember what I'm *supposed* to be doing. Which is *not* lusting after a woman I've only just met.

Raelynn drags a decorative screen away from the far corner of the room. The heater—a metal behemoth that's bigger than I am—looms all the way to the ceiling. "Wow. How old is this thing?"

"Older than dirt in dog years." She blows on the hot tea, and I can't tear my eyes away from her lips.

Get it together. You're supposed to be looking at the furnace. Not trying for a hook up.

Setting my mug down on a storage trunk, I run my hand over the belly of the metal beast. "My pops was a handyman. We lived in Seattle for a few years when I was a teenager, and he'd bring me with him on the weekends. These old Howells were his specialty. Along with knob and tube wiring."

She snorts. "Got plenty of that. It's all through this place. I'm savin' up to have it replaced next year." She shivers, her shoulders hunched. It's too cold down here for someone who was hypothermic only twenty minutes ago.

Popping the cover off the control unit, I scan the electrical panel. "Looks like all the fuses blew. Probably a power surge. See these wires here? They're melted."

"Well, shit." She draws the word out, one hand on her hip. "This place is gonna bankrupt me. If it don't kill me first."

Frustration and despair edge her tone. I set the panel on the floor and brush my hands on my jeans. "I can't do anything without my tools. And some research. But I can probably get her running again with a little work." Raelynn stares at me, disbelief arching her brows. "I promise I know what I'm doing."

"I met you *yesterday* for all of two shakes," she says. "But for some reason, I invited you down to my basement late at night. I'm actin' a damn fool." She stalks over to the stairs. "You should go, Nash."

"West knows me," I offer. "And Adam. He runs Broadcast Coffee. They'll both tell you I'm not a serial killer."

"Adam?" She's slightly less wary now, but still ushers me ahead of her back to the living room. "How do you know him?"

After she shuts the door to the basement, she leans against the hearth, as close to the fire as she can. Dammit. I knew she was still cold.

Instead of wrapping my arms around her like I want, I mirror her position on the other side of the bricks. "I live in the little studio over Broadcast. When I got to Seattle—a few months ago—I was staying at a hostel downtown. But it took me a while to find work." A sip of tea surprises me with how good it is, and I take another. "So I started sleeping in my car."

"Your car...? Sheeeit, Nash. This is supposed to make me trust you?"

"You might if you let me finish," I offer with a smile. She holds her mug close to her chest, long fingers fluttering over the design of the Space Needle. "I move around a lot. Hostels are cheap. Usually safe. And a great place to meet people. Get the lay of the land. One of the things you learn there? What streets to park on to get a good night's sleep. The Green Lake neighborhood is safe, and as long as you move your car every night, no one's likely call the cops."

"Still waitin' for the part where I trust you," Raelynn mutters.

Chuckling, I set my mug on the mantle. "I picked up a couple of odd jobs right after I left the hostel. And since I wasn't spending money for a bed every night, I started treating myself to coffee."

By the time I finish explaining how I came to live above Broadcast, she's relaxed a little. I even get her to smile when I tell her about fixing one of the barstools right under Adam's nose. "I sat on the floor with my wrench for ten minutes before he noticed."

Despite her grin, she leans against the hearth like it's the only thing holding her up. "He's so amped on caffeine, he's on a higher plane of existence. At least that's what West says about him. I've only met him a handful of times, but the two of them go way back."

Shit. Why didn't I notice how tired she was? I run a hand through my hair, finding it only slightly damp. "I should go. It's late. But...your heater? Will you let me take a crack at it?"

With a sigh, she picks up my mug. "Okay. If you think you can get her running..."

"I can." I pull out my phone. "Tomorrow, I'm patching a roof up in Lake City. But after that, I'm free for a few days. Give me your number and I'll text you to arrange a time for me to come over."

Warmth spreads through me when she rattles off the digits and adds, "So...this weekend?"

The promise in her tone is intoxicating, and if I thought she'd let me, I'd wrap my arms around her one more time before I go. Instead, I shove my hands into my pockets and nod. "This weekend."

CHAPTER FIVE

Raelynn

"What can I get you?" the barista asks with a perky smile that makes me want to stab myself in the eye.

"Double espresso." It's almost eleven, but after last night, I'm dragging, hard.

"Coming right up!"

I fight my cringe. It's not the poor girl's fault I'm in a shitty mood. That my shoulder aches every time I move. That I had to take a Lyft here because my bike tire rim is bent beyond my ability to fix. Or that I had more than one dream last night about Nash—all featuring him shirtless.

The single glimpse of his back when he stripped off his sweatshirt affected me more than I wanted to admit. But then I saw Brooks's flannel shirt in his hand—the shirt *I* offered him—and I had to leave the room.

Trudging off to the end of the coffee bar, I pull out my phone and scroll down to the text message he sent less than five minutes after he walked out the door.

Stay warm tonight. I'll talk to you soon.

I read it half a dozen times when I got into bed. Almost responded. But I don't *want* anything with him. Or...I shouldn't. At least that's what I keep telling myself.

So why am I here with his sweatshirt tucked in my bag? I could have kept it until he came to fix the heater. I'm sure he has more than one.

The espresso sends a jolt through my system and gives me the courage—or stupidity—to ask the barista how to get to Nash's apartment.

But before I take two steps toward the stairs, the man ambles through the back door.

"Raelynn? What are you doing here?" He runs a hand through his hair, and I'm drawn to the way his bicep flexes. And the tattoo of a flock of birds winding all the way down to his elbow. Why couldn't he be wearing a sweatshirt again? His t-shirt is *way* too distracting.

"Your...uh..." My words fail me. Digging in my bag, I come up with the dark blue fleece. "I washed it."

His full lips twitch into a half smile. "I haven't been to the laundromat yet. Your shirt is still upstairs, but I can run up and get it. If you want."

"I don't need it back." My heart screams at me. I didn't keep much from my old life. Our rings are in a box in the basement. Along with the pictures from our wedding. Everything else—except for a couple of Brooks's heaviest flannels—I donated to charity after I sold the ranch.

"Are you sure?" He drapes the sweatshirt over his shoulder and leans against the wall. "I can bring it over this weekend."

"No. I mean...yes. I'm sure." Flames crawl up my neck, all the way to my cheeks. I'm not this person. Flustered and insecure ain't words I would *ever* use to describe myself. Yet with Nash, I can't find my footing. "It belonged to my late husband."

Shock plays over his features. "Shit. I'm sorry, Raelynn. When did he—?"

"Four years ago." The lump in my throat feels like it's cutting off my air, and I swallow hard. "He was struck by lightning. In a bad storm."

The understanding in his eyes breaks me. Pinning my gaze to my boots, I fight for control. "I'm already feelin' as low as a bow-legged caterpillar. Can we change the subject? I don't want your sympathy."

"No sympathy. Got it. What about a latte? Or an espresso. That's why I came down. I need the jolt before I climb onto a steep, moss-covered roof. Can I buy you one?"

"I gotta get to the dojo. We've got a new session of the Horizon program startin' this afternoon. Accessible classes for all abilities. It's a big deal. This time of day, it could take me an hour to get a Lyft, so I'm walkin'."

"You have to be sore after last night." He glances me over like he's looking for evidence. "Let me drive you. It's on the way."

Say no.

The last thing I need is to be trapped in a car with this man...again. It might be sunny, but he still smells divine. My brain and body are fighting like two hound dogs over the last soup bone, and common sense loses. "Thanks. I'd like that."

"I'd like that?" What the hell? You sound like a teenager who just got asked out by the star quarterback.

It's a damn good thing the barista calls his name. Lord knows what I'd say next.

Nash

Raelynn sidles up to the counter next to me while I wait for the oat milk latte. "You said you did 'odd jobs'? Like…handy-man-type shit?"

I can smell her shampoo—or perfume, though she doesn't seem the type—and the light orange scent draws me in.

"Yep. I put flyers up everywhere I can when I settle in a new city. Doesn't usually take more than a week or two before I have enough work to pay the bills. My pops used to do the same thing. When you only stay somewhere for six months to a year, it's too hard to find a full-time gig."

"How come you move around so much?"

Warning bells go off in my head, tension radiating down my spine. This is why I don't let myself make friends. It's never very long before they start asking questions I can't risk answering.

Shrugging, I offer the safe, practiced response I've honed over the years. "My pops liked it. He'd pick a place on the map every year—at most—and we'd hit the road. Start fresh somewhere new."

"Wasn't that hard on you and your sister? Leavin' y'all's friends all the time?"

Fuck.

"Mae…died when I was fourteen," I say quietly. "She would have hated that life. Pops and I didn't start moving around until after…"

The look on Raelynn's face about does me in. Until I realize it's probably the same damn look I had when she told me about her husband.

"It was a long time ago." I hike my backpack higher on my shoulder, pausing for a second to squeeze the bag. Yep, Bandit's safely tucked inside.

Raelynn's eyes hold so many questions, but she snaps her mouth shut, then turns to stare out the front windows while Frank's voice plays on a loop in my memories.

"Don't ever talk about your family, Nash. Anyone you confide in could sell you out to the DeLuca family. Or worse. You'll make them a target too."

I'd scoffed at him for the warning. The DeLucas don't care about me. Why would they? I was fourteen, and they think I'm as dead as the rest of my family.

In almost twenty years, I've never said a thing about the horrors of my childhood—to anyone—and I'm just now realizing how lonely of a life that's given me.

I want to tell Raelynn *everything*, but not even two decades on my own will make me that reckless. Still, now that I've started talking about Mae, it's hard to stop.

"She was eight. Took after our Mom. Red curls, freckles, dimples." I pop a lid on the to-go cup and take a sip of the latte. The rich flavor centers me, and my next breath is easier. "She *loved* playing hopscotch. Every couple of days, I'd draw a fresh grid for her in front of the house. She had a special rock, and no one was allowed to touch it unless they were playing with her."

A smile curves Raelynn's lips as she studies me. "I bet she won every time."

"Damn straight. She was undefeated." Setting my bag on the closest table, I dig into the side pocket for my keys. "I haven't thought about that in years."

"Do you have a picture of her?"

All the lightness in my heart is sucked out so fast, I can practically *hear* the *whoosh*. "No."

Her brows shoot up, one hand molding to her hip. "What in tarnation...? Why not?"

Change the subject! Now!

I shrug, hoping she'll leave it alone. "One of the hazards

of moving so much. I guess they all got lost over the years. We should get going. I'm parked on the next block." Once we're outside, my palm finds its way to the small of her back. "Did you sleep okay?"

Raelynn hesitates for a moment, squinting up at me in the morning light before she scans the street with a sigh. "Not great. Six weeks ago, I about dislocated my shoulder. The crash jacked it up again. If the doc makes me restart my physical therapy, I'm gonna be in a real horn-tossin' mood."

I almost spit out the sip of coffee. "Where do you come up with this shit?"

Her laugh is like a slow, languid, kiss—so damn sexy, my jeans feel tight. Until a guy in a dark gray suit bumps into me. I manage to hold onto the latte, but he isn't so lucky, and a full cup of dark roast from Siren Coffee spills down his shirt.

"Shit. Sorry." I stop, unsure what the hell to do as he blots at his chest with a green handkerchief. "I didn't see you—"

"It was my fault," he says, balling up the wet silk. "I wasn't watching where I was going..." Brows drawn together, he looks from me to my cup and back again. After a pause so long, it crosses the border into uncomfortable, he clears his throat. "You live around here?"

The edge of my key digs into my palm. I don't like the intensity of his stare. Or how he takes a step closer when I don't answer right away. "In Seattle? Yeah. Why?"

The guy doesn't move until Raelynn clears her throat. "We got a problem?"

He spares her a quick glance before he smiles. "I only packed one suit and now I need a dry cleaner. You don't know a place, do you?" With a shrug, he tugs at the bottom of his jacket. "Big meeting tomorrow."

"No idea. Sorry." His accent is familiar, but I can't place it. Hazards of moving as much as I do. Hell, everything about the guy makes me nervous, though he's being friendly enough. But Frank taught me to be forgettable. To blend in. And this is anything *but* blending in.

Fumbling for Raelynn's hand, I urge her toward the corner. But it's not until we're in the car that my heart rate returns to normal.

THE ROOF JOB only took me four hours, so on the way home, I pop into a mom-and-pop hardware store in Maple Leaf. Half a dozen customers roam the aisles, but it's not busy. It never is. Mitchell, one of the supervisors, waves when he sees me. "New project this week?" he asks.

"Yeah. Doing some work for a friend. She's got one of those old Howell heaters and a serious electrical problem." I toss a pack of fuses into my basket, then drop to one knee so I can check out the store's wire supply.

"She?" Mitchell leans against the shelf, playing with the ID card hanging from his belt. "Is *she* hot?"

My knuckles crack, and anger flares at the hungry look in his eyes.. "*She* is a friend. And I doubt she'd want me to answer that question. Have a little respect." Once I find the right spool of wire, I push to my feet. "You don't have sisters, do you?"

"Two brothers. Why?" He follows me to the next aisle, puffing out his chest like he's ready for a fight. "You got something to say?"

Shit.

The last thing I want is a brawl with a guy who thinks women were put on this earth for his amusement. I should find another hardware store, but the owners, Bert and Martha, have been in business since I lived here with Frank, and he always said they were good people.

"Pretty sure you've got a line forming at the register, Mitch. Might want to go check on that."

He turns, swears under his breath, and rushes up the aisle.

Unfortunately, when I finish shopping, he's the only one working checkout. By the time I pay for all the shit I need to fix Raelynn's heater, I want to punch the guy in the face. But that would make me memorable—and probably get me arrested—so I keep my mouth shut and hurry out to my car with a bag in each hand and the spool of wire tucked under my arm.

Tires squeal as I close the trunk, and I turn toward the sound.

A black blur speeds toward me. "Look out!" someone shouts.

I scramble over the back of the car. My foot slips, sending me crashing to the ground. Throbbing pain radiates from the back of my head. Metal screeches. The old Honda shudders. An engine roars, then fades, leaving a silence so consuming, it's like the whole world suddenly...stopped.

Until Bert shouts, "Call 911, Martha!"

"No!" I shake my head—big mistake—and try to get up. I don't make it, collapsing against the car behind me. My whole body trembles.

He didn't slow down. Didn't stop.

Thin fingers wrap around my bicep. "Come on, son. Let's get you back inside." Bert tugs on my arm. "You can lean on me."

Spots swim in front of my eyes for a second. Fuck. Do I have a concussion? My hip aches, and the world isn't entirely level anymore. Or steady.

"Martha, where the hell are you?" Bert calls. "This boy needs an ambulance."

"No ambulance," I protest. "I'm fine."

Martha pats the pockets of her *Gray's Hardware* apron as she crosses the parking lot. "You are *not* fine, young man. You're bleeding!"

I reach up, finding a cut on my temple sticky with blood. "Did you see the other car?" My trunk looks like a wrecking ball slammed into it. But I'm alive, and all I want is to get the hell out of here.

"It was black," Bert says.

Martha jabs him in the shoulder. "You need your eyes checked. It was green."

"You lost your glasses a week ago. It was black!" The two bicker over the color, which direction the car went, and whether I have a concussion for so long, I start limping away.

My hands are still shaking, but I unlock the door and start the engine before they notice. One of the tires wobbles a little, but I manage to back out of the space without the rear bumper falling off.

Bert calls after me. Hitting the gas harder than I should, I peel out of the lot.

"It was an accident. That's all." I say it a dozen times, but that doesn't make it true.

No one knows who you are. You've been careful. The driver was texting. Or drunk. That's the only explanation.

But is it? Was it really an accident? Or did someone *try* to hit me?

By the time I get close to home, my heart has stopped hammering against my ribs. Years of Frank's training help me focus.

Check for a tail, get somewhere safe, and then decide what to do.

Rather than park on the street, I pull into an underground parking garage half a mile from my studio. I can't afford the twenty-dollar-a-day rate for long, but with its crumpled rear end, my car is way too noticeable now.

I'm still a little dizzy, but I limp around five different blocks, checking behind me at every turn until I'm sure I'm not being followed. One of the first things Frank taught me was to always pay attention to my surroundings. Just in case.

AFTER A HOT SHOWER, I crack a beer and open my ancient laptop. It's slow as fuck, but half an hour of searching the internet and I'm satisfied Nash Grace is still as off the grid as he can be.

But what about Nathan Rossi?

Holding my breath, I type the name I was born with and click *Search*.

Half a dozen results pop up. An article in the *Chicago Tribune* about my junior high track team going to the state championships. Another one when we dominated, and I came home with a handful of medals.

And four separate links to obituaries. I've read them so many times, I could probably recreate them from memory—and every word is a lie.

Angelo Rossi was killed on March 30th, when the car he was driving veered off the road and hit a power pole. Also in the car were his wife, Stella, and their two children, Nathan, age twelve, and Mae, age six.

The forty-two-year-old real estate agent...

I slam the laptop shut and reach for my backpack. Bandit's floppy ears are looking the worse for wear, and every time I pick him up, I worry his days are numbered. But I need to feel close to Mae. To try to remember my mom's smile. Or my dad's laugh.

My phone rings, and I jerk up. I fell asleep holding Bandit. His side is damp from my tears. Setting him next to me, I flip open the ancient device. "Hello?"

"Hey. It's Raelynn. Are we still on for tomorrow?" Her honeyed voice chases the grief into the dark corners of my mind. "If not—"

"I'll be there first thing. I should have called you earlier. I meant to, but...something came up." I card my fingers through my hair until I hit the swelling behind my ear. "Shit."

"Nash? Is everythin' all right?"

"Fine." The answer comes too quickly. Too sharply. "Sorry. The roof job today was a real headache." The lie comes easily after all these years, but this time, the guilt hits hard. "I was about to turn in. Is 9:00 a.m. too early for me to show up tomorrow?"

"That'll be just fine. You sure you're...?" She pauses, and I'm hanging on her quiet little inhale, desperate for her next words—whatever they are. "Have a good night, Nash. I'll see you in the mornin'."

The call drops, and I'm left wondering how the hell I'm already in too deep. We've known each other for three days, and every time I'm around her—or even hear her voice—I want more. It shouldn't matter that I never date. That I haven't hooked up with anyone in years. My dick doesn't get to call the shots.

My hand skims the bulge in my sweatpants, and I groan. Maybe a cold shower will help.

But as soon as I strip out of my clothes in the bathroom, I know I'm fucked. Palming my length, I picture Raelynn's smile. I can practically *feel* her pressed against me.

"Nash..."

I tighten my grip, my other hand braced against the shower door. In my fantasy, she's naked under me, her skin flushed, her hair tangled and spread over the pillow. Thrusting faster, I lean down so my lips are against her ear. "What do you want, sweetness?"

"You," she gasps. "Only you, Nash."

With a shout, I lose control, my release hitting the back of the shower and sending me to my knees.

"Enough." I struggle to my feet and turn on the spray. The frigid water does its job, washing away the mess and calming me so I don't think about Raelynn again until I crawl into bed.

If only it could stop her from invading my dreams.

CHAPTER SIX

Raelynn

DOC REYNOLDS DIGS his fingers into my shoulder. For a split second, my vision goes white. I try to focus on his wrinkled brow, clenching my jaw.

"When you told me about the bike accident, I expected to find you in a lot more pain," Reynolds says. "You didn't do any additional damage that I can see. I'll tell Ryker you're cleared to resume training, but you have to promise me you'll take it slow for the first couple of workouts."

"I promise. Thanks, Doc." Snagging my sweatshirt from the back of the chair, I slip it over my head. The slight twinge doesn't bother me. On Sunday, I'll be back on that climbing wall *without* a two-minute head start.

I'll never beat West. Or Ryker. The man's so tall, he can sprint faster than all of us—even *after* the Taliban broke fifty-four of his bones and left him with arthritis and permanent nerve damage.

But Graham is fair game. So's Tank. He's not used to these intense workouts. I'll leave him in the dust.

"I mean it, Raelynn." He zips up his bag—the damn thing looks like it's straight out of the 1950s—and squares his shoulders. He carries himself with the authority of a man who's served, but Ryker warned me not to ask him *any* questions. Part of the deal he made with Reynolds years ago. "You were lucky in Utah, and you've healed well. But in my experience, luck eventually runs out."

His brown eyes are bloodshot, the bags underneath them darker than I remember. Ignoring Ryker's orders ain't smart, but I don't care. The man is hurting. "You okay, Doc?"

He composes himself with a single, hard blink, and it's like a mask slides back into place. "I shouldn't have said anything. You just remind me of someone I used to know. Take care, Raelynn."

A stiff breeze ruffles my hair as I walk him out to the porch.

"A little advice," he says, pausing at the bottom of the steps. "If you're going to stay in Seattle long term, get a car. Just because you *can* bike everywhere, doesn't mean you should."

I frown, though I know he's right. Ryker's said the same damn thing to me a hundred times.

"I pay you enough you can buy a car, probie."

"Thanks, Doc. Don't take this the wrong way, but I hope I don't see you again for a long time."

He chuckles as he crosses the street to his shiny silver SUV. With his brusque bedside manner and complete loyalty to Ryker, I doubt I'll ever find out who I remind him of. Or why the memory made him so sad.

Nash's beat-up Honda turns the corner, instantly brightening my mood. Until he pulls into the driveway. The trunk of his car has a dent in it the size of hell's half acre.

"What happened?" It rained again last night, and icy water soaks into my wool socks as I jog over to him, but I don't care. *This* is why he sounded off on the phone last night. Bad roofing job, my ass.

Dark circles brace his eyes. He hasn't shaved, and when he shuts the door, he winces.

"Are you hurt?" I reach for his arm, but he stiffens.

"I wasn't in the car," he says, the rough edge to his voice sending my mood plummeting. "I'm fine."

"Bullshit." I give him the once over, zeroing in on the slight angle to his shoulders and the way he's favoring his left leg. "Don't lie to me, Mr. Fix-it."

I'm tempted to call Doc Reynolds back. He can't be more than a couple blocks away, but then I'd have to explain a doctor making house calls and never asking about insurance.

With a sigh, Nash leans over to grab a toolbox and his backpack from the passenger seat. "Some asshole came flying through the parking lot at the hardware store. I had to jump out of the way and fell. It's nothing."

"Jump out of the way? Shit." I point to the large dent. "That could have been you!"

"It wasn't," he snaps. But two seconds later, he shakes his head. "Sorry. I'm being an ass. I didn't sleep well last night. If it's all the same to you, I'd like to get started."

I shouldn't care so much. I barely know him. But Nash came to my rescue when I needed it. I'd like to return the favor. If he'll let me.

Biting my tongue before I tell him what I *really* do for a living, I nod at the house. "Come on, then. I just made a fresh pot of coffee. You look like you could use some. After that, I'll leave you be."

Relief softens his features, even brings a smile to his lips. "Thanks."

I toss a glance over my shoulder as I lead him inside. The limp is subtle, like he's trying to hide it, but the lines of pain tightening around his eyes give him away.

"What did the police say?" Kicking off my wet socks, I make a beeline for the kitchen.

"Nothing." If his tone didn't tell me everything I needed to know, the way he's staring down at his boots would. He didn't call them.

Coffee pot in hand, I give him my best Texas side-eye. "Someone almost runs you down and pancakes your car, but you just shrug it off like it never happened? I didn't take you for an idjit."

Nash's toolbox hits the ancient linoleum with a loud *thud*. I set the pot down as he throws his shoulders back and stalks over to me. "Drop it, Raelynn. It was an accident. I didn't see the driver or get the license number. I'm fine. My car's...fine. If you really do think I'm an idiot, then I'll leave. But you owe me forty-three bucks for the parts."

I tilt my head up to meet his gaze and almost take a step back. There's a darkness churning in his eyes that should frighten me. But I can hold my own in any fight, and I sure as shit ain't backing down in my own damn house.

"Where'd it happen? Which hardware store?" I jam my hands on my hips, daring him not to answer.

"It doesn't matter because I'm not reporting it."

He moves to sidestep me, but I grab his left hand. His palm is scraped, and when I skim my fingers down to his wrist, I find a bruise darkening the skin. "So, this is nothing? You're limping. Did you hit your head too?"

He stiffens when I touch his temple. A couple of inches back, there's a knot three fingers wide. "For fuck's sake. You could have a concussion!"

"I'm done with this conversation." Nash takes a step back, grabs his toolbox, and edges toward the door. "I should go."

If I push him any harder, he'll bolt and I'll never see him again. Or have a working heater. "Wait. Cold front's comin' in next week. Will you stay? I'll drop it."

He touches the thick scar over his left brow and sighs. "I don't like the idea of you living here without heat. So, yeah. I will."

I scoot around him, fully intending to flee to my bedroom, but pause after a beat. "Help yourself to coffee. I'll be upstairs if you need...anything."

Nash

It's a good three hours before the basement door opens and Raelynn calls down the stairs, "I made lunch. Come up if you're hungry."

I shouldn't. She'll want to talk. Or worse. She'll remind me why I can't file a police report or go to a hospital or call my non-existent insurance company. But it's fucking freezing down here, and if nothing else, I could do with a fresh cup of coffee and a few minutes of daylight.

I laid awake half the night replaying the hit-and-run. The driver was wearing sunglasses. It was a black car. A sedan, I think. It's all a blur outside of those sunglasses.

The scent of something rich and spicy leads me into the kitchen.

"Chili," Raelynn says, handing me a steaming bowl. "Jalapeños and cheese are in the fridge."

I follow her lead, piling on the sliced peppers and shredded cheddar. "This smells great."

"My mama's recipe." She shrugs, fills both of our coffee cups, and gestures to the living room. "Got the fire goin'. Reckon you need to warm up a bit."

"These old basements never get much above sixty. I should have brought my coat." I follow and take a seat next to her on the faded blue sofa.

Sun streams through the windows, and with the logs burning in the hearth—and a bowl of chili in my hands—the room feels so much more inviting than it did the other night. Awkwardness sets in, the silence broken only by the scrape of spoons and the crackle of the flames.

"I overreacted," I say, desperate to fix whatever I broke between us this morning. "I didn't call the police because what would I tell them? I didn't get the guy's license number or see his face. My car's fifteen years old. It's not worth fixing. If I filed a claim, insurance would just total it. I can't afford to buy a new one."

She sets her bowl on the side table and turns, bending one leg so she's facing me. The early afternoon light turns her eyes the deepest shade of blue, and I can't look away.

"I don't mean to get all up in your business. You came to my rescue the other night, and I...shit. This," she gestures between us, "ain't somethin' I'm good at."

"*This?*"

With a sigh, she starts fiddling with the hem of her sweatshirt. "I can talk a blue streak about nothin', but I'm shit at makin'...friends. Hell, I haven't told anyone but my doctor about the other night. Sooner or later, West is gonna notice I'm not bikin' to the dojo, but he won't say anythin', and neither will I."

All those feelings I buried last night come rushing back. I shrug, giving her a small smile. "I move around too much to make friends. Can't really get to know people when you never stay in one place for more than six months."

"So why don't you put down roots? Seattle's as good a place as any."

The hint of longing in her voice surprises me. Is she just making conversation? Or does she *want* me to stick around? There's a spark between us I can't deny—despite how little I actually know about her. Does she feel it too?

I don't have an answer. Not an honest one, anyway. "I've thought about it. I loved living here when I was a kid. But Seattle is too damn expensive for me to stay long term. Picking up odd jobs here and there is good enough to pay my grocery bill, but not to afford rent in this town. If it weren't for Adam letting me live above the shop for free, I'd have left weeks ago."

Raelynn frowns, and damn if I don't want to take it all back and find a way to stay.

She rubs her shoulder, and I wonder if it's still hurting her. "I've lived in this house for six months. Rehung those French doors, painted the kitchen and dining room, and replaced the bathroom sink. But every day, I find somethin' else that's broken or worn out. If you have extra time on your hands...I can fill it. And pad your bank account a little."

My mouth goes dry, shock stealing my words until she says my name. "Nash? Does fifty bucks an hour sound like a fair rate?"

A fair rate. To fix things. Damn if I didn't think for just a minute that she was referring to...other activities.

"I'm not licensed," I sputter. "If I fuck things up—"

"You won't." She scoops up the bowls and pushes to her feet. "After you finish with the heater, we'll talk about what's next."

A LITTLE AFTER FOUR, I give up for the day. The entire electrical panel needs to be replaced, and I don't have the tools or the equipment to do it.

"Raelynn?" I call, finding the living room empty. "You upstairs?"

A shadow moves outside the big picture window. Every muscle in my body tenses until I see a flash of her long, blond hair. She's crouched next to a set of chairs making some high-pitched noises I can't understand.

I open the front door, and she jerks to her feet. "Christ on a cracker, Nash. You scared me."

"Is everything okay?" I shove my hands into my pockets as her cheeks turn bright red.

Shoulders heaving, she drops into one of the chairs. "I don't know. The cat's missin'."

"You have a cat?"

She huffs and shakes her head. "No. He ain't mine."

"Then...how is he missing?" I ask.

Raelynn tucks a lock of hair behind her ear. "Were you in town at Christmas?"

For a beat, I don't answer. I spent the twenty-fifth at the hostel trying to ignore the ache in my heart from yet another holiday alone.

"I got here in early December. Wanted somewhere warmer than South Dakota."

"Remember that snowstorm? Six inches on Christmas mornin'. The next day, I went out to shovel the sidewalk, and I spooked this scrawny cat hidin' under the laurel bushes. I gave him some leftover chicken, and he's been comin' around ever since. Until last night."

As if the cat knows she's talking about him, he leaps up onto the porch with a scratchy yowl.

"About damn time," she says, nothing but relief in her tone.

"Hey there, little guy." I drop to one knee and hold out my hand. He's all black except for a small patch on his chest of pure white, and he looks up at Raelynn and meows loudly.

"Keep an eye on him? I'll go get some fresh food."

Easing myself down onto my ass, I stretch my legs out slowly while Raelynn disappears back into the house. "You got a home?" I ask the cat, who eyes the door like he knows exactly where it leads. "Looks like you want one. Can't say I blame you."

He inches closer until his little wet nose presses against my fingers. In under a minute, he's rolling on the ground while I scratch him behind the ears.

"Here you go." Raelynn slips through the door and sets a small plate under one of the chairs. The cat attacks the chicken, purring the entire time. "I was worried about you, kiki."

"Kiki?"

She shrugs. "Growin' up, my mama called all the ranch cats 'kikis.' Since this guy doesn't have a name..."

"Kiki" finishes his meal and starts winding around Raelynn's ankles.

"I think he wants one."

She snorts. "He's gonna have to make do with kiki. I ain't adopting a cat." Despite her words, she crouches down next to me and runs her hand over the animal's back.

"Why not? You've been feeding him since Christmas. If he were feral, he wouldn't let you pet him like that."

The way she looks at him, I think she's about to scoop him up and take him inside. For all of two seconds before she jerks to her feet and makes a beeline for the door. "He shouldn't stick around. Not if he knows what's good for him."

She's back inside before I can say another word. Kiki paws at my leg, whining until I pick him up and settle him in my lap. "Give her a little time. I think she needs you as much as you need her."

Sanchez leads the beginner class through the last of the cooldown stretches, and I stagger off to the corner, spent. Coming tonight was a mistake. Though my head stopped throbbing after lunch, my hip sports a deep purple bruise. My wrist isn't a hundred percent either.

But after being around Raelynn all day, I needed to work off some steam. Or...something.

Dropping down onto the mat, I cross one leg over the other, my foot planted firmly on the outside of my knee. The spinal twist feels like heaven.

At the back of the room, West works with a small group of women teaching advanced self-defense.

I'm mesmerized as he lets one of them wrap duct tape around his wrists.

"Tighter, Marisol. I'm a Navy SEAL. You won't hurt me."

The petite dark-haired woman finishes two more rounds, and then steps back.

"Duct tape and zip ties are a lot weaker than you think. If you know what you're doing. Leverage and force are your friends. Spread your fingers wide, extend your arms in front of you, and then drive your elbows back as hard and as fast as you can."

West demonstrates, and the tape rips easily. He grabs one end with his teeth and pulls it from his skin. "You *will* lose some arm hair. But you'll be free."

As I finish my stretches, he asks another woman to tie him up again, this time with a length of rope. But she can't get it tight enough, and after three tries, he calls, "Nash? Can you come help us for a minute?"

I shuffle over to the group. "What do you need?"

"As tight as you can." He passes me the rope and holds out his wrists, totally at ease. "The rest of you, watch closely."

As I pull the ends of the rope—hard—West balls his hands into tight fists. Finishing the knot, I step back. It looks painful, but the former SEAL is smiling.

"Anyone catch what I did?"

The redhead next to me clears her throat. "You made yourself bigger."

"Right answer." West relaxes, and the ropes, which looked inescapable, loosen. He twists his hands enough to capture the ends, then starts to work them toward the knot. In under thirty seconds, he's free. "Angle your fists, force your hands apart—even a quarter of an inch makes a difference—and tense your muscles. Then, when you're alone, relax."

He claps me on the shoulder. "Thanks for the assist."

"Thanks for the lesson." I head for the lockers, retrieve my backpack, and escape into the crisp, evening air.

Maybe it *was* a good idea to come tonight. West gave me a hell of a discount on the eight-class package—Adam's doing, I suspect—and I always leave feeling better than when I walked in.

I didn't think about the car accident once. Or worry I should get the hell out of town. No time. Not with Sanchez repeatedly throwing himself on top of me so I could learn how to escape something called a "mount."

Passing the Siren Roastery, I inhale the rich scent of coffee. Before I came to Seattle, instant was my go-to. Now, I'm spoiled forever.

My toe catches on the uneven sidewalk, and I stumble, shaking loose a thought that's been rattling around in my head all day.

"You live around here?"

The man who ran into me yesterday...his accent was from Chicago. The home of the DeLuca family.

I walk faster, breaking into a jog for the last few blocks. It's not until I'm back inside my little studio that I start to relax. Coincidences happen every day. I haven't been back to Chicago in more than twenty years. I'm wrong about his accent. I have to be.

CHAPTER SEVEN

Raelynn

SUNLIGHT WARMS THE PORCH. I step outside with my morning coffee and a bowl of gourmet kibble. The cat bounds up the steps when he sees me, meowing the whole way.

I should never have fed him all those months ago. Nash is right. Kiki thinks this is his home, and if I let him in, he'll never leave.

If only I could make him the same promise.

As soon as he finishes his breakfast, he jumps into my lap. I barely hold on to my coffee cup. "I'm not a good bet, buddy. Every time I go out with Hidden Agenda, there's a chance I won't come back."

My shoulder aches—but the memory of the injury is a hundred times worse than any lingering soreness. Kiki gets right under my chin, rubbing his head along my jaw, purring the whole time. "You deserve someone who'll love you and won't fuck it all up."

He flops over, showing me his belly. "Way to make me feel guilty," I grumble.

I could call one of the local animal shelters. They'll be able to find him a good family. He's young—I think—maybe a couple of years old. Now that he's not starving, he *looks* healthy. Before I take him to a shelter, I should make sure.

The cat settles down for his post-breakfast nap, and I pull out my phone to call a vet. I'll get him checked out, then find him a new home.

It's the right thing to do. So why do I feel like shit over it?

It doesn't take me long to book an appointment for Tuesday morning. "I'll get you a carrier tomorrow," I say, stroking my hand over Kiki's sleek black coat. "You're gonna make some family very happy."

My eyes start to burn. I haven't cried in four years. Not since I buried Brooks. So why does the idea of this stray cat finding a home with someone else hurt so much?

Get over yourself. He'll be better off. And so will you.

As if God herself disagrees with my plan to spend the rest of my life alone, my phone vibrates with a new text message.

Nash: Leaving my place now. I hope you haven't had breakfast yet.

He ends the message with a donut emoji. Oh, God. That better not be code for some weird sex thing. The one time I tried an online dating app, my messages were filled with eggplants, peaches, tacos, bananas, and baguettes. I still don't understand that last one.

I spend a full five minutes staring at my phone, agonizing over my reply. Nothing sounds right.

Can't wait!

Too excited.

Haven't eaten yet.

Too boring.

There better be a maple bar in there.

What if there isn't? Or worse? What if he's not actually talking about donuts?

Finally, I send him a single coffee emoji. That's safe. Casual. Nothing he has to respond to. Nothing too needy. Nothing too serious.

Despite my uncharacteristic chattiness yesterday, I know the score. Nash and I aren't *friends.* We're not dating. He's my damn handyman. So why did I just spend all that time worrying over what to say to him?

"Shee-it." I scare the cat, and he jumps off my lap, his tail twice its normal size, then stares at me from the edge of the porch. I should try to calm him down, but my hands are shaking. I doubt my voice is much steadier.

I care what Nash thinks because I want us to be...*something*. Friends, at least. But maybe more.

Four years is a long damn time. Any woman in your position would be lusting after a guy like him.

Works with his hands. Check. Has a smile that lights up his whole face. Check. Has already seen you at your worst and didn't run away. Check.

Nash is safe. He's a good guy who won't be around long enough to get clingy. Or demand more than I'm willing to give. And he's damn fine to look at.

Ain't no surprise I want him. Hell, it'd be strange if I didn't.

By the time Nash arrives, I'm almost calm. Until he gets out of the car. It's warm today, and he's wearing a dark blue t-shirt that molds to his arms and shows off every curve and dip of his muscles. "Give me a hand?"

"Good mornin' to you too," I say, leaning against the mangled trunk and appreciating the view as he reaches into the backseat.

He straightens and hands me a white box with a wink. "Be careful with these. I had to go all the way to Mill Creek for them."

God. He smells so damn good. His hair curls over the

collar of his shirt, and as he stretches to snag his backpack, I catch a whiff of spice. And a glimpse of smooth skin.

I have to put some space between us before I say—or do—something I'll regret. Like grab the back of his neck and kiss him until he can't remember his own name.

"Raelynn?" Nash touches my shoulder, and I jerk back to the present. If I didn't have a death grip on the box of donuts, they'd be in the gutter. "You *do* like donuts, right?"

"Of course, I do." I take a quick peek into the box. "But you're damn lucky you got two maple bars. I'd hate to have to fight you for one."

"I'LL TRADE you the rest of my maple bar for another cup of coffee." Nash nudges the donut box closer to me with a hopeful grin.

"Rookie move." Not waiting for him to change his mind, I snag the rest of the prized confection, holding it just out of reach. "The coffee pot is full—and unguarded. You could have kept this *and* refilled your mug."

"Maybe I just wanted to see you smile like that."

Flames race up my cheeks, and I can't remember the last time I blushed. Or spent an hour with a guy, enjoying his company and just...talking. "Get to work, Mr. Fix-It. I'll keep you in coffee all day long."

"Promise?" His blue eyes sparkle as he clutches the cup to his chest. "Because I have to cut into your drywall today to connect a whole new electrical panel. It's not going to be pretty. Or quick."

"Will my lights stop flickerin' for no reason whatsoever? Because if so, you can make as much of a mess as you want, and I'll be happy as a pig in shit." Shoving the last of the maple bar into my mouth, I move to the cabinet next to the sink and pull out the bag of coffee beans. "If you get my heater workin' at the same time, I just might kiss you."

His mug lands on the counter with a rattle. I didn't notice him get up. Or move so close, we're practically touching. He stares at me, the intensity in his eyes almost feral.

Oh, shit. What did I—?

Nash grabs me, one hand cupping my neck, the other molding to my waist. His lips are the stuff of legends. Soft, yet strong, with a hint of stubble scraping against my skin. I can't think. Not with the way he tastes. With the heat of his body setting me ablaze.

Lord have mercy, this man can kiss.

And I'm kissing him back.

He traps me against the counter, but escape is the last thing on my mind. The low rumble in his throat and the growing bulge in his jeans make my heart race and heat gather in my core.

Scoring my lip with his teeth, he tugs at the swollen flesh until I moan, then touches his forehead to mine.

"Rae..." he whispers. "That..."

The fire burning through my veins cools in an instant. "Let me go." I shove at him, twisting out of his hold. "Don't call me that. Don't *ever* call me that."

Tears make the room shimmer. My chest tightens. I have to get out of here before I lose my shit.

I race through the house and up the stairs. Nash calls after me, telling me to wait, apologizing, asking what he did wrong. But I can't answer. All I can do is slam my bedroom door in his face.

My tears soak into the pillow. I don't even remember falling onto the bed. He knocks repeatedly, but eventually, his footsteps echo on the stairs, and I'm left with the sounds of my own grief amid the silence.

I wish I knew what to say to him. Or how to explain what

he did. It's been four years since anyone called me Rae—since *Brooks* called me Rae. For so long, I heard his voice every time I closed my eyes. As much as that hurt, it was also a comfort. A reminder that once...I'd been loved by someone who treated me like I was his whole world. That once I'd loved someone who was my everything.

But now...the memory scratches and skips like one of those old records Brooks loved so much and will never play again.

Nash

After an hour, Raelynn still hasn't come downstairs. No footsteps. No creaking floorboards. Not a single sound.

Parked on her couch, elbows on my knees, I stare down at my boots, wondering what I should do. I've been here so long, it would be weird to leave now. Wouldn't it? She didn't tell me to get out. Just...let go. But why?

My backpack and toolbox sit next to the door. I could head down to the basement and get to work. At least then, I'd have something to stop me from replaying that kiss over and over again.

Raelynn came alive in my arms. That first day when I caught her at the dojo, I saw the fire in her eyes. But the storm broke her somehow. It doesn't matter that I'd only exchanged a few words with her before that night. I knew. She lost something after the panic attack and found it again—briefly—over donuts and that one, passionate kiss.

I can't just sit here. But disappearing into the basement doesn't feel right either. So, instead, I head for the kitchen and clean up from breakfast. It doesn't take long—two plates, Raelynn's empty mug, a few crumbs scattered over the table in the breakfast nook—and when I'm done, I stare at the coffee pot, wondering how much of an ass I'd be if I poured myself another cup.

"You're still here."

I whirl around, almost dropping my mug. The sight of Raelynn's swollen eyes and splotchy cheeks makes my heart hurt. "I'm sorry. I don't know what I did, but I'm—"

"Brooks used to call me Rae." Her voice holds none of its usual strength. She won't look at me—focusing just over my shoulder instead—and pulls a heavy flannel shirt tightly around her body.

"Brooks?" The truth registers the moment the name leaves my lips. "Your husband. God, Raelynn. I'm so sorry."

A single tear glistens on her cheek. If I thought she'd let me, I'd wipe it away.

"You didn't know." With a deep sigh, she drags the cuff of the shirt across her cheek. "It's been four years. I thought... ain't nothin' gonna bring him back. But..."

The hitch in her voice smashes my resolve. In two steps, I'm right in front of her, and she melts into my arms like it's the most natural thing in the world. But when she rests her head on my shoulder, I know however much pain I caused her, it's nothing compared to what she lives with every single day.

"You're not supposed to 'get over' losing someone you love. You learn to live with the pain of missing them until it's...part of you." My words sound heavy and awkward as I close my eyes and try to picture Mae. But after all these years, I can only remember her red curls. The freckles she hated. Everything else about her is mostly...gone.

We stay locked together for what feels like an hour but is probably only minutes before Raelynn straightens and I let her go.

"I can't have you here right now, Nash." She pins her gaze

to the floor and backs up until she hits the counter. "Can you come back tomorrow? Maybe then..."

"I can be here at eleven." I wish she'd look at me. Give me some indication she'll be all right alone. But she doesn't answer. Only nods and tugs at her shirt.

Shit. Can I really leave her like this?

"I don't have any right to ask, but will you text me later? Just to let me know you're okay?"

Her head jerks up, shock arching her brows. She presses her lips together, and I can't tell if she's angry or trying not to cry. Until she whispers, "I will."

CHAPTER EIGHT

Raelynn

THE AFTERNOON SUN warms my back as I drop into a forward fold. I'm the only one at Hidden Agenda's warehouse—for once—so my favorite, *Queen,* blares through the speakers along the wall.

After Nash left, my house felt so...empty. The moment he walked out the front door, I knew I'd made a mistake. Hell, a whole mess of them.

His kiss rocked my entire world, but then I had to go and fuck it all up.

Now the only way I'll sleep tonight is to push my body to its limits.

The climbing wall taunts me from the corner of the room. As desperate as I am to prove I'm back to full strength, Ryker would kick my ass if he found out I tried it alone. Though there aren't any cameras inside the warehouse, he'd still know. Somehow.

Once I finish my warmup stretches, I jog over to the start of the indoor track. Last week's pitiful running splits are still on the whiteboard. Beating them might make me feel less like a worthless piece of shit who can't handle her own damn emotions.

On the fourth lap, I hit a wall. My entire body aches and all I want to do is curl into a ball and go to sleep. Shit. My hour-long crying jag left me dehydrated, and I haven't eaten anything since I stole the last of Nash's maple bar this morning.

The fridge is stocked with Gatorade, yogurt, and fresh fruit, and I crack the seal on one of the bottles. The fake "blue raspberry" flavor threatens to turn my stomach, but the brain-freeze gets to me first.

"Ow, ow, ow..."

"Ry sets the fridge just shy of Arctic winter."

I jump, splashing cold, sticky blue liquid down my shirt. "Shee-it, West. No one was supposed to be here today."

The former SEAL drops his rucksack on the table and shrugs. "Tank wanted a refresher course on the new cell phone tracking program. He should be here in twenty." He braces an elbow on the counter, studying me.

My once-white tank clings to my chest. The sugary sweet scent doesn't do shit for my nerves. Neither does West's intense stare. Dammit. Why did he have to show up today of all days? He's gonna want to talk, and I just...can't.

"You look like someone stole your puppy. What happened?"

"Nothin'." The word slips out before I realize there's no fucking way he'll believe me.

"Dammit, Raelynn," he snaps. "This is your last chance. If you can't be honest with me, I'm benching you."

I square my shoulders, meeting his steely gaze with all the confidence of a June bug who just escaped the chicken coop. "We're not on mission, asshole. And you know my history.

You want to bench me for havin' a bad day? Go for it. I gotta clean up."

I hightail it for the lockers before West can stop me. So much for a hard workout. Coming here was a mistake.

The hot water soothes a sliver of my battered heart—or maybe that's the fresh tears I couldn't hold back once I stepped under the spray—and I feel almost human again when I emerge from the showers in a clean sports bra and leggings.

Until I spot West leaning against my locker, his arms crossed over his chest. "Give me a fuckin' break, will you? I'm benched. I got it. Call me when you think I've learned my lesson."

He doesn't move or react in any way, holding my gaze like he's daring me to have a go at him. "Didn't take you for an idiot. Or a coward."

A ball of rage gathers in my chest, burning so hot, I can't control it. Shoving him, I expect him to move, but the SEAL is two hundred pounds of solid muscle. He doesn't budge.

"Want to get it out of your system? We can step into the ring right now. But if you don't want to fight me, you'll sit your ass down and listen."

If I'm gonna keep this job, I don't have much of a choice. Doc Reynolds gave me the all clear to resume training, but sparring with West isn't in the same *universe* as "taking it easy." If we tried, I'd be flat on my back in under two minutes. "Move so I can get a clean shirt. I ain't havin' this conversation in just my bra."

He inclines his head toward the couches next to the kitchen. "Do what you need to do. I'll be waiting."

Though I'm tempted to drag out every single step—fumbling my locker combination, repacking my go bag, taking the time to put on some foundation—I can't. Better to rip off the Band-Aid and find out how badly I fucked up.

A steaming mug of coffee waits for me on the side table when I sink down across from him. "Thanks."

He nods. "You look like you need the jolt." After a pause, he stares me down. "I *do* know your history, Raelynn. That's why I was concerned. You didn't need to cry on my shoulder for an hour. That's not you. But I didn't expect you to flat-out lie to me either."

The denial dies on my lips. That's exactly what I did. What I'd keep doing if I thought I could get away with it.

"I didn't set out to lie. I ain't good at talkin' about my problems. It slipped out, and I'm sorry."

West sets his coffee cup down and leans forward, his fingers steepled. "When Ry handed me your dossier, he said you were looking to move somewhere no one knew your history. We gave you that. He and I are the *only* ones who know what happened back in Texas, and it'll stay that way unless you decide to open up to the rest of the team."

I choke down my sip of coffee. "You didn't tell anyone else?"

"No." After a beat, he frowns. "Why does that surprise you?"

Sputtering, it takes me three tries to form a coherent thought. "N-no secrets. Complete honesty. Your words. And Ry's. Ain't that a damn big secret to keep?"

His gaze softens, and though West never loses that patented SEAL intensity—the one designed to make even the most hardened criminal wither under his stare—this is a side of him I haven't seen before.

"It is. For you. But it isn't my secret to tell. As long as it doesn't affect you on mission, it's nobody's business but yours."

"So why the hell are you givin' me the third degree here?" I ask.

"Because ever since Salt Lake City, you've been in a shit

mood, and it's only a matter of time before we all pay the price. Why do you think I've been riding your ass since we got back?"

Any other person—any other time—with this much sympathy in their voice would send my anger boiling over. But West ain't done, and I'm just too tired to fight any more.

"You're a damn good operator, Raelynn. You follow orders —most of the time—you've got great instincts, and you're so stubborn, you don't give up even when you probably should. But keep your pain bottled up for too long, and it's going to explode like a rusty IED. While we're on mission."

It already has. If only I were brave enough to tell him that.

"I can't make you talk to anyone. Not me, not Ry, not a shrink. But if you don't find someone, you're going to burn out sooner rather than later."

Six weeks ago, I would have laughed in his face. Or behind his back—I don't have a death wish. But after our last mission...

Wyatt glares at me as Hope whimpers from the basement of her ex's compound. "If it were the love of your life down there —" he says.

"The love of my life died in my arms. Bring him up again, and I'll break my foot off in your ass."

Maybe it wouldn't be the worst thing to tell West *something.* Just enough to get him off my back.

"Brooks and I were high school sweethearts," I say quietly. "He took over his daddy's cattle ranch while I was in the Air Force. We ran it together after I retired. Almost ten years of the hardest work I've ever done."

"Clearly, I need to step up my training game," West says with a dry chuckle.

"You do that, ain't none of us gonna be field ready for a month. You and Ryker are fuckin' sadists."

West lets loose with a rich laugh that practically has him

doubling over. It feels good to relax—even a little—after the day I've had.

I finally found someone I like who likes me, who excites me in a way I haven't felt in...forever. And I'm going to ruin it if I can't find a way to open up to him. What the hell is wrong with me?

West takes a sip from his mug, still watching me. I could probably get him to leave me be now. But if I tell him the *real* problem, could he actually help?

"My barbaric training regimen aside, why is this all comin' up now?" he asks.

I don't look at him, choosing to stare down at the floor. "That guy in your beginner class, Nash?"

"Yeah? What about him?" West leans back against the cushions and drains the last of his coffee.

"He's fixin' my heater. Damn thing broke a week after I closed on the house. It's been a couple of days and we've... gotten to talkin'. He's nice. Funny."

I swallow hard and take a deep breath.

"We kissed this morning. But then he called me Rae." My emotions threaten to drown me, and I scrub my hands over my face.

"Rae?" West tugs at his short brown hair like that'll help him figure out the puzzle I just dropped in his lap. "I'm going to need a little more to go on here."

"Brooks was the only one who ever called me Rae. It...*hurt*. And I lost my shit." Gesturing to my face, I shrug. "Acted a damn fool, kicked him out, and now I gotta find a way to face him. This is the first time in four years I've wanted to get to know a guy in *that* way, and I've fucked it right up."

West snorts. "He's into you, Raelynn. You didn't see how many times he checked you out during class the other day. He's not going to give up on you because you had one moment of grief. And if he does, he's not good enough for you anyway."

I'm older than West by a couple of years, but he's actin' like I always imagined a big brother would. Patient. Protective. Encouraging. Even if I do want to kick his ass half the time.

"Are you sure?" I ask. "Because the way he looked at me when I told him to leave..."

Tank pushes through the outer door, startling me into silence. His fancy jacquard shirt shimmers over tight black jeans and heavy motorcycle boots. "How you doin', bro? Ma'am?"

"He gets 'bro' and I get 'ma'am'? I ain't that much older than you are."

The big man chuckles. "I respect my elders, ma'am. Dax will kick my ass if he hears otherwise."

West pushes to his feet, shooting me a quick, pointed look that clearly says, *"We're okay. For now."*

"Get your laptop," he says, motioning for Tank to meet him at the table in front of a group of massive flat-screen monitors. "We've got three hours until I have to pick Cam up for date night, and there'll be hell to pay if I'm late."

Tank heads for the tech center in the front of the warehouse, and the SEAL leans down and clasps me on the shoulder. "Talk to him, Raelynn. If he's worth it, he'll understand."

I meet the SEAL's gaze for all of a second before I have to look away. "Thanks, West. For not givin' up on me."

He holds on for a beat, then straightens. "This is a family, Raelynn. And family sticks."

Nash

A fresh breeze ruffles my hair as I walk along the waterfront. After Raelynn kicked me out, I drove around for an hour, then headed down to Georgetown to work on the chairs for Broadcast. But I couldn't focus.

I thought we had a real connection this morning. One that might keep me in Seattle for more than a few months. But with a single careless word, I fucked it all up. I shouldn't care. Moving on is smarter. Safer. I can't stop thinking about the guy who bumped into me the other day. About the hit and run. Twice last night, I even started to call Duncan. The former U.S. Marshal has been retired for years—since before Frank died—but he still has connections.

Would he know if the DeLucas are still after me?

I kick a rock into the gutter. We should have been safe in Chicago. Even safer in Minnesota. My father wasn't involved in his family's *business* and the DeLucas knew that. Yet they came after us anyway.

Dammit. Tension tightens a band around my forehead. I have to stop. Going down this road usually ends with me passing out after a hell of a lot of tequila. Not this time.

I check behind me and turn down a different side street. I'm safe. No one's following me. I should relax. It's a warm, spring day. The sun's shining, and though the morning turned into a shit show of epic proportions, there's been no sign of trouble since the hit and run. Even so, "Uncle" Duncan would tell me to get gone. "Better safe than sorry." I can almost hear his voice now.

I'll finish the work on Raelynn's heater tomorrow, then walk away.

If only I could forget her as easily.

If I'm honest, I don't want to leave Seattle. Not now. Maybe not for months. Or longer. For the first time in years,

I'm putting down roots. I don't know when it happened, but I consider Adam a friend.

And there's Raelynn. Despite how we left things this morning, the spark between us is too powerful to ignore. If she can forgive me, I want to see where this goes.

I keep walking, almost on autopilot, until I find myself just up the hill from one of my favorite places in Seattle.

Olympic Sculpture Park spans several city blocks, and as I approach the outdoor art installation, a sigh escapes my lips. Years ago, Frank and I would come here once a week—if it wasn't raining—sit on the benches that overlook Puget Sound, and watch the ferries go by.

One speeds across the water, headed for Bainbridge Island. "Wish you were here, Pops. Even if you *would* tell me to get the hell out of town."

The paved path winds around half a dozen different works of art, and I take my time, averting my gaze from a group of people following a tour guide through the park.

My favorite piece—a thirty-foot Eagle sculpture made of red steel—soothes the last of my raw nerves. Raelynn promised she'd text me later, and I don't get the sense she's one to lie.

Unlike me. One of these days, I'm going to disappear, and I won't be able to tell her a damn thing.

I don't have a choice. Hiding the truth has kept me alive for twenty years. But I'm so fucking lonely. God, I wish I had *someone* to talk to. Someone who knows my secrets. Who understands why I have to be so careful.

A loud beep startles me, and I pull out my old flip phone.

Raelynn: Little Red Hen in Green Lake has line dancing every Saturday at 7.

I stare at the screen, confused. Is there another message coming?

Something like:

Come on down.

Want to meet me there?

Let's go.

But after five minutes, the phone is still silent. Fuck. Do I just show up at seven and hope for the best? No. Not after this morning.

This ancient hunk of plastic doesn't have a full keyboard, but I manage a short reply that I hope will get a rise out of her.

Nash: Good to know. Maybe I'll check it out sometime.

I return my gaze to the water. Puget Sound is as smooth as glass today. Unlike my emotions. I shove my phone into my back pocket and head down to the very edge of the park where a gentle breeze slaps the water against the rocks. With each step, I wonder if I did the right thing. Until I hear another loud beep. My phone's so old, its silent mode broke a year ago.

Raelynn: Tonight, Mr. Fix-it. Unless that kiss meant nothing to you.

I almost drop the phone. So I didn't fuck up as badly as I thought. But what's a guy supposed to wear to go line dancing?

CHAPTER NINE

Raelynn

I CAN'T TELL if I feel more like myself than I have in years, or if a complete stranger has taken up residence in my body. I've been to the Little Red Hen half a dozen times since I moved to Seattle, but never once dug out my vintage red cowboy boots. Or put on a dress.

It's been a day of firsts. First kiss since Brooks died. First time I let another person see me cry. First time I shared my problems with West. First time I asked a man out.

And, assuming he shows, this will be my first date since high school.

Shit. What am I doing?

"Living."

My inner voice is right. So why is this so *hard?* Brooks would want me to be happy. Hell, *I* want me to be happy.

"He's into you, Raelynn."

West better be right. Otherwise I'm gonna make a damn fool out of myself tonight.

I agonized over what to say to Nash for an hour after I left

Hidden Agenda. Until I looked at the calendar. Line dancing is safe. A crowd. Loud music. Little to no touching. We'll either have a good time and put this morning behind us, or it'll be so awkward, I'll never want to kiss him again.

My black leather jacket slides over my shoulders like butter, and I feel more like *me* than I have in a long time.

Kiki meows at the big picture window. "Dinner time?" I ask. Snagging the bowl of kibble from the table by the door, I try to slip outside quickly, but the cat darts around my ankles faster than greased lightning.

He jumps onto the couch, sitting up proudly, and kneading his little paws as his purrs fill the room. "Git," I say, pointing to the door. "I'm goin' out, and you can't stay here by yourself."

As if he understands me—and doesn't like what I'm saying one bit—the cat extends one of his legs and starts cleaning himself.

"Absolutely not. You might be cute, but the last thing I need is to come home and find a puddle of cat piss in every room."

When the little freeloader shifts to give me a prime view of his ass, I huff and stalk out to my rental car. I stopped at the pet store for a carrier on the way home. Even looked at litter boxes—food bowls and toys too—but I couldn't bring myself to admit the truth.

I don't want to drop Kiki off at a shelter on Monday. I'd miss the little fluff ball too much.

In five minutes, I have the carrier set up on the porch with its door latched open and one of my sweatshirts folded inside.

Crouching down in front of the couch, I run my hand over the cat's sleek fur. "You can't stay inside tonight, little guy. I don't have a litter box for you yet. But I'll get one tomorrow. Deal?"

He gives my hand a tentative lick, then rolls over to show me his belly.

"Nice try. And you better not have fleas."

After another few minutes of belly rubs and scritches, I pick up the food bowl and shake it. The cat jumps up and follows me back outside with only a single meow of protest. Tossing a few pieces of kibble into the open carrier on top of the sweatshirt, I hope he gets the hint.

"I still don't think this is a good idea, you little monster, but you ain't gonna give me a choice, are you?"

He ignores me, his face buried in the bowl. Before I lose my nerve, I pull out my phone to order a litter box and the most expensive litter I can find to be delivered tomorrow. When Kiki finishes eating, he looks up at me like he knows he's home.

I just hope I don't fail him like I've failed everyone else in my life.

My dark thoughts threaten to drag me so far down I can't see my way clear, so I push to my feet and rush down the steps to the car.

Nash

Country music spills out onto the sidewalk from the old building just east of the lake. The bouncer checks my ID, pockets the cover charge, and waves me inside. Looks like my jeans and black t-shirt weren't a terrible choice. Though a few of the men on the dance floor look like they just stepped out of Cowboy Monthly. I don't see any spurs or chaps, at least.

The press of people around the bar is overwhelming, so I stick to the edge of the crowd, scanning the booths for any sign of Raelynn. The whole way here, I wondered what the fuck I was doing. Going on a date? Even if this ends well—with another kiss that will feed my fantasies for days to come—I'm still fucked.

Either I fall hard and disappear on her one day without a word, or I say the wrong thing and screw up the only *real* connection I've had with a woman…ever.

Dumbass. Why would she even bother with a thirty-four-year-old man who's never been in a serious relationship?

I know what I see in her. Raelynn is gorgeous, independent, and funny. But also sad. Lonely. Desperate for something I don't think even she understands.

When I step around a pillar, my jaw hits the floor. She leans against a two-person booth, long, bare legs crossed at the ankles. Red cowboy boots. A floral print dress that ends only a couple of inches below her ass. Blond hair flows over one shoulder in a waterfall of wavy curls.

She reaches back for her margarita glass, and I'm mesmerized as she takes a drink, then licks a bit of salt off the rim. One foot bounces in time with the music, and I might never get the fantasy of Raelynn in those cowboy boots—and nothing else—out of my head.

Stop acting like a stalker and go talk to her.

The song ends as I approach, and the handful of folks on the dance floor applaud and high-five one another. "Hey." I scan her face, looking for any sign of the lost, broken woman who kicked me out of her house this morning. But the spark is back in her eyes. Is it genuine? Or is she putting on a show for me—and for herself?

"About damn time." Raelynn grabs my belt, pulls me against her, and crushes her lips to mine. The brief, hard kiss tastes like salt, tequila…and something sweet. My dick rockets to attention. If I didn't need to know we were on solid ground first, I'd suggest we get the hell out of here right now. "What do you want?" she asks. "It's on me."

The urge to say *I* want to be on her is almost overwhelming. But that would probably get me kneed in a rather uncomfortable place, so I swallow hard and fumble for a more acceptable answer.

"Uh...well, you taste amazing, so...whatever you're having. But it's going to take an hour to get through that crowd."

She winks at me. "Be right back."

I take her place, my hip against the table, and wait. Raelynn strides to the far corner of the bar, leans in, and shouts to someone hidden behind the throngs of people. Less than two minutes later, she returns with a pair of large, pink margaritas. "Shit. How did you do that so fast? You have to tell me your secret."

"No secret, darlin'," she says as she takes a seat. "I know the bartender."

Darlin'?

I slide into the booth across from her, still unable to tear my gaze from her face—even when I lift the glass to my lips. The drink is strong, a hint of watermelon mixing with the salt and tequila.

"Do you come here often?" I ask. The DJ announces the next song—and some dance step I've never heard of before—and more than a dozen men and women form two lines down the middle of the room.

"Once or twice a month." Raelynn takes a long sip of her drink, her tongue flicking some of the salt off the rim. If she keeps doing that, even my tight jeans won't be strong enough to hide how much I want her. "Have you been dancin' before?"

"Not like that." I'm in awe of how each person on the dance floor seems to know exactly what to do—and when—in time with the music. "There's no way I can keep up..." I wave my hand at the perfectly coordinated steps, "with that."

Her laugh has the power to send me to my knees. I'd do

anything she asked just to see that look on her face a second time. "If you want another date, Mr. Fix-it, you'll try."

The single word—date—rattles around in my head until Raelynn lifts the margarita to her lips once more. The motion highlights her toned arms and the way her dress clings to her body.

I clear my throat. "Does that mean I didn't completely fuck up this morning?"

Raelynn flinches but recovers quickly. A hint of sadness lingers in her gaze until she pops a tortilla chip into her mouth and stares at the lines of folks performing a complicated sequence of steps I'll *never* be able to master.

"What happened wasn't your fault, Nash. It was mine. But we're not talkin' about it tonight." She drains the rest of her margarita and sets the glass down with enough force, the last of the salt hits the table. "Drink up. Next song, you're dancin' with me."

I NEED a hell of a lot more liquor to move my feet like I'm supposed to. Flubbing my way through the simplest of the dances—something called the Cupid Shuffle—I bang into the guy next to me more than once before Raelynn pulls me out of the line to the back of the crowd.

"You're gonna hurt someone. I should start callin' you Mr. Two-Left-Feet. We're doin' this next one alone." Raelynn moves directly behind me, molding her hands to my waist.

"We could go somewhere a hell of a lot more private," I say over my shoulder. "And work on some *other* moves."

She's a tall woman—at least five-foot-seven—and levers up on her toes so her lips are close to my ear. "Not until you get through one dance without steppin' on anyone else's toes."

I groan. "We're going to be here all night."

"You want to get out of here?" she purrs and presses a kiss to my neck. "Pay attention."

The DJ announces the next song, but I can't focus on the name with the way she's holding me. My jeans are strangling my dick. If I make it through the night without doing permanent damage, it'll be a miracle.

"We'll start slow. Right foot." She nudges my knee with hers, and we step forward together at an angle. "Left behind the right, then repeat."

With her guiding me, we manage two out of every four moves. Enough to dial my arousal up to eleven and leave us horribly out of sync with the rest of the dancers. Raelynn laughs whenever I miss a step—and finds some new way to touch me. But despite how close we are, every time I try to reach for her, she stops me.

By the last song of the night, I'm ready to beg. And sit my tired ass down. But I manage to get through the whole dance without my size thirteens crushing Raelynn's toes, and when the DJ thanks everyone for coming, she drapes her arms around my neck. "You did good, city boy."

"How good?" My hands mold to her waist, and for once, she doesn't pull away. "Good enough you'd consider coming back to my place? Or...take me to yours?"

She smiles at me, and it doesn't falter—not even when I slide my hands down to cup her ass. "Oh, you're comin' home with me, Nash. And we'll see what other *moves* you have to show off."

CHAPTER TEN

Raelynn

"So, did I do well enough for a second date?" Nash asks when I start the car.

I pull away from the curb, then flick my gaze to his for a split second. "Before you step out on the dance floor again, darlin', I'm givin' you private lessons."

"Private...lessons?" His voice is half an octave higher than normal, and he shifts his hips like his jeans are suddenly very tight.

"By the time I'm done with you, you'll be dancin' in your sleep."

I don't know what came over me this afternoon. The Little Red Hen is one of the few places I feel like *me*. Line dancing is in my blood. I tried five different bars when I moved to Seattle, but the Little Red Hen is my favorite.

Only one member of Hidden Agenda knows what I do every other Saturday night. The first time I saw Graham behind the bar, I almost walked right out the door. But the guy's perceptive well beyond his years and he's never said a damn thing to anyone.

I pull into the driveway, suddenly so nervous, my hands shake as I pocket my keys.

Nash rests his hand on the small of my back as he walks me up to the house. It makes me feel...wanted. I can't remember the last time I felt wanted. Or felt much of anything, really.

"That's new," he says, nodding at the open cat carrier on the porch, with a sleeping Kiki still inside.

A flush creeps up my cheeks. "Quiet. If you wake him up, he'll be through the door in two shakes, and his litter box ain't comin' until tomorrow."

To his credit, he doesn't say a word. Not "I told you so" or "finally" or "about damn time." He just smiles at Kiki while I open the door.

We make it inside without the cat noticing, and as soon as I flip the locks, Nash slides his arm around my waist and pulls me against him. "What are we doing here, Raelynn?" His lips travel from the curve of my neck up to my ear, sending a shiver through me.

Tipping my head back, I stare into his deep blue eyes. "Havin' a little fun."

That must be enough for him, because he backs me against the door. Rough fingers skim over my throat, setting my core on fire.

"Nash..." It's been so long since anyone touched me—since I *wanted* anyone to touch me—I don't know how to ask for what I need. "Upstairs..."

He pins me with his bulk, one hand cupping my neck, the other tangling in my hair. "I need a taste first."

His lips feather over mine, gently to start, then with so much raw passion, my entire body comes alive. I grab his hips, tugging him closer. I need to feel him. All of him. Not just the hard bulge in his jeans against my stomach. Not just his fingers on my neck. Not just his stubble against my jaw. I want every part of him.

Nash groans when I deepen the kiss, pulling his bottom lip between my teeth and swiveling my hips as best as I can with his weight holding me still.

"Hang on to me," he grits out, then lifts me enough for me to wrap my legs around his waist. I lock my arms behind his neck, a thrill racing through me when he manages to carry me up the stairs without breaking a sweat.

Nash lowers me to my feet next to my bed. The same bed where I lost my shit this morning. For a single moment, I wonder what the hell I'm doing with this hot handyman who kisses like it's an Olympic sport and he's a gold medalist.

But then his hands mold to my ass, and nothing else matters but getting both of us naked faster than a duck on a June bug.

He tugs his t-shirt over his head, and I run my hands along his abs. Smooth skin, all those delicious ridges, and a deep *v* that disappears into his jeans.

Nash skims his fingers under the hem of my dress, teasing my inner thighs. "So soft," he murmurs. He stops just short of the silk covering my mound. "Tell me what you like..."

"You're doin' just fine."

I reach for his belt, but he stops me. "Not yet, sweetness. I'm gonna take my time with you."

The last thing I want is slow. My core has been clenched half the night, and my panties are soaked. "I need—"

Nash slants his lips over mine, silencing my plea. At the same time, he tugs on the tie at my waist. His kiss leaves me breathless, and when he lifts my dress over my shoulders, my nipples tighten to hard points under my bra.

"God. You're fucking gorgeous." Dropping to his knees, he kisses a line from my breasts to my navel, then stops to press his nose to my mound. "Do you taste as sweet as I think you do?"

"Until you lose the jeans, Mr. Fix-it, you'll never find out." I sidestep him, rounding the bed with a grin.

This isn't how I expected tonight to go. A little dancing, a lot of flirting, a quickie to break the tension between us, and then I'd send him home. But after watching him try his damnedest to nail more than eight different line dances, all those plans flew out the window.

Nash kicks off his boots, shucks his jeans, and stands before me in just his boxer briefs.

"Those too, darlin'." I flick open the catch on my bra but hold it in place and give him my best innocent smile. "Tit for tat."

"Or...tits for dick?" he counters.

I double over with laughter but manage to maintain my grip on my bra until I come up for air. And see Nash standing naked at the edge of the bed.

I work with some of the fittest men on the planet, and they've got nothing on the man in front of me. His dick juts from a patch of dark blond curls, and that six pack might just be an eight. But there's a softness to him that's *real*, that tells me he doesn't spend every waking moment at the gym, but still takes care of himself.

"I held up my end of the bargain. Your turn." The gleam in his eyes excites me, and I let my hand fall.

He looks at me like it's Christmas morning, but doesn't make a move to touch me.

"You like what you see?" I can't help the tremble in my voice. I've never been self-conscious about my body. Until now. I'm forty-three. And despite Hidden Agenda's rigorous training program, parts of me ain't as...*tight* as they once were.

He's on me in a single breath. Hands smoothing down my

arms, his cock pressing against my navel. His arousal scents the air, salty and a little sweet. God, I've only ever done this with one other man. What if I'm...bad at it?

But then Nash sucks one of my nipples into his mouth, and I can't think about anything but him. And what he's doing to me.

My body catches fire. Every nerve ending sparks to life under his touch. His fingers tease my mound. I'm ready to beg, but I don't have to, because Nash backs me up until my legs hit the mattress.

"Lie down." It's not a request. More like an order.

I don't want to let go of him long enough to comply, but I'm desperate for more. "Make me."

Nash scoops me up in his arms. "Never been one for that sort of thing, but I'd give it a shot. For you."

I wrap my legs around him, wriggling my hips until his dick nestles between my ass cheeks. "As long as you don't stop touchin' me, you can do whatever else you want, darlin'."

He lays me down like I'm a fragile, delicate, precious thing. Feathering kisses along my collarbone, he whispers all the things he wants to do to me. I'm not inexperienced. But I still blush knowing what's coming. I rake my short nails over his skin until he turns his attention to my lips. Our tongues battle for dominance, and I win. Flipping our positions, I straddle him with my hands on his chest.

"You ain't the only one with moves." I reach for my nightstand drawer—for the box of condoms I bought on the way home from Hidden Agenda—but he stops me.

"We're not there yet." Nash palms my breast, his thumb skating over one hard nub. "I still need to know what you taste like, and I want you so wet for me, you're begging."

"I don't beg." Even as I say the words, I know I'm lying. He's grinding his hips against me. Heat builds in my core, so hot, I'll catch fire if he doesn't strip me of my panties soon.

He chuckles. "There's a first time for everything." I silence him with my kiss until he plunges two fingers deep inside me and swallows my cry.

Fuck.

I thought my little black vibrator was the best invention on the planet—and maybe it still is—but it can't hold a candle to the man under me. He finds my clit with his thumb, rubbing circles over the tight bundle of nerves.

"Oh, God!" I come hard and fast, riding his hand like it's a prized bull until I can't take any more and collapse onto him.

Nash bands one arm around my back, the other still wedged firmly between my thighs. "I didn't think my 'moves' were *that* good," he says, a hint of amusement tinging his words.

My breath stutters with the last of my tremors, and I wriggle until I'm pressed to his side. Tipping my head, I find him staring down at me. "You're a damn genius with that hand. If you're half as good with your tongue..."

He crushes his lips to mine, and my brain short circuits as he proves his fingers aren't the only part of his body capable of bringing me to the very edge of the abyss. When he finally pulls away, I'm panting—and ready for more.

"These have to go," he says, tugging at my black silk panties. He sucks his fingers into his mouth—the same fingers that were just inside me—and light dances in his eyes. "We're just getting started."

Nash

Raelynn cries out, her back arching as I find her g-spot. She tastes like a rainy day, and her body comes alive with each flick of my tongue. My dick, trapped under me, aches in time with my heartbeat.

"Goddamn, Nash." Trembling fingers card through my hair, and I finish lapping at her essence and lift my head. "Are you goin' for a merit badge or somethin'?"

"Maybe." I get to my knees and wrap slick fingers around my length. Even the light touch is almost too much. I'll be lucky to hold out for a minute once I'm inside her. "How am I doing?"

"You passed. With flyin' colors." She tries to push up onto an elbow, but she's still shaking and collapses back against her pillow. "Shit."

"Easy, there." Gathering her in my arms, I try to maneuver her under the blankets, but she stops me with a hand to my chest.

"We're not done." Her deep, sultry tone dials my need up to a thousand. "Drawer."

I yank on the handle and find a box of condoms. Still sealed. "Fuuuuck." I shred the cardboard. Raelynn plucks one of the foil packets from my hand as I sit back on my heels.

"Easy now, darlin'. I've got you." She tears the wrapper with her teeth, and I'm so far gone, I can only watch as she strokes her hand over my shaft. Until her thumb traces a circle around my crown and my vision goes white. "Nash? Look at me."

I blink hard. Her entire body is flushed. Cheeks bright pink, rosy nipples begging to be pinched, her sex glistening from her release. "You're so damn beautiful," I whisper as I take the condom and roll it over my length. "Keep your eyes on me."

She sucks in a breath but doesn't look away. Not even when I slide halfway home and find her so tight, I'm afraid I'm going to break her.

"Tell me to stop," I manage, though I don't know what the hell I'll do if she does. Jerk off in her bathroom? Limp home with my balls so blue, they might as well be purple?

"I ain't fragile, Nash." She digs her short nails into my ass and pulls me closer. Deeper. She feels like heaven. Her heat brands me, and I'm not sure I'll ever be the same again. "Fuck me."

I don't know how long I'll last, but I can't refuse her anything. Not when she's staring up at me like I'm the only person in the whole damn world. "Hold on, sweetness. And remember..."

"Eyes on you."

After a single thrust, my lids flutter, and a whimper escapes Raelynn's lips. She's still holding on, and the pinpricks of pain so close to my crack are like lightning shooting straight to my dick.

It takes me more than a single breath to get myself under control, but I grit my teeth and fight my desperate need to come. "Want to make this last," I grit out.

"We have all night, darlin'." Raelynn wriggles her hips—as much as she can with me balls deep inside of her—and winks at me. "Show me what you can do."

As if I could resist a challenge like that.

Bracing my hands on either side of her head, I start to move slowly, hoping to draw this out as long as I can. But after only a few seconds, I know there's no fucking way I'm going to be able to hold back.

Despite my order—to keep her eyes on me—I wish I could look away. The connection between us scares me. This isn't just sex. I don't care that we barely know one another. This...is something more. Something my life has been missing for a very long time.

Raelynn hooks one leg around my thigh. The shift in

angle lets me go deeper, and my God. She's perfect. Wild and assertive and—for this one, brief moment—mine.

The pressure builds. Her slick heat, the way she whimpers with each thrust, and her unwavering gaze are so fucking hot, I can't hold on.

"Raelynn..." I manage.

She slides a hand between us, her palm skimming over her stomach and down...lower.

The quiet, keening cries turn to moans as she starts to play with herself. "God. I'm close, Nash..."

Thank fuck. It takes everything in me not to give in right now. My balls draw up tight, and my dick swells until her inner walls threaten to strangle me.

"Come for me, sweetness." I swivel my hips once, and the motion is enough to send her flying. Her entire body bucks against the mattress. The sight of her lost to her own pleasure is intoxicating.

With a shout, I give in, thrusting until I have nothing left, and all I can do is collapse onto my side, taking her with me.

CHAPTER ELEVEN

Raelynn

NASH SLIDES FROM THE BED. Relief washes over me, making my skin tingle. He'll leave now. I'll call him a Lyft. Hell, I'll drive him back home if he wants. Even if my muscles do feel like overcooked spaghetti.

The floorboards creak. Is he leaving without saying a word? I don't know why the thought makes my heart ache. Pillow talk is for people in a relationship. Not whatever we are.

Friends with benefits? Barely.

Strangers with chemistry? Closer.

Something in between?

I can hear him moving around downstairs. I should care what he's doing. But instead, I let my eyelids drift closed and pull the blankets up to cover my chest. It's been so long since anyone touched me. I didn't realize how much I missed it.

I'm almost sad this has to be a one-time deal.

Heavy footsteps on the stairs startle me awake, and I sit

up. Nash ambles back into the room, still completely naked, carrying a glass of water and one of my washcloths. He sinks down onto the bed with a sheepish smile, then pulls back the blankets.

"What the hell are you doin'?" I ask as he swipes the warm cloth over my inner thighs.

He freezes. "Taking care of you?"

"Why?" I snatch the cloth from his hand, suddenly feeling terribly exposed, despite how many times he made me come tonight. "I can take care of myself, Nash."

"Did I say you couldn't?" With a sigh, he scoots back, then grabs his briefs off the floor. Disappointment weighs me down when he pulls them on. He'll leave now, and that's for the best. At least that's what I tell myself.

But after a beat, he skirts the bed and slides under the covers next to me. "Everyone needs to be taken care of sometimes, Raelynn. It doesn't make you weak. Just...human."

Conflict churns in his eyes, like *he's* the one who needs tending, and I brush my fingers over the thick scar at his temple. "What happened here?"

Nash shies away from my touch, his gaze pinned to a spot on the wall behind me. "Car accident when I was a kid."

Liar.

"When?" I ask. He *wants* to tell me. Hell, I think he *needs* to tell me. But if I press him too hard, he'll shut down.

He runs his fingers through his hair, tugging the sandy locks down to cover the old wound. "You know when."

Shit.

"Fourteen. When your sister died." I squeeze my eyes shut, desperate for something to talk about that won't trigger his grief—or mine—until he settles closer to me and links our fingers over his heart.

"We were all together. I don't remember what happened.

Just Mom screaming. Dad..." He swallows hard and looks away. "I should have died too."

The raw edge to his voice is the God's honest truth, so why did I think he was lying before?

Pushing the thought aside, I cup his cheek, lean in, and brush my lips to his. "I spent a long damn time wishin' I'd been the one...in that godawful storm."

"Tell me about him," Nash says. "Brooks. What was he like?"

"I...can't. Not when I'm naked in bed with...you." Tears prick at my eyes. Thinking about the man I loved for half my life when I'm starting to fall for someone else ain't right.

Shoving my emotions down so deep they can't hurt me is getting harder every day.

Nash gathers me in his arms. I could get used to his warmth. To his scent. To the way he holds me. "Raelynn, when was the last time you let anyone *see* you? The real you."

I can't give him an answer. Not one I'm proud of, anyway.

"I've been alone most of my life," he says quietly. With my head tucked under his chin, I can't see the anguish on his face, but it bleeds through his tone. "I haven't been with anyone in...five years? Maybe six." He tightens his hold, and I don't protest the closeness. "I know what it's like to pretend you don't need anyone."

"We could stop."

Fuck. Why did I say that?

He sucks in a sharp breath. "I...can't."

Shifting so I can meet his gaze, I find panic. Fear. Pain. Everything I'm feeling, but so much more.

"If I can try...so can you. Stop runnin'. Put down roots here. We could...see where this goes."

"You don't know how much I want that," he whispers. "But it's not possible."

"You're a grown-ass man, Nash. Pretty sure you're capable of decidin' where you hang your hat and for how long."

He looks like a lost puppy. All sad eyes and sorrow. He can't even meet my gaze when he stands and starts hunting for the rest of his clothes. "I...uh...don't have a smart phone. Can you call me a taxi? Or a Lyft? I have cash. I can pay you back."

"No. Get back in bed." Turning away, I shut off the light and lie down. The lump in my throat warns me I'm about to break. I tried to let him in—I would have told him anything he wanted to know—and he won't do the same for me. "I'm tired, Nash. I'll drive you home in the mornin'."

He doesn't move. In the darkness, I can barely make out his profile. But his shoulders slump and I think I hear his jeans hit the floor. A few seconds later, the mattress dips.

I should keep my distance. But his heavy sigh does me in. Rolling over, I drape my arm around his waist and rest my head on his shoulder. "What are you runnin' from, Nash?"

His entire body stiffens for a single breath before he gets himself under control. "Nothing."

I could call him on the lie. I *should* call him on it. But he feels so good next to me, I can't. Not tonight. Maybe not ever. If this is all I can have of him, I'll take it. Until I wake up one day, and he's gone.

Nash

Dawn's gray light illuminates the room when I open my eyes. Raelynn's tangled locks tickle my chin. She's tucked against my chest, wrapped tightly in my arms.

I woke up once in the middle of the night to find myself curled around her lithe, warm body, and despite knowing I should leave, I couldn't force myself to let her go. Even with her words playing on a loop in my head.

"What are you running from, Nash?"

My past. My future. A real connection with this woman who's everything that's been missing from my life for more than twenty years.

This was a mistake. One hot, mind-blowing, perfect mistake. And I want it to happen again and again and again.

Harsh beeping makes us both jerk, and Raelynn groans. Swiping her phone from the nightstand, she taps the screen and blinks up at me, her lids heavy from sleep. "Sorry..."

Fuck. Her voice is a thousand times sexier first thing in the morning. "How long do we have?"

With a chuckle, she slides her hand over the bulge in my briefs. Her fingers are soft, warm, and gentle. So unlike mine. "Just long enough."

She straddles me, the sheets rustling around us. "You got anythin' against mornin' breath?"

Cupping the back of her neck, I pull her down so I can taste her lips.

"That answer your question?" I ask when I finally let her come up for air. Before she can reply, I roll one of her nipples between my thumb and forefinger. Her eyelids flutter. Her hips grind against me, and fuck. This is going to be better than last night. "On your back, sweetness."

She stretches out next to me. I can't get enough of her scent. Or the way her body responds to my touch. Trailing my lips from her collarbone to her mound, I ignore the ache in my dick.

Her heels dig into the mattress when I position myself between her legs and part her slick folds. She's already glistening for me. "So sweet," I say against her clit. "Never going to get enough of you..."

Raelynn sucks in a breath. Shit. Too much. Too soon. I

start tracing patterns over the tight little bundle of nerves, desperate to distract her from a promise I'll never be able to keep.

By the time she's panting, I'm barely holding on. "Inside me," she rasps. "Now."

I almost fall off the bed trying to shed my briefs. Rolling the condom over my length takes all my control. With a grin, Raelynn pushes me onto my back. "My turn to ride *you*."

Holy hell, I didn't think I could want her more than I did last night, but when she pins my wrists to the mattress, I realize how wrong I was.

She rolls her hips in such a way, I grit my teeth so I don't shoot my load in under a minute. Our gazes lock, and time stands still.

Until she releases my right hand. "Touch me, Nash. Make me come with you."

I find her clit as she squeezes her inner walls around me. My balls tighten, white hot pleasure consumes me, and when she cries out, I let myself fall along with her.

AFTER A SHOWER—WHERE we barely managed to avoid major injury with round three—I watch her pull on a pair of black leggings, a bright red sports bra, and a gray sweatshirt. "I've got somewhere to be in an hour. But I'll drop you at home first."

"When should I come back to work on your heater? Tomorrow? Tuesday?"

She tosses a glance over her shoulder. "I'm at the dojo from noon to six tomorrow. But if you get here by ten, I'll leave you a key to lock up when you leave."

I gape at her. "You'd trust me with a key...?"

"Some reason I shouldn't?" Raelynn finishes braiding her long, blond locks and turns to me, brows raised.

"Uh...no..." I take a step back under the power of her stare. "But you've only known me for a week."

She gives me the side eye, her hands on her hips. "I'm a good judge of character. And after yesterday," her voice softens, a hint of longing creeping into the tone, "trustin' you? It ain't a choice. I just...do."

CHAPTER TWELVE

Nash

"CAN I buy you a coffee before you go...wherever...?"

The ride from Raelynn's house was almost completely silent. Her confession seemed to confuse her, and she's been uneasy since we left.

Her gaze pings from the car's clock to me. "If I'm late, West will kick my ass."

I offer her a hopeful smile. "Looks pretty empty in there right now. And Teresa's working. She'll have you on your way in less than five minutes. Park around the back. There's always a space."

I can't read her. This morning, she was all sex and sass. Now, she wears her uncertainty like a second skin.

In the alley, I wrap my hand around hers, then lead her through the back door into the shop. A couple shares a scone at a corner table, and a woman with a laptop stares off into space by the windows, but it's otherwise quiet. Sundays usually are.

"Morning, Nash!" Teresa says with a wide smile. "What'll it be today?"

"I'll take a double espresso. Raelynn?" I squeeze her fingers, hoping the promise of caffeine will ease the discomfort between us.

"Quad shot Americano." Glancing around, she pulls her hand from mine when the bell over the front door jingles.

I gape at her. "And I thought *I* was addicted."

We both laugh, and suddenly, it's like the awkward drive never existed.

"If I show up to work one wheel down with the axel draggin' I'll never hear the end of it. I'm already on thin ice with West for—get *down!*" Raelynn shouts, shoving me, hard.

Teresa screams. Something grazes my cheek, stinging just below my right eye. I stumble, slamming my knee into the counter, and hit the ground.

By the time I look up, she's halfway across the shop, racing straight for a man in a black suit. He ducks around one of the tables, picks up a chair, and throws it at her.

Her slide is worthy of Major League baseball. The chair sails over her head and hits another table. With a whimper, Teresa scrambles into the stock room. Someone else—the woman with the laptop?—screams. I think the couple escapes out the front door. Raelynn tackles the guy and grabs his arm.

Something in his hand clatters to the floor. She lunges, but he punches her in the stomach, then shoves her onto her back. Wrapping his fingers around her neck, he growls, "Fucking bitch." But she escapes with one of West's signature Krav Maga moves—slamming her hands against his wrists while her knee crushes his nuts.

The guy falls over with a high-pitched yelp. "Ain't too bright, are you, asshole?" She flips him onto his back, but before she can pin one of his arms, he jerks the other up and catches her in the shoulder.

She goes down, and fear tightens a noose around my heart. "Raelynn!"

"Stay the fuck back!" In the second it takes her to glance over at me, the guy scrambles to his feet, grabs for something I can't see, and sprints for the front door. "Don't follow me!" she orders and takes off after him.

Like hell I'll stay here. I think...in his hand...he had a *gun*. But as soon as I hit the sidewalk, Raelynn jogs back around the corner.

"I told you to *stay inside.*" She takes my arm and steers me back into the coffee shop. It's empty. "Sugar? You still there?" she calls. "Teresa?"

The barista peeks her head out from the back room. Tears stain her cheeks. She's shaking so hard, I grab a chair and carry it over to her. "The police are coming," she manages.

I can hear Frank in my head.

"If trouble finds you, run."

He warned me so many times. Don't go over the speed limit or get a parking ticket. Don't talk to the police. No hospitals. Free clinics only. Nothing that could leave a trail.

Nash Grace might have a birth certificate, social security number, and expired driver's license, but he's a figment of "Uncle" Duncan's imagination. None of my paperwork will hold up if anyone looks too closely.

I edge toward the side door, three quick steps before I stop myself. What the fuck will Raelynn think if I bolt? And Teresa is still crying. I can't just walk out on her.

"Nash?" Raelynn fastens her hands around my biceps and holds my gaze. "I can't help you once the police get here."

"Help me?" I'm confused. "With what?"

She gives Teresa a sideways glance, then lowers her voice. "That idjit tried to kill you, and I think you know why."

My world grinds to a halt with all the grace of a semi truck. "No. That's not possible." Shaking off her hold, I take a quick step back. No one knows I'm alive. He couldn't have been after me.

First the car accident. Now this.

She stares at me, disbelief shining in her eyes. "If he'd been a better shot, you'd be dead." After a beat, she shakes her head. "You want to keep your secrets? Fine. For now. Go upstairs and lock the door. I'll come get you when I'm done."

I don't move until she forcibly turns me toward the back door and gives me a light shove. Duncan. I have to call Duncan. He'll know what to do.

He'll tell you to run.

Every step feels like I'm carrying a thousand pounds on my shoulders. Raelynn's voice carries after me, and I stop to listen. "When the police show up, sugar, you tell them that asshole came in, shot at *me* and you went to hide. We clear? I don't know where the other folks got off to, but everythin' happened so fast, they probably didn't see shit."

"You don't want them to know Nash was here?" she asks with a tremble to her voice. "Why not? Is he in trouble?"

"I don't know. But you can be damn sure I'm gonna find out."

Shit.

I can't stay here. She let me have my secrets last night, but now, they've put her in danger too.

Flipping the lock, I sink down onto the floor and clutch my backpack to my chest. My hands shake, but I find my old flip phone and dial the number Frank made me memorize twenty years ago. I hope to God it still works.

Raelynn

The sirens get louder as I text West.

Raelynn: Got some trouble brewing. Won't make it to the warehouse today.

Three dots dance along the bottom of the screen. In less than two minutes, I'll be elbow deep in cops, so he better be quick.

West: What kind of trouble? And where?

My first instinct is to tell him I can handle this on my own, but after our *talk* yesterday...I have to give him something.

Raelynn: The kind that walks into a coffee shop in broad daylight with a silenced pistol. And takes a shot at Nash.

Lights flash along the ceiling from the black and white pulling up to the curb.

West: I'm on my way with Ry. Fifteen minutes.

Raelynn: I want to talk to Nash first. Alone. I'll meet you at Ry's when I'm done here.

The dots start bouncing again, but I slide my phone into my back pocket as the officers push through the doors. West is gonna be pissed at me, but there ain't much I can do about that. Once I unravel *this* mess, I can try to salvage a single scrap of the SEAL's trust.

Half an hour later, I trudge up the stairs to the studio. Teresa did great talking to the police. Despite how shaken up she was, she didn't say a word about Nash. It helped that she fled into the back room after two shakes and hardly saw a thing.

Nash opens the door, his hair sticking up at all angles, and ushers me inside. "They don't know about me. Right?"

I tilt my head and give him the side-eye. "If they did, don't you think they'd be up here by now? They think the guy came after *me* because I cut him off on the freeway. Just some deranged idjit with anger management issues. Barely worthy of filin' a report."

Some of the tension leaves his shoulders. "Thanks. Is Teresa okay?"

"She will be. Adam just got here. He closed the shop and he's gonna take her home. And he doesn't know you were there either. You can thank me for coverin' your ass by tellin' me why someone would want you dead. And why you're scared of the police."

Nash shoves his hands into his pockets and moves to the window, peering out a small crack in the drapes. "I'm not... wanted or anything."

"Well, that's a start. But if you believe that guy was shootin' at anythin' but you, you're a damn fool."

"I'm nobody," he says. His voice might be only a whisper, but I can still hear his desperate need for the words to be true.

"Sure. And I'm Elmo." With a huff, I glance around the studio. There's nothing personal here. A plate standing up in the rack next to the sink, two shirts and a pair of jeans hanging in the closet, and his backpack sitting on the small couch. The rest of the space is pristine.

"Do you even live here? Because this," I say, gesturing around us, "ain't sellin' the 'I'm not wanted' bullshit you're feedin' me."

He flinches, shoulders hiked halfway up to his ears. "I move around—"

"A lot. I know." Anger simmers just under my skin. After what we shared last night—and this morning—I can't believe he's still lying to me. "I shouldn't care *what* you are, Nash. But I do. And I can help. If you let me."

A black strap peeking out of the closet catches my eye. I cross the room in three steps and find a small duffel bag almost full to the brim. Right on top? The shirt he was wearing yesterday morning.

"You're runnin'." Those two words scare the piss out of me. I'm about to lose him, and I don't know why. "We have somethin'. I know you feel it too. But you're about to throw it all away."

He strides over to the door, pain rolling off him in waves. Staring down at his feet, he pauses with his hand on the knob. "I have to. Please, Raelynn. Just go. I'm sorry I didn't get a chance to fix your heater. Or...spend another night with you. But...it's better this way."

"Better?" I gesture to the cut on his cheek from the ricochet. "A couple of inches to the left and I'd be mournin' you..." The lump in my throat swallows my words. I can't do this again. Losing another person I...care for would put me in the ground faster than a prairie fire with a tail wind. "You think runnin' is gonna keep you safe? That asshole wasn't some amateur. You're up shit creek, Nash, and I've got a goddamn boat."

"If you get involved..." He shakes his head, still refusing to look at me. "I'll call you. In a day or two. But right now, I need to leave." The sorrow in his voice is like a knife to my heart.

In my back pocket, my phone buzzes incessantly. West, I'm sure. Or Ryker. I'm shocked they haven't burst into Nash's apartment in full riot gear already.

Fuck this. He might not be willing to fight for us, but I am.

I dig into my bag for my house key, stalk over to him, and shove him until his back hits the door. "You've got two options. One. You pack up the rest of your shit and go to my place. You've clearly been runnin' for a long damn time, so I reckon you know how to check for a tail. Make sure you're not bein' followed, park at least three streets away, get inside, lock the fuckin' door, and wait for me there."

He lifts his gaze to mine. "And two?"

"Come with me and pray the men I'm gonna introduce you to don't kick both of our asses six ways from Sunday."

He'll be as welcome as a skunk at a lawn party at Ryker's condo, but at least there, I know he'll be safe.

Nash's shoulders slump, all the fight leaving him so suddenly, I can almost *hear* it.

"You should let me go, Raelynn." He cups my cheek, skimming just under my eye with the rough pad of his thumb. Leaning closer, he kisses me with such tenderness, tears threaten.

"Yellow don't suit me one bit," I manage when he pulls away. My voice wobbles, and I clench my free hand so hard, it shakes. Pressing the key to his palm, I hold his gaze. "I don't think it's your color either. So what's it gonna be?"

The fear in his eyes twists my stomach into knots, but eventually, he closes his fingers over mine. "Your place. For one night only. Tomorrow, I'm gone."

I tighten my jaw until my teeth scrape against one another. "We'll see about that. If anyone comes knockin' but me, there's a false wall in the back of my closet. Leads to a reinforced crawlspace. Hide there and don't make a peep until you hear me say 'wildflowers.' You understand?"

His brows furrow, and he takes a step back. "A false wall? Who the hell are you?"

I press my fist over my heart, needing to soothe the ache in my chest. "Someone who can help." My phone keeps vibrating, and I groan. "Get your things. We're swappin' cars, and I need my bag out of the trunk first."

We don't speak again until Nash has thrown his duffel bag and backpack into my rental. The late morning sun doesn't leave many places to hide, but I'm still on high alert. "If you spot a tail, call me immediately. Got it?"

He nods, slides behind the wheel, and peers up at me. "What you said earlier...about trust?"

If we have this conversation now, I'll lose my shit, and that won't keep him alive. Slamming the door, I pin my gaze to his. "Trustin' and believin' ain't the same thing. I trust that you're a good man, Nash. But lie to me again, and we're through."

CHAPTER THIRTEEN

Raelynn

My phone stops buzzing just before I get to Nash's car. That ain't a good sign, but I don't bother checking the messages. In one half less than no time, Ryker and West can cuss me out in person.

Less than ten minutes later, I pull into the underground garage and stop at the heavy gates. It takes a twelve-digit code, a fingerprint scan, and a ridiculously complicated passphrase for the system to let me in, but I find a parking spot right next to the elevator.

Ryker owns this whole building, and the man is fanatical about his security. I have to repeat the process—with a completely different passphrase—before I can access the top floor where he and Wren live. Half of Hidden Agenda calls this place home. Graham and Q—his boyfriend—Ripper and Cara. Wyatt and Hope. Some days, I wish I'd taken Ry up on his offer to move into the last empty unit on the seventh floor. But I wanted a back yard. A porch. Privacy.

I don't have to knock. The second I step off the elevator, the condo door opens.

"About damn time," Ry snaps. "Unless you're dead in a ditch somewhere, you answer your fucking phone."

"Give me a goddamn break. I'm here, ain't I? Had to get the cops to believe my bullshit story and convince Nash not to rabbit first." I stalk into the large, open concept living room and move directly to the floor-to-ceiling windows looking out over downtown.

"Raelynn?" West comes up behind me and touches my shoulder. I jerk away, but my foot lands on something soft—and squeaky.

With a yelp, I stumble and crash into Graham. The younger man wraps an arm around my waist to keep me upright.

"Whoa. It's just one of Pixel's toys," Graham says. "You okay?"

No. Not even close. Okay is a thousand miles from here. Or more. Somewhere I don't have to face these men who insist we're family and admit the guy I *just* slept with is in trouble—and a liar.

I push Graham away, sidestep West, and narrowly avoid the fluffy, white dog who came running when I stepped on her stuffed ducky.

"Sit down." Ryker stands between me and the sofa, his arms crossed over his broad chest. At almost seven feet tall and more than three hundred pounds of hard, scarred muscle, he leaves me no way to get around him. "And talk."

"Fudgesicles. Give the poor woman some space." Wren shuffles into the room, one hand rubbing her *very* pregnant belly, and the other pressed to her lower back. "She's not the enemy, remember?"

"You're supposed to be resting." Ryker reaches for his

wife's arm, but she shoots him a look that could cool the fires of hell.

"If you had your way, I'd never do anything *but* rest. I'm fine. My doctor said the baby and I were both perfectly healthy just two days ago." Wren gives Ryker a little shove. "Get Raelynn some coffee. She looks like she needs it."

The big man stares down at her like she's his whole world, presses a kiss to the top of her head, and ambles into the galley kitchen, grumbling the whole way.

"I'm...fine," I protest. But I'm suddenly so tired, my knees threaten to buckle, and I sink down onto the couch.

"You're obviously not." Wren lowers herself to the cushions next to me. "Ry said someone shot at you?"

I shake my head. West and Graham take seats across from us. Ryker sets a cup of coffee in front of me. I can't look at him. At any of them. If I do, they'll see everything. The anger. The hurt. The betrayal.

"I wasn't the target," I say softly, staring into the dark brew. "The guy was aimin' at Nash's head."

"Who's Nash?" Wren asks.

My cheeks catch fire. God, I wish this mug were bigger so I could hide from West's stare. "He lives above Broadcast. I, uh, drove him home this morning. That's the only reason he's still alive."

West chokes on a sip of his coffee. "You drove him *home*—"

I straighten and set my mug on the polished wood coffee table. "If you're gonna give me shit, you can go straight to hell."

The SEAL holds up his hand as Graham asks, "You bought a car?"

Ryker's chuckle sounds more like a hoarse grunt than anything else. "*That's* your first question? 'You bought a car?'"

Graham glances from me to West to Ry and back again before understanding dawns in his eyes. "Oh. Never mind."

"You're going to tell me all about this guy and how you met him later," Wren says, her lips quirking into a smile for a hot second before she reaches for her laptop. "But right now, I need his full name."

"I...*fuck*." Dropping my head into my hands, I kick myself so hard, I'll be sore for a week. "He's just...Nash. I never..." My eyes start to burn. "Goddammit!"

Wren wraps her arm around my shoulders. "Raelynn, breathe. We'll figure this out. What *do* you know about him?"

"Nothin' worth spit, apparently. He can fix things. Moves around a lot. Drives a Honda that's older than dirt. And is currently parked in the garage downstairs. He's got my rental car." I rattle off Nash's license number. "And he's runnin' from somethin'. Or someone. But that's all I've got."

"Nash Grace," West says, and I lift my gaze. He's holding his tablet and shows me the intake paperwork from the dojo.

"Did he list an emergency contact?" Wren's fingers fly over her keyboard, and in under a minute, Nash's expired driver's license photo appears on screen.

"Nope. All I've got is his address above the coffee shop." West sets the tablet down and runs a hand through his dark hair. "You didn't leave him there, did you?"

I jerk up straighter and glare at him. "I got enough sense not to spit downwind, y'know. I sent him to my house. The shooter took off in a black BMW—I didn't catch his plate number."

"He make it to your place yet?" Ryker asks. "You *do* have cameras set up, right?"

My patience is about gone, but I manage not to roll my eyes at the man. "Yes, I have cameras. No, he's not there yet. It's a twenty-minute drive." Blowing out a breath, I give voice to the fear that's settled like a stone in my gut. "Assumin' he ain't on his way to Canada right now."

Ryker pulls out his phone. His big fingers move over the screen with a grace he shouldn't possess. "Tank? I'm sending you Raelynn's address. Set up a perimeter—two blocks in every direction should do it—and report anything suspicious." Hanging up, he cuts his multi-hued eyes to mine. "Gut answer, Raelynn. How much trouble is this guy in?"

I'm so tired, so utterly worn out, all my defenses fall away. "More than hell and half of Texas? I don't know much about his past. One sister, died when he was fourteen. His folks are gone, from what I can tell. God, I'm such an idiot. I got no right to ask y'all for help—"

"Are you a member of this team?" Ryker asks, pushing to his feet so he's towering over me. Anger lends a harsh edge to his tone and a muscle in his jaw ticks.

"Yes." I jerk up to put us on equal footing, though I'd have to stand on the couch for us to be even close. Ryker stares at me, brows raised, daring me to challenge him. No one else moves. Even Wren's stopped typing. "What do you want me to say? That I feel somethin' for Nash? That I don't know his last name, but he needs our help? That I'm scared he won't be there when I get home and I'll never see him again?" My voice fails me on the last word, and I'm barely holding on to a shred of control.

Ryker McCabe is the toughest man I've ever met, and I'm about to break down in front of him. He'll never trust me again after today. I wouldn't trust me either.

Just when I expect him to snap, he presses his lips together and sighs. "I want you to understand you can say all of it. Or none of it," he adds, his voice almost gentle. "This team *works* because when one of us has a problem, we all have a problem. You might think you're keeping us at arm's length, Raelynn, but when you needed help, you came here. So stop with the 'I got no right' bullshit and let's get to work."

All I can do is nod. Shock muddles my thoughts until Ryker takes me by the shoulders and turns me back toward the couch. "Sit. While Wren does a deep dive into Nash Grace's background, tell us everything you can remember about the guy who tried to kill him."

Nash

I flip the last breaker and hold my breath. The overhead lights flicker briefly before there's a loud *pop* and I'm left shrouded in semi-darkness lit only by a battery-operated floodlight in the corner of the basement.

"Shit." I shouldn't be working with electricity, but what the hell else am I supposed to do? Duncan hasn't called me back, Raelynn is still God-knows-where, and I have no idea who she's talking to or what she's telling them.

It doesn't matter that she can take care of herself. That she tackled the gunman like a professional football player. If he works for the DeLuca family, he'll be back. And he'll bring friends.

Kiki meows from the stairs. He darted inside as soon as I unlocked the door. Raelynn's going to be pissed. Though I found a delivery from the local pet store on her porch when I got here, and the new litter box is all set up in the corner of her living room.

"I know. I'm an idiot," I mutter. "I should get in the car right now. I could be in Coeur d'Alene by dinner." With another meow, the sleek black cat turns and races up the stairs, leaving me all alone.

I sink down onto one of the storage trunks along the west wall. Coming here was a mistake. The more time I spend with Raelynn, the more I want to stay in Seattle—long term. By tomorrow morning, will I be able to let her go?

You have to. She deserves so much better than a guy whose entire life is a lie.

The truth hits me like a tidal wave, pulling me under and sapping the strength from my body. I slump back, wishing I'd never left my apartment the night of the storm.

But then...what would have happened to Raelynn? Alone with a busted bike, a sore shoulder, and a fear of thunder and lightning?

"You can wish all you want, but what's done is done. It's up to you now—what you do with the life you have."

One of Frank's favorite sayings. Especially when I was a kid. Mad at the world. At him. At my parents. At...myself.

I have to stop wishing and start *doing*. Leaving is going to hurt, but it's the only way to keep her safe. Pushing to my feet, I make it two steps before I remember the blown circuits.

It's barely noon. Disconnecting the heater won't take me long. I can fix what I broke and still be on the road in half an hour.

As I reach for a screwdriver, my phone rings. I don't recognize the number. "Hello?"

"This is Duncan." The connection crackles, but even after all these years, I recognize his voice.

"It's...uh...your nephew from Chicago."

He pauses, static the only indication the call hasn't dropped completely. "Shit. This is a secure line, kid. What's wrong?"

I tell him everything. Except there's not much to tell. The hit and run in the parking lot of the hardware store could have happened to anyone. And despite Raelynn's take on the shooting, maybe the guy *was* just a robber looking for an easy target.

"Am I overreacting? It's been twenty years. Why would they come after me now?"

"Are you somewhere safe?" Duncan asks.

My mind is still racing through all the different ways the DeLuca family could have found me. Not a single one of them makes any sense.

It's only when Duncan says my name that I realize he asked a question. "I think...yes. I'm safe."

"Good. That's a start. I can send a marshal to your location, but I'd rather keep this 'off the books.' I'm in Italy with my wife, and it's almost 8:00 p.m. here. I can get a flight first thing tomorrow. Where are you?"

"Seattle. Should I leave? I can start driving right now."

"No. As long as whoever shot at you this morning doesn't know where you are, stay put. It'll take me at least eighteen hours to get to you, but once I'm there, we'll figure this out. Together." His voice takes on that patient, placating air all fathers seem to master—though I don't think he has kids of his own.

The low-level panic I've carried with me for the past few hours starts to fade away.

Duncan promises to call when he lands, and after I apologize for ruining his vacation, his voice softens. "Frank would never tell me much about your life, Nash. We both agreed it was safer that way. But I never forgot about you. I'll see you soon."

I swallow the thick lump in my throat as the call disconnects. Kiki pads down the stairs and starts winding around my ankles. "You lonely, little guy?" He's purring so loudly, I can *feel* it. "You're not the only one."

Leaving Raelynn tomorrow won't be easy. But I'm going to

make the most of the time we have left. One more night to last me a lifetime.

Raelynn

Inara—who showed up half an hour ago with four bags of burgers, french fries, and shakes from Dick's Drive-In—puts the finishing touches on the charcoal portrait. "This the shooter?"

I lean in to peer over her shoulder, impressed. "Damn close. Where'd you learn to draw like that?"

"Needed something to keep me sane while I was deployed." She shrugs and adds some shading to the man's neck. "One of the guys in my unit was an art major before he enlisted. Another used to take the comic books his mom would send and trace every panel over and over again. I stuck to landscapes for the first couple of years, but somewhere around my fiftieth kill..." She stares out the window and shakes her head. "I don't regret a single shot. But I wanted to remember their faces."

"Why?" I shouldn't ask. The former Army Ranger sniper carries the weight of the dead every single day. She never told me her number, but it's got to be north of a hundred.

Inara passes me the sketch, sorrow lending a shimmer to her gray eyes. "Because they were people. Terrible, violent people who would have killed me, my unit, and thousands more, but still...people."

I wish I knew what she needed me to say. We've never really *talked* outside of our missions together. Hell, I've never done much more than shit talk over a game of foosball with anyone. I thought it was better that way. But in this moment, I wonder if I've been wrong this whole time.

West is at Broadcast, getting the security camera footage from the cafe. Wren moved to a plush, zero-G recliner with her laptop and just found some of Nash's high school records—from Denver, Colorado.

"That was Graham," Ryker says, shoving his phone back into his pocket. "By the time the sun goes down, he'll have eyes on every inch of the building. If anything bigger than a mouse gets within half a block of Nash's apartment, we'll know. Ripper's still with his shrink, but as soon as he gets back, he'll be all over the security camera footage."

I sink against the cushions, staring at the face of the shooter. Ry's memory palace lessons are tedious as fuck, but without them, I'd be holding a blank page. Or at best, looking at a stick figure in a black t-shirt and black leather gloves. Carrying a silenced Nighthawk Custom GRP.

"Pass me the drawing?" Wren asks. At Ryker's pointed glower, she sits up and reaches for his hand. "You know I'd be climbing the walls if I couldn't work, right?"

"Doesn't mean I have to like it." Despite his words, his voice gentles, the tone reserved just for Wren. Until I met her for the first time—a few weeks after I joined Hidden Agenda—I couldn't imagine anything or anyone softening Ryker McCabe.

Seeing them together has always reminded me of everything I've lost. But now, I realize what I've found is more important. The entire team dropped everything to help me. Wyatt and Hope are even on their way back from his cabin in the mountains—just in case.

Every time West talked about family, I pulled away. Family was for the rest of them. They'd been together longer. I was the probie. The outsider.

But now, I'm starting to realize they never saw me that way. They shared parts of their lives with me, pulling me in so deep, I'll never escape. But for the first time since I joined Hidden Agenda, I don't want to.

Nash could be my second chance at happiness. Though we're still new, though we both have secrets that could destroy whatever we're building, there ain't a damn thing I won't do to keep him safe.

Even if he walks away.

CHAPTER FOURTEEN

Raelynn

I STARE at a wall of food and water bowls, not truly seeing any of them.

"I don't think Nash Grace actually exists."

Wren's words play on a loop in my head. *"He's got the smallest electronic footprint of anyone I've ever seen. No tax records. No credit cards. Bank accounts will take me some time, but I'd expect at least an email address or two."*

All the little inconsistencies I ignored in our conversations are giant red flags now. He moved around a lot, but his mom had a stove like mine. His dad looked for a replacement "for years."

His "Pops" would pick a new place on the map every year, but "we were all together" in the accident that killed Mae. *"Mom screaming. Dad..."*

So, instead of going straight home, I'm agonizing over whether Kiki's gonna care if his food bowl is covered with tiny fish or paw prints.

Cowardice ain't a good look, so I grab the closest set of

matching bowls and head for the cashier. What the hell am I supposed to say to Nash when I get home?

Hi. I'm part of an elite group of mercenaries who travel all over the world to save people who need it. So, do you need savin'?

Or maybe something more direct.

You've been lyin' to me from the day we met. Nash isn't even your real name, is it?

"That'll be thirty-two-fifty," the woman behind the counter says. "Are you a member of our rewards program?"

"No. And I don't want to be." Cringing when the cashier's smile fades, I rush to add, "Sorry. I'm havin' a day. I'll sign up next time."

The twenty-minute drive to my house feels like it takes an hour, but when I see the rental car in the driveway, I start to relax for the first time since the shooting.

So why can't I go inside?

Because once I do, I could lose him.

You could lose him anyway. Stop stallin' and talk to him.

I sit in Hidden Agenda's SUV for another few moments, forcing myself to breathe deeply. I can do this. I have to.

It's quiet when I finally work up the nerve to go in. Until Kiki comes racing up the stairs from the basement, meowing the whole way.

"Nash took pity on you, didn't he?" The cat rubs against my ankles, purring up a storm. The stress of the day hits me —hard—and I scoop him up and bury my face in his soft fur.

When a pair of strong arms wrap around me, I swallow the sob welling in my throat.

"I was worried." His lips brush my cheek. "Are you okay?"

Kiki wriggles free, and I turn in Nash's embrace. "You're the one who almost died." The cut on his cheek is bright red, and I brush my fingers under the wound. "This is gonna get infected. Come with me."

Leading him into the kitchen, I point to the breakfast nook. "Sit. I'll get my first aid kit."

"Raelynn..."

I silence him with a single look. "Let me do this, Nash. Before I have to ask you why the best hacker on the planet can't find any evidence you are who you say you are."

He drops his head into his hands. "I didn't want to lie to you."

"But you did." Sliding onto the bench next to him, I wait for him to look at me before I dab an antiseptic pad over the cut. To his credit, he barely flinches. "What's your real name?"

"I've been Nash Grace for twenty years. That *is* my real name."

Two butterfly bandages close the wound but now that I have him trapped by the built-in table, I don't make a move to get up. "Not the one you were born with."

"Nathan," he says, his voice barely above a whisper.

"Nathan...what? I can't help you if you don't talk to me." If I could stop, I would. The pain etched on his face is enough to break me. Or break us.

"You can't help me at all. Not with this." His fingers flutter over the thick scar at his temple. "You have to let me go, Raelynn. If you're right, and that bullet was meant for me, staying in Seattle is a death sentence. For both of us."

"It doesn't have to be." Slamming the lid on the first aid kit, I get to my feet. It doesn't surprise me when Nash—Nathan?—scoots out from behind the table and edges toward the door, but a part of me aches that he's so ready to give up on what we have.

One perfect night and a handful of lies. That's all you have, and he knows it.

"I don't work at the dojo." The admission tumbles from my lips. He stops, a deep furrow between his brows. In the afternoon light streaming through the kitchen window, he looks so much older than his thirty-four years. The sun highlights a few strands of gray in his stubble and casts shadows on the exhaustion lines around his eyes.

"Then why are you there almost every time I take a class?" He rubs a hand over his chin, fear churning in his eyes. "Oh, fuck. You were watching me."

"No!" I reach for him, but he turns and sprints for the front door. "Nash! Wait!"

Kiki darts in front of him, nothing but a black blur. Nash skids on the rug and goes down, landing on his ass with a rough, "*Oof.*"

I'm beside him before he can scramble to his feet, grabbing his arms and straddling him. "If I were gonna hurt you, I'd have done it last night."

All the fight leaves him, and he stares at me, equal parts defeated and...turned on. Canting my hips, I find the hardening bulge in his jeans.

"Raelynn..."

I push him down onto his back, my hands straining over his biceps. His lips part in an invitation I should refuse, but after the truth comes out—mine and his—we might not get another chance.

He's not gentle. Catching my lower lip between his teeth, he bites down hard enough I gasp. Heat floods my core, desire burning even hotter when I see the feral, raw need in his eyes.

"Let go." His voice is a low rumble, one I feel more than hear with the way my heart's pounding.

"Not if you're fixin' to run."

In a move he must have learned from West, Nash hooks his leg around mine, throwing me off balance so he can flip our positions. Rough fingers scrape over my neck. "Not running."

His hand at my throat is the hottest thing a man has ever done to me. I have the button on his jeans undone in a heartbeat. "Take these off. Right now."

Nash shifts so he can kiss a line from my jaw to my collarbone. "Tell me what you want me to do to you."

"Fuck me," I manage.

"Not good enough, sweetness. I need more." He grinds his hips against me, and Lord have mercy, I'm wound tighter than a fiddle string.

"I want your tongue against my clit." I moan when he pinches my nipple, and arch my back for more. "You make me so damn wet."

"How wet?" His hand slides down my body, into my pants to tease my soaked folds.

"You did that to me, Nash. And I'm the one who needs more." Pushing up his shirt, I rake my short nails over his back. "Off. Now."

The flannel hits the floor, followed by his shoes, jeans, and tight black briefs. I'm still in my sports bra and leggings —too many damn buttons and hooks to keep up—but Nash takes over, stripping me of the rest of my clothes in just a few seconds.

The coarse fibers of the rug scrape against my back. Nash grabs my thighs and jerks me closer. The first sweep of his tongue pulls a moan from my lips.

"That's it. Let me hear you," he says, scoring his teeth over the small bundle of nerves at the apex of my thighs. Time starts to blur as he takes me to the very edge of my control time and time again.

"Nash...please."

He tightens his grip on my legs. "Please...what?"

"Let...me...come!"

With a low growl, he sucks my clit between his lips. The

vibrations send me flying. Before I can come down, he's on top of me, swallowing my whimpers with his kiss.

I dig my fingers into his ass cheeks, trying to get him inside of me. It's the only thing I want. All I can think about.

Nash stops me with that damn hand to my throat. His fingers skim my jaw, almost gently, and he touches his forehead to mine. "I don't have a condom. We can go upstairs—"

"Are you clean?" I should put a stop to this. Or agree to take this to the bedroom. But, I need him to answer me. Even in the haze from my release, I'll know if he's telling the truth.

Pulling back enough he can look me in the eyes, he nods. "I got tested a couple of years ago. Haven't been with anyone since."

"I have an IUD and I'm clean. Let me feel you, Nash. All of you."

His eyes turn feral, and his crown nudges my entrance. "Be sure, Raelynn."

Wrapping my legs around him, I urge him deeper. "I am."

Nash

Staring up at the ceiling, I can't remember how we ended up in the living room. "That was..."

"Hot as hell?" Her voice is rough. Raspy. I close my eyes and replay the words on a loop, memorizing everything about her. All those Texas sayings that mean nothing and everything at the same time. Her smile. Her rich, sultry laugh. The way she bites her lip right before she comes.

Nothing's changed. After tomorrow, I'll never see her again. Whatever we do now...tonight...is for the last time.

My muscles feel like Jell-O, but I manage to pull up my briefs and stagger into the kitchen. Running warm water over a dish towel gives me a moment to think, but it's not until I return to the living room and swipe the cloth gently over her thighs that I feel steady.

"This is important to you, ain't it?" she asks. Her hand covers mine. "Takin' care of me after?"

"Yes. It is." I ball up the damp towel and toss it onto the concrete in front of her fireplace. "Why does it make you uncomfortable?"

"No one's ever tried..." Her eyes shine, a single tear threatening to spill over. "But even if they had, I would have stopped them. I ain't good at this."

"At what?"

She shrugs into my flannel, then finds her panties. "Bein' with someone. Trustin'...anyone."

We're the same. More than I thought—definitely more than I want to admit—but maybe that's why we found each other. If only that were enough to keep us together.

Her phone buzzes twice, pulling a sigh from her lips. "There's a whole lot we need to talk about, but doin' it naked...ain't a good idea." She tosses my jeans at me, then levels me with a hard stare. "I'll put on a pot of coffee. Don't leave."

Without waiting for a reply, she gathers up the rest of her clothes and stalks into the kitchen.

Kiki watches at me from the couch as I tug on my pants. "If I didn't know better, I'd say you *tried* to trip me." The cat meows once before he rests his head on his paws and starts to purr. "Thanks," I add. "Make sure you watch out for her, okay?"

I don't expect an answer. I *definitely* don't expect him to jump down and pad into the kitchen. Raelynn starts talking to him, her voice softer and a little higher pitched than usual. I'm glad she won't be alone anymore. Even if I do wish *I* were the one moving in.

Warm air flows from the ornate vent on the wall. A few seconds later, Raelynn's startled, "Holy shit! You...fixed it?" makes me grin.

"What else was I supposed to do while I waited for you?" I take the mug she hands me. Once she sinks down onto the sofa, I grab a seat next to her.

Her smile fades, and she stares into her cup. "Nash? Or... should I start callin' you Nathan?"

My mug wobbles as I take a sip, and hot coffee burns my tongue. After I choke it down, I swallow the lump in my throat. "Nathan died a long time ago. Even if I could bring him back, I don't know that I'd want to."

"Why did...he...die?"

"It's better if you don't know." We're swimming in dangerous waters with this conversation. Any hope she'd let me have my secrets dies when she sets her coffee cup down hard enough the table rattles.

"We are *not* doin' this again. You don't need to protect me, Nash. Not when I'm tryin' to protect *you!*" The fire in her eyes would be enough to convince me she could—if I didn't know just how ruthless the DeLuca family could be.

"You can't. No one can."

Raelynn jerks to her feet and holds out her hand. "Come with me."

"Where?" I don't know why I'm asking. My fingers are already linked with hers, and I let her lead me up the stairs to her bedroom. "Not that I mind another round, but—"

"We ain't here so you can hang your hat on the door." She sweeps a handful of dresses and shirts to the side of her closet, then presses on the dark wood wall. It pops open to reveal a space big enough for a person to hide in. And...is that metal lining the panel?

I didn't even *think* to come up here while I waited for her.

Though if I had, I might have taken off for Idaho immediately.

"When I told you about this earlier, you asked who the hell I was. I've been tryin' to tell you ever since." Moving the clothes to the other side of the closet, she presses a finger to the lock on a five-foot-tall safe. Inside are two large black bags, half a dozen pistols, four rifles, and several stacks of cash.

"Holy shit."

A few wisps of hair have escaped her braid, and she tucks them behind her ear as she locks the safe and starts to pace. "Protectin' people is my job, Nash. I *don't* work for West at the dojo. I work *with* him—and a whole mess of other folks—doin' K&R."

"I should know what that means..."

"Kidnap and ransom. We save people. From some of the worst som'bitches in the world. The guy who brought us all together, Ryker, is retired Special Forces. Same with Ripper. West and Wyatt were SEALs. Inara and Tank were Army Rangers. Graham did a stint in the Coast Guard. Wren's the best hacker in the world. And that's only the team we have in Seattle.

"I can protect you, Nash. It don't matter if you're runnin' from one man or a whole country's goddamn government. I'll keep you safe."

CHAPTER FIFTEEN

Raelynn

WHILE THE CAT devours his first indoor meal, I pull a cube steak out of the fridge. After I told Nash what I do for a living, he only asked one question.

"Do all of those people—the ones you work with—know about me?"

My answer—yes—wasn't what he wanted to hear. He said he needed space, so for the past two hours, he's been down in the basement, putting my electrical panel back together.

Ryker's number flashes across my phone screen, and I pop in one of my earbuds. "Yeah?"

"Tank is set up at a hotel two miles away. He and Graham will take shifts watching the traffic cameras in your area. If your security system goes off, they can be there in under five minutes. West and Inara are staying at Nash's place tonight in case the shooter comes back. You got anything new?"

I angle a glance into the living room—at the basement door. "He's scared, Ry. If I push him too hard, he'll run."

"So that's a no."

"It's a maybe." Pulling out the flour, seasoned salt, and pepper, I try to decide how much to tell him. "Wren was right. He wasn't born Nash Grace." Ryker's silent long enough, I finish beating the eggs before I crack. "No. I don't have his real name."

"When this is all over, you're getting a refresher course on interrogation. From Trevor."

I cringe. The former CIA assassin is one of the only men in the world scarier than West and Ryker. Last week, I would have cussed Ry a blue streak for implying I'm not doing my job. But instead, I ask, "Do you trust me?"

He doesn't hesitate. "Yes."

"Then give me until tomorrow. He'll talk to me. But it has to be his choice. When *he's* ready."

Ry grumbles something unintelligible, then sighs. "I'll check in at oh-eight-hundred. But if you don't have anything by then, I'm paying you a visit. With *both* the SEALs."

He hangs up before I can say another word. "That went well."

"What has to be my choice?" Nash asks. I drop the large piece of steak, and it hits the counter with a *splat*.

"Shee-it. I didn't hear you come in." I nod at the fridge. "Lettuce, tomatoes, cucumbers, and ranch dressing. Take care of the salad, will ya'?"

"Answer my question first."

"That was my boss." I fiddle with the knob on my ancient stove until the flame catches, then slide the cast iron skillet onto the burner. "He asked for an update. I didn't give him one. Not one he wanted, anyway."

Nash stares at me for a beat, then moves to the fridge. "So my name...?"

"I'm walkin' a very narrow line, Nash. The folks I work with are a family. One I didn't ask for. But they all dropped everythin' to help me—and you—today. I didn't ask them. I didn't have to. Until you give me the okay, what you told me stays between us. But we can help you. If you let us."

I finish dredging the steak and wipe my hands. Nash is quiet as he washes the lettuce and cuts the vegetables.

"Bring all that to the table. I got beer and Dr. Pepper. Help yourself to whatever you want. The gravy takes ten minutes."

He twists the cap off a bottle of Shiner Bock and leans against the wall, watching me recreate another of my mama's recipes. "Nathan Rossi. Son of Angelo and Stella Rossi."

"That name supposed to mean somethin' to me?" I steal a sip of his beer and pull the steak from the pan.

"Twenty years ago, the Rossi family controlled more than fifty percent of all illegal gambling in Chicago."

I whistle. "Organized crime. So the car accident...was a mob hit."

"There was no car accident," he says, shaking his head. "That was a cover story. My family was murdered."

Nash

She doesn't push. Doesn't demand I tell her everything. Just ladles thick gravy over the chicken-fried steak and carries the plates to the table. "Grab me a Dr. Pepper, will you?"

This isn't how I imagined the conversation would go. "You're not surprised."

"Darlin', there ain't nothin' in this world that surprises me anymore. Not since I joined Hidden Agenda."

I cut into the steak, unsure how to process the past twelve hours. I haven't thought about food all day, but I'm suddenly ravenous. "Nothing?"

"My first mission, we had to go rescue Graham's boyfriend. His ex kidnapped him, drove him to Utah, locked him in a basement, and kept him drugged out of his mind for two full days, all to steal his company. A few months later, a French cartel ordered a hit on one of their former members. She had enough evidence to put the leaders away for a dozen lifetimes, but they got to her first. Tortured her for more than twenty-four hours. We stopped them."

"Stopped them?"

Raelynn pauses, a piece of steak halfway to her mouth. "Yes. They made their choice."

Shit. She killed them.

Uncertainty tightens her expression. "What we do—what *I* do—is dangerous. We go up against the worst of humanity, and sometimes, people end up dead. If you can't be with me knowin' that, I'll understand..."

Leaning across the corner of the table, I cup the back of her neck and brush my lips to hers. It's barely a kiss. The briefest of touches. But when I sink down again, some of the worry has faded from her eyes.

"My father was the oldest son. He had a younger brother who was all in with the family. But Dad...he didn't want anything to do with it."

"How well did *that* go over?" she asks.

I take a long pull on my beer. "Better than you'd expect. My mom was pregnant with me, and my grandfather just... agreed. Dad went into real estate and until I was twelve, everything was great."

Raelynn's tongue darts out, swiping a drop of gravy from her lips, and for a moment, I forget all about the danger I'm in. "What happened then?"

"I don't know all the details. But a member of the United States Marshal's Service showed up at our house in the middle of the night, and suddenly, we weren't the Rossis anymore. Two days later, we moved into a rental in

Minnesota with new names, new schools for me and Mae, and a whole new life."

Peeling the label from my beer bottle, I shake my head. "Mae hated every minute of it. She was too young to understand. Hell, we both were. But Dad told me a little about the family 'business' when I started acting out at school. He said he needed me to understand we couldn't go back. Things had just started getting better when..."

Raelynn reaches for my hand. I twine our fingers, holding on tight. If only her touch could keep the nightmares away. Or stop the DeLucas from coming after me.

"Mae started having night terrors after we left home. When they got bad, she'd come into my room and ask me to tell her a story. I heard her cry—just for a second—and got up, but she'd left Bandit on the floor, and I stepped on him."

"Bandit?"

My backpack sits on a chair a few feet away. I don't know why showing Raelynn the old stuffed animal is suddenly so important. Maybe it's a way to delay the inevitable. Or maybe I need her to know what the little guy means to me.

Gently, I pluck the sloth from his special pocket. "This is Bandit. He's...all I have left. I never go anywhere without him. It's stupid. But..."

Raelynn's face shimmers as my tears threaten.

"I slipped on him. There was this shadow, and then my head hurt so much. Mom screamed, and Dad...he was begging for our lives, but..." My fingers brush over the thick scar at my temple. "Two bullets. I was lucky." The word tastes bitter on my tongue. "The shooter thought I'd died. Dad's handler found me—found all of us, he said—and didn't tell anyone I was alive. I woke up in the hospital three days later."

Raelynn scoots her chair close enough she can wrap her

arms around me. It's too much. I don't deserve her comfort. Not with Mae's cry echoing in my memories.

"I wish I'd died with them."

"Nash..." She rubs circles over my back, Bandit squished between us. "You have to know they wouldn't have wanted that."

I jerk away, knocking my chair over with a loud *crack*. Bandit tumbles to the ground, but Raelynn rescues him and cradles him to her chest. "What about what *I* wanted? Dad's handler was so worried the DeLucas would come after me, he didn't put me back into the program. Instead, he convinced his old partner to adopt me. To run. And to *keep* running for the next twenty years. That's who Nash Grace is. A figment of someone's imagination. With a fake social security number and a perfect backstory, but no friends. No family. No home. Nothing that makes life worth *living*."

Raelynn rises and presses the stuffed animal into my hands. "You have this. And you have me."

"Not if the DeLucas have anything to say about it."

"Did you miss the part where I'm gonna help you?" she asks. "Because I thought I was pretty damn clear about that."

"This is *the mob!*"

"Oh, for fuck's sake." She pulls out her phone, fingers flying over the screen for half a minute before she offers me the device. "*This* is Hidden Agenda."

Venezuelan President Manuel Farias Ousted in Overnight Coup. Infamous Prison La Crypta Emptied and Destroyed.

The news story is vaguely familiar. I'd been living in New Mexico when it happened. One of the guys I hung out with at the local Home Supply Emporium had grown up in Venezuela, and he'd told me how bad the former president had been for his country.

"This...?"

"Happened eight months before I joined." She purses her

lips and swallows hard. "About a year after Brooks...died. It was Ryker, Austin—he's got his own group of badasses now—Ronan, out of Boston, Dani, Graham, and Leo. Along with Wren and Ripper workin' from here."

"You took down the government of Venezuela."

She offers me a grim smile. "Damn straight. You ain't alone, Nash. And you don't have to run ever again. You just have to trust me. And my...*shit*. My family."

Raelynn

Tucked against Nash's side with Kiki stretched out over our legs, I feign interest in the movie he chose—some horror flick about a robot doll who goes on a killing spree—so I can play our earlier conversation back in my head to get the details straight.

He doesn't have any idea how the DeLuca family could have found him. He's been careful his whole life, and there's nothing tying Nash Grace to Nathan Rossi—at least nothing he knows about.

If there is, Wren will find it. I texted Ryker an hour ago and told him we'd be at the warehouse by 9:00 a.m. so Nash can meet the rest of Hidden Agenda.

Unless he sneaks out of the house in the middle of the night.

Nash twirls the end of my braid around his finger while, on screen, the cute little robot with the human face decapitates the babysitter. "Sweet Jesus."

He chuckles, presses a kiss to the top of my head, and pulls me closer. "Not a horror fan?"

"Give me the first *Halloween* movie any time," I whisper. "This...is somethin' else."

Pausing the film, he shifts so he can meet my gaze. "It's been so long since I've had *this*."

"What?"

Longing creeps into his voice, the emotion so strong, I can *feel* it. "Someone to sit with. To watch a movie with. In a place that felt like...a home. Not since I was a kid."

He's about to break, and if I'm honest, so am I. Kiki meows when I ease him onto the cushion next to me so I can wrap my arms around this man I'm falling for.

"You can have it here," I whisper.

He holds onto me like I'm his whole world. "I called Duncan. My dad's handler. I didn't know what else to do. He'll be here tomorrow. But...he'll tell me to leave. I know he will."

Tears prick at my eyes. "You don't have to. We can keep you safe."

"Raelynn..."

"No," I say sharply, pulling back to glare at him. "Don't give me that self-sacrificing bullshit. *You* get to decide what happens with the rest of your life. Not the DeLucas, not this Duncan idjit, not even me. So what do *you* want?"

He's silent for the longest time, and I can't breathe until he squeezes my hands. "To see where this goes."

It takes a full minute for the lump in my throat to fade away. "Me too. When Brooks...died—and I couldn't save him—I decided bein' alone was for the best. I was wrong."

"Tell me about him. Please?" There's no pity in his eyes. No judgment. He truly wants to know about my life...before. Steeling myself for the painful memories, I think about the man I fell in love with at seventeen. To my shock, my heart doesn't feel like it's about to crack in two. Instead, a warmth blooms in my chest, spreading through my limbs. We lived a lifetime in twenty-two years, but he's my past. And my future—Nash—is right next to me.

"Brooks and I started datin' in high school. He asked me to marry him on our graduation day." I smile at the memory. "Got down on one knee and everythin'. I was hell bent on goin' to the Air Force Academy, but he'd torn his ACL twice playin' football and couldn't pass the medical exam. We had a quickie ceremony the day before I left and he went to work on his daddy's cattle ranch. Every chance I got, I came home to Texas to be with him."

"How long did you serve?" Nash settles against the cushions, but his eyes never leave mine.

"Ten years. I missed him too damn much to stay in another day longer. By then, he'd taken over the ranch, so we ran it together. We were happy—doin' what we loved every day, even tried to start a family."

"You wanted kids...?"

With a nod, I snuggle back against his side. "A whole mess of them. But we both had some...issues...and cattle ranchin' ain't a rich man's game. IVF was too expensive, so we made our peace with it bein' just the two of us."

Nash's warmth, his scent, the way he holds me like I'm the most precious thing in the world...everything's easier with him. Even talking about Brooks, who was once my everything, with the man who's becoming all that and more.

"The night he died..." I shudder, and Nash tightens his arm around me. "The storm was a real toad strangler. Pastures flooded, and one of the fences came down. He was fixin' it while I rounded up the herd. I didn't see him get hit. Thunder spooked his horse and I was chasin' him down. By the time I got back to Brooks, he was barely breathin'." My tears spill over, and I don't try to stop them. Not this time. "He died in my arms."

I don't know how long we stay locked together. Long enough for me to stop crying, for my eyes to burn. For the gaping wound in my heart to scar over.

"I thought I was doin' fine here," I say quietly, tipping my head so I can look him in the eyes. "But I was wrong. What I feel with you...*for* you...it's like I'm livin' again for the first time in years."

His rough hand cups my cheek, his fingers sliding into my hair as he leans down to claim my lips. The kiss is tender, gentle, and everything I need in this moment.

"There's a difference between living and being alive," he murmurs. "I'm not sure I realized what it was until I met you."

CHAPTER SIXTEEN

Nash

South Seattle is full of warehouses like this. Big. Gray. Nondescript. Some have stripes of color. Others...nothing but broken, boarded-up windows and weeds poking through cracks in the asphalt.

Hidden Agenda fits right in. Paint peeling in spots, more than one of the dozens of windows along the roofline covered in plywood, and most of the white lines in the parking lot worn clean off.

Raelynn takes my hand, and I wonder if she's as nervous as I am. Or if she's worried I'm going to bolt.

"We'll keep you safe," she murmurs as we approach the door. "It's what we do, and we're damn good at it."

More than once last night, I woke to find her staring at me in the darkness. Every time, I told her I wouldn't run, but what if I don't have a choice?

Inside, I stop short. "Whoa. This is..."

Every inch of the place is sparkling clean. A climbing wall stretches all the way to the ceiling directly in front of me, with a boxing ring, a complete set of free weights, and two pull-up bars next to it.

In the far corner, three men and a woman banter in a kitchenette with stainless steel appliances and shiny black counters, while a dozen feet away, a petite redhead leans against the biggest man I've ever seen, his hands spread across her very pregnant belly.

Almost as one, they turn toward us.

"Welcome to Hidden Agenda," Raelynn says quietly. "Come on. I'll introduce you."

I clutch my backpack tighter. Bandit, my cell phone, and five hundred dollars in cash are tucked safely inside. She doesn't know about the cash. If I have to run, I have what's most important to me.

Except her.

She'll stay here. With her family. Where she's safe.

It's obvious who's in charge. The massive, scarred man who looks like a mountain with an attitude problem. But every single one of the men and women standing in front of me look like they could kick my ass. Even the pregnant redhead.

"Nash." West steps forward, offering me his hand, and though he *should* be a friendly face, all I can think about is how I lied on the dojo's intake form.

"Hey."

The big, bald one stares me down, and between that and West's iron grip, I'm starting to think this was a very bad idea.

Raelynn starts with the introductions. "Inara," she says, gesturing to a woman with short black hair and pale gray eyes. "Then there's Graham, and Tank, out here from Boston."

One by one, the others step forward to shake my hand or meet my gaze with a nod.

"Wyatt is the big lug with the beard. But don't be

surprised if we all start callin' him 'probie.' Right?" She shoots West a look.

The former SEAL grumbles what might be a "yes" and I glance at Raelynn, confused.

"Rite of passage," she says. "Newest member of the team gets hazed for *at least* a year. Or until someone else joins. I've been the goddamn probie for way too long."

"I'm Wren," the redhead says. Her giant protector softens his gaze, staring down at her with such adoration, it's obvious they're completely in sync. "And the grumpy, yet lovable mountain of granite behind me is Ryker."

"I thought we agreed," Ryker grumbles, "you weren't going to use the words lovable, teddy bear, or 'puddle of goo' to describe me in public anymore."

"*You* agreed." Wren tips her head back to smile up at the big man. "*I* merely agreed not to tell anyone what happened when you saw the ultrasound for the first time."

She winks at Raelynn and traces a single finger down her cheek.

"Little bird..."

The last man in the room steps out from behind the couple, a big German Shepherd at his side. He's bulkier than West, but shorter than Wyatt and Ryker. His dark eyes shift between me and Raelynn, and he sticks close to the mountain of muscle with an attitude. "That's Ripper," Raelynn says, but stops me when I offer to shake. "He doesn't..."

"Oh." I shove my hand into my pocket. "Sorry, this is all kind of overwhelming. I haven't met this many people at once in...years." If I hadn't promised Raelynn I'd listen, that I'd give this family of hers a chance, I'd have been out the door two seconds after we walked in.

My admission seems to ease Ripper's discomfort, and Ryker gives the other man a terse nod before turning back to me. "So, Nash Grace...want to tell us who you really are?"

West clears his throat. "Ry, maybe we move this to the command center? Pretty sure Wren would like to get off her feet."

"Fuck. Sorry, little bird. Sit down and relax." Ryker slides his arm around Wren's shoulders and guides her to a plush recliner. Several couches, low tables, and lamps give the area a comfortable, lived-in look—if it weren't for the three large flat screen monitors along the wall.

Wren sinks down with a sigh. "I only have another month of this," she says, her green eyes flicking to mine as she rubs her belly. "Then it's all sleepless nights and diapers and watching this one," she pats the big guy's hand, "turn into a—"

"Don't say it," Ryker warns. "Or I'll cancel tomorrow's ice cream delivery."

She tips her head up and bats her eyelashes at him. "You and I *both* know you'd never do that. You love me too much."

He leans over to press a kiss to her lips. "This kid is going to ruin my reputation. Let's get started before West has to scrape me up off the floor."

Wren aims a remote at the wall, and two of the three screens flicker to life.

Oh, shit.

The first one has my driver's license, records from my last two high schools, and a grainy, live video feed of the alley behind my studio. On the middle screen, there's a sketch of the man I think *might* be the one who came after me yesterday alongside a mug shot of him from years earlier.

"What is all of this?" I ask.

"Everything we were able to find about you," Wren says. "Which isn't much."

"High school transcripts? How the hell did you get those?"

"Took me all of ten minutes." Wren picks up a keyboard

from the side table. "But in twenty, I should have been able to find your bank accounts, credit cards, email addresses, lease agreements, and job history."

"I don't have any of that stuff." I turn to Raelynn, confused. "Why was Wren searching for *me*?"

"Because you're the one that asshole shot at," Ryker snaps. "Diego Ruiz. Arrested in Rockford, Illinois ten years ago for assault with a deadly weapon. But before the case went to trial, the evidence mysteriously went missing."

"So, he walked?" Raelynn asks. "Where is he now?"

Wren and Ryker exchange glances. "We don't know. Diego's been off the grid for more than a year and a half. His last known place of residence was an apartment on the south side of Chicago."

My gut clenches, and ice fills my veins. "The DeLucas lived on the south side of Chicago."

"Who?" West sits up straighter, and the whole team is suddenly *very* interested in what I have to say next. Time to come clean and hope it doesn't backfire on me.

"I was born Nathan Paul Rossi. Son of Angelo and Stella Rossi. Grandson of Giovani Rossi, head of the Rossi crime family."

Raelynn

I pull a can of Dr. Pepper from the fridge and pop the top. Nash talked for two hours—amid all the questions Ryker and West had for him—before Wren needed a break. Graham and Tank are picking up Thai takeout, but they won't be back for at least another twenty minutes.

Nash wanders over to the climbing wall and runs his fingers over the lowest of the handholds.

"Want to go up?" I ask when I'm only a few feet away. "I can give you a lesson."

"You climb this thing?" Nash turns to me and shakes his head. "Of course you do."

"Three days a week for over a year. Before I jacked up my shoulder. Only been up a handful of times since then." Grabbing a harness, I toss it to him. "We've got a few minutes. And safety gear."

He glances over at his backpack sitting next to the couches, his shoulders suddenly hiking halfway to his ears.

I cup his cheek, urging him to look at me. "No one's going to mess with your stuff here, Nash. Rip might scan it for bugs later, but we have a wand for that."

His eyes widen. "Bugs?"

Shit. That was the wrong thing to say. Clasping his shoulders, I hold his gaze. "Just a precaution. Like West and Inara stayin' at your place last night."

As if he's suddenly realizing the lengths I'll go to in order to keep him safe, Nash surges forward, his arms banding so tightly around me, I stifle a yelp. "Thank you."

"Put me down," I hiss. "Before someone notices."

"No." He backs me up against the climbing wall, kissing me until one of my team—Wyatt, probably—whistles loudly.

Flames lick up my cheeks, but I don't push him away. "They're all gonna tease me about this for months."

"Oh?" He closes his teeth over the shell of my ear and tugs until I shiver. "Do you care?"

"Not one bit." Sliding my hand up to his neck, I touch my forehead to his. "I know this is a lot. Bein' here. Trustin'... anyone after so many years. But you're doin' great."

"I don't know how I'm going to explain any of this to Duncan."

Shit.

I'd almost forgotten about the former U.S. Marshal Nash

called yesterday. "Do you know when he's landin' yet?" Ryker's gonna be pissed—and there's no way in hell he'll agree to bring the man here.

Nash pulls out his phone and checks the screen. "No service?"

I take his arm and guide him to the door. "Signal jammers. We have to get outside."

Anger radiates from his entire body as he stalks after me. Sunlight blinds us for a moment until we round the corner of the building.

"What the fuck, Raelynn? I can't stay here without my phone. Duncan's on his way, and if he can't reach me when he lands—"

"Calm your shit. The jammers only work on outsiders' phones. Ours...are special. Text him and give him my number. He can call me when he lands. It'll ring through, and you'll be able to talk to him."

Nash stares at me for so long, I start to worry. He doesn't know which way is up, so far out of his comfort zone I wouldn't blame him for snapping like a fiddle string at any moment. But he cracks open the phone and sends the message.

"He said he'd be on the first flight. How long does it take to get here from Italy?" The man looks like a lost puppy, and the confusion in his eyes twists my heart into a knot.

"Goin' west, you got headwinds to consider. But with the time change, you make up time. There ain't many direct flights from here to Italy. Wren might be able to work some magic if he's already gone through customs. Let's go back in."

Before we make it to the door, a motorcycle roars to life. Inara speeds past us, a large duffel bag strapped to the back of the bike. "Inside. Now." I grab Nash's hand and pull him with me as I take off at a run.

"What's wrong?"

"That's Ry's bike. He don't lend it out on a whim. Inara needed to get somewhere fast. Either somethin' happened with her husband or there's shit goin' down..."

We burst through the door and make a beeline for the command center. The rest of the team is huddled around the large table. Tension hangs so thick in the air, I can taste it.

The monitors along the wall show different views of Nash's studio. On the center screen, Diego Ruiz opens the closet and curses.

"You have...cameras in my apartment."

West looks up, his blue eyes devoid of all emotion. Shit. "As of last night, yes. And it's a good thing we do. Keep the chatter to a minimum. I'm calling Adam."

He sets his phone on the table and puts it on speaker.

"West! What's up?"

"Listen *very* carefully. Pretend I'm an old friend you haven't talked to in years. And don't let anyone hear my side of the conversation. Got it?"

Adam pauses for a moment, then clears his throat. "The last time I heard from you was...the summer after graduation."

"Do *not* react to what I'm about to say. A man just broke in to the studio upstairs. Nash is with me, but when the asshole doesn't find him, he'll probably come back into the shop. How many customers do you have right now?"

"Uh...maybe half a dozen."

This is gonna go south faster than greased lightning if Adam doesn't get his shit together. He's not trained for this.

West glances up at Ryker, who mouths, "Eight minutes."

"I've got someone on the way. Until she gets there, I need you to do exactly what I say. We're talking about our upcoming high school reunion. Got it?"

"What the hell is she going to do about...the decorations?" He whispers to someone else to take over, then mutters under his breath, "This is fucking ridiculous. Tell me what's going on."

"Can't. Not yet." On screen, Diego stalks out the door. "He's leaving the studio. I'd lay odds he's on his way back to you. Tell him you expect Nash any minute. Give the dude a free coffee. Suggest he wait upstairs. Be friendly, don't let on you know what he was doing, and get him out of the shop and away from your customers."

"Fine. But you're going to tell me—hang on a minute," Adam says. He must cover the speaker, because his next words are muffled. "He wasn't up there? Sorry, man. He said he was just going to the drugstore. Hang out in the stairwell. Otherwise you might miss him. Shouldn't be more than another five minutes."

The seconds drag out for what feels like an hour before Adam swears under his breath, the sound suddenly clear again. "I think he's going back upstairs. Who is he and what the *hell* is going on?"

"Put the phone on the counter but don't hang up," West says. "Inara will let you know when she's neutralized the threat. But until you hear from her or me, do *not* go back upstairs."

Adam calls his name more than once, but West jabs the mute button as Ryker tosses me a comms unit. The device is so small, it all but disappears in my ear. A second one sails through the air for Nash. "Listen only," he says sharply.

I tap his earwig once, muting the sophisticated bone-conduction mic, then hand it to him. "What's Inara going to—"

"One minute away." Nash flinches at Inara's tense whisper in his ear. "Golf? Tango? Status report."

"Right behind you," Graham says.

"Take him alive, Indigo." West cuts his gaze to me for a split second. "If you can."

Nash's fingers dig into my forearm. "If she can?"

I tap my own earwig so I can talk to him without distracting the rest of the team. "She ain't goin' for a walk in the park. This guy tried to kill you. Hush up." Any other time, I'd pull him aside to explain, but she's less than thirty seconds away from the stairs. So I take Nash's hand and hold on tight, all the reassurance I'm able to give in this moment.

"Stairway's clear," Inara says quietly. "Is the target inside?"

"Negative." Ryker slams his fist down on the table, rattling Wren's laptop and West's phone. "He bolted. Golf, Tango, perimeter check. Three blocks in every direction."

"That's it? He's...gone?" Nash looks from Ry to West to me, all the color draining from his cheeks. "Maybe he was just a thief. You can't be sure he's working for the DeLucas."

"Oh, we're sure." Wren points to the center monitor. "Inara just sent this picture of your front door."

The screen flickers, the camera feed dissolving to reveal a switchblade pinning a piece of white paper to the wood, the point dead center of the single hastily scrawled word.

Nathan.

CHAPTER SEVENTEEN

Nash

A LARGE DOOR swings open at the far corner of the warehouse, and Inara rolls Ryker's motorcycle inside. "Your back tire caught a nail," she calls over her shoulder. "*Before* I took her out. Pressure's still good, but you'll want to fix it ASAP."

"Son of a bitch," Ryker mutters. "Wyatt, you good with driving my truck home when we're done here?"

"Don't you mean 'probie'?" Raelynn asks.

"Not yet." Wyatt ambles over to the kitchen—it's the only word for his slow, loping gait—and pours himself another cup of coffee. "I'm here in an advisory capacity only. For now."

Raelynn gives him the side eye. "What the hell does that mean? And I'll take a cup if you're pourin'."

"Hope's having a bad week." He fills a second mug and sets it in front of her. "She's still having a lot of pain from the cracked vertebrae. The doc's coming over in the morning. Until he takes a look at her, I'm sticking close to home."

"Shit. Sorry." Raelynn cradles the coffee to her chest and inhales deeply before glancing over at me. "You doin' okay, darlin'?"

"No." Pulling out my phone, I check the screen. I keep forgetting about the signal jammers. "Dammit. Why hasn't Duncan called yet?"

"Who the hell is Duncan?" Ryker asks, suddenly appearing right next to me.

I take a step back so I can stare up at him. Both of the big men are terrifying in their own way. Wyatt's been quiet. One or two word answers, delivered in a gentle South Carolina twang that would reassure me if it weren't for his steely-eyed stare. But Ryker...he's lethal. In every way.

"You gonna answer me, *Nathan?*"

Raelynn slides between the two of us, shoving at Ryker's chest. "His name is Nash. Nathan died twenty years ago. And you need to back off. He's here, ain't he? Cooperatin'?"

"Then why is this the first I'm hearing about some guy named Duncan?"

I can't let Raelynn fight my battles for me. Not all of them, anyway. "He was my dad's handler. I told you about him."

Ryker stares down at me. His eyes are the oddest mix of colors. Hazel, blue, green, even a few streaks of bronze, and they change with the light. "Not his name."

"You're wrong—" The second the words leave my mouth, I know they're the wrong thing to say. So does everyone else. West straightens and slaps a hand against Wyatt's chest so the other man doesn't move, and Wren swivels in the plush recliner.

"Wrong?" With a single step forward, Ryker makes me feel like I'm only two inches tall. "I remember *everything*, Nash. Your mother's maiden name was Meadows. You lived at 231 Millstein Avenue back in Chicago. At the Junior High State Championships, you took first place in the four hundred meters with a time of forty-six point five-two seconds, and this—" he points to a jagged scar along his cheek "—came from a Kershaw Launch 1 blade on day three hundred and ninety four of my time in Hell."

Holy shit.

"So I know for a fact you never mentioned Duncan's name. 'My dad's handler showed up in the middle of the night and told us to pack enough clothes for a week.' Your exact words. And now you're saying not only is this handler still alive, but you *called* him?" Ryker cuts his gaze to Raelynn. "And you knew about it?"

I step in front of her so his wrath is centered on me. "What the hell else was I supposed to do? Someone took a shot at me. I was alone and scared. I didn't know what Raelynn did for a living or that you all," I wave my hand toward the men and women standing behind Ryker, "would be willing to help me. Duncan was the only person in this world I could think of who still gives a damn about me. So yes. I called him."

By the time I finish my tirade, I'm shouting. Not smart as Ryker could snap my bones without breaking a sweat, but I'm so sick of feeling like a bystander in my own life, I can't hold back my anger.

"About fucking time," he snaps.

"F-for...what?" I shoot Raelynn a look, but she's as confused as I am.

"For you to show some goddamn backbone. Raelynn's half gone over you, and until now, I couldn't understand why."

West sidesteps Ryker and claps a hand on my shoulder. "When was the last time you felt in control of your life, Nash?"

"Never." The truth hits me, hard. My first instinct is to bolt. Take off out the door and run until even *I* don't know how to find myself again. But then I catch sight of Raelynn out of the corner of my eye. She's holding onto that coffee cup like it's a shield, her expression equal parts pride and fear, and I know running isn't the answer.

I want a life here.

"What Ry's trying to say—"

"For fuck's sake, Sampson. I don't need a goddamn translator." He runs his palm over his bald head. "Not anymore." Staring down at me with both hands on his hips, he arches a single brow. "Every single one of us—including Raelynn—fought to be here. To survive. She deserves someone in her life who'll do the same."

"I've got food!" Graham calls from the door. "Get it while it's...nowhere near hot?" His arms are laden with two large paper bags from one of Seattle's best Thai restaurants. "No trace of Ruiz. Tank's sitting on Broadcast in case he comes back. I'll go relieve him in a couple of hours."

"Oh, thank Goldilocks," Wren says. "The baby wants curry."

I turn to Raelynn. "Goldilocks?"

"Wren doesn't swear." She smiles, some of the light returning to her eyes. "Not like the rest of us. You get used to it. Fudgesicles is my favorite. And spitsnacks. You'll figure it out. Eventually."

Everyone beelines for the kitchen. As soon as no one's looking our way, she reaches up to cup my cheek. "Ry...wasn't wrong. He never is. Annoying as fuck."

"You're 'half gone over me'?" Sliding my hand down to cup her ass, I give it a quick, hard squeeze. Her smile lights up my whole world. "Good. Because I'm falling for you too."

"This him?" Ripper angles his laptop toward me. "Duncan Wilder?"

The years haven't been kind to the man I once called "Uncle Duncan." His white hair is styled in a terrible combover, and heavy bags gather under his eyes. "Yes. How'd you find him?"

It's after four. Wyatt took Wren home an hour ago. West and Inara spar in the boxing ring, while Tank races Raelynn up the climbing wall. Ryker's on his way back with the motorcycle after getting the tire fixed.

The haunted man across the table from me shakes his head. At his feet, Charlie, a big German Shepherd with a mangled ear, whines until Ripper reaches down to scratch the dog's head. "Wasn't easy. Hacking the Marshals Service would take a week—even for Wren—so we've been working with approximate age plus what little you could remember about his visits and hitting the DMV in every state on the eastern seaboard."

"What about his flight?" Raelynn's phone sits between us, completely silent. I checked it five minutes ago, but that doesn't stop me from tapping the screen again. No messages. No calls.

"There are a hundred ways to get from Italy to Seattle. I set an alert for customs, but if he's in the air, he'll land before I can hack my way into even a single airline." Ripper meets my gaze for a split second before he returns his focus to his screen. This is the most he's said all day, but he's clearly uncomfortable. With me? Or with everyone?

Raelynn lets out a triumphant yell as she slaps the ceiling at the top of the climbing wall. "Hot damn. Pick up the pace, probie!"

Ryker, who walked through the door moments ago, stares up at her. "Tank's only here for another week, you know."

Pushing off the wall, she floats to the ground—some sort

of rappelling system controlling her descent—and brushes her hands on her thighs. "He's one of us, ain't he? That makes him the probie even if he does work for Second Sight. All y'all can start callin' me by name any time now."

"Second Sight?" I ask.

Ryker strips off his leather jacket and drops down into a chair next to Ripper. "You all right, brother?"

"Fine. Answer the man."

So Ripper doesn't like talking to anyone.

With one big hand on Ripper's shoulder, Ryker leans in and lowers his voice to a whisper. I pick up Raelynn's phone and turn away, giving the two men some privacy. In one of the quieter moments after lunch, Raelynn told me they served together but that Ripper "went through some shit" before he came home. Given the scars covering every inch of Ryker's exposed skin, I can't imagine what additional hell would qualify as "some shit."

"Getting some coffee," Ripper says. He sways when he pushes to his feet, and I think his right hand shakes until he balls it into a fist. But he recovers quickly and strides to the kitchen. Charlie trots after him.

Ryker stretches his legs out and crosses them at the ankles. "Eight years ago, my ODA team was captured. They held us for fifteen months." He gestures to his face. "Fuckers couldn't stand how handsome I was."

Am I supposed to laugh?

"You weren't handsome," Ripper calls from the coffee pot. "You were pretty."

"Asshole." One corner of Ryker's mouth twitches. "Three of us survived. Rip...got the worst of it. For another six years. Thanks to a sadistic fuck in Afghanistan and a couple of low-life JSOC shitstains. Dax and I didn't talk for a long damn time. He started a security firm in Boston, and I came out here. After we got Rip back, we realized we could do more—save more people—if we merged our two companies."

The phone buzzes on the table, and I scramble for it.

"Huddle up!" Ryker says sharply. "And put the call on speaker."

Raelynn slides into the chair next to me and rests her hand on my thigh.

"Duncan?"

"Whose number is this?" He sounds tired. Wary.

"It's...a friend's. Are you in Seattle? Tell me where and I'll come to you."

"I got a room at The Pinnacle Hotel. But we shouldn't meet here. It's too dangerous for you to be moving around. I rented a car. Give me your address."

I look from Ryker to West. What the hell am I supposed to say? I can't bring him *here*.

"Mr. Wilder." Raelynn leans closer to the phone. "Nash is stayin' at my place. I can have him to the Pinnacle in twenty minutes, and I guarantee no one's gonna find out he's there."

"You told someone about me? About the DeLucas? Dammit, Nash. Frank taught you better than that." He mutters under his breath, his words too muffled to hear. After a heavy sigh, he continues. "Fine. I need to check around the area first. Give me an hour. The elevators are locked unless you have a keycard. I'll be in the lobby when you get here and we'll go up to my room. But leave your lady friend at home."

"Lady friend?" West chuckles when the call drops. "He's going to regret that."

"Damn straight. Nash? You're ridin' with me. I'm gonna give Duncan a piece of my mind."

Raelynn

The lobby of the Pinnacle Hotel has seen better days. "Ain't no one here," I say quietly, trusting my comms unit to relay the update to West and Ryker.

"Not even the target?" West asks.

"Nope." Taking Nash's hand, I give it a reassuring squeeze. "Whiskey, you find his rental car? I got a bad feelin'."

"Whiskey?" Nash stares down at me, confusion furrowing his brow.

After a quick tap to my earbud, I drape my arms around his neck. The only people here are the front desk clerk and a twenty-something woman at the bell desk who can't weigh more than a hundred and ten pounds soaking wet. "We only use code names in the field. Whiskey, Romeo, and I'm Sierra."

"So that makes me November?"

"You're bright as a new penny, darlin'." After I turn my mic back on, I add, "Base, any chance you can hack the hotel database and find out what room our smooth-talkin' Mr. Wilder is in?"

"Not without their IP address. But even if I had it, you'd be faster," Rip answers.

I'm still holding on to Nash, and slowly turn him in a circle so I can scan the lobby. A single, tired vase of flowers sits in a corner by a small collection of books helpfully labeled "Guest Library."

Planting a hard kiss to his lips, I allow myself a single moment to enjoy the taste of him. His body responds to me in seconds. The quiet groan is music to my ears—or would be if we were alone.

It's harder than it should be to step away. "Follow my lead."

I pluck a single rose from the vase and snap off the soggy

part of the stem. With the flower clutched in one hand, I slide the other into the crook of Nash's arm and plaster a wide grin on my face.

"Come *on*, baby. We'll just ask this nice man here to help us."

For a split second, Nash looks at me like I'm one bubble off plumb. But to his credit, he follows me without protest.

"Howdy, sugar," I say to the man at the front desk. "This here is my *fiancé*. We just got engaged not fifteen minutes ago. Can you believe it? I've been waitin' for him to pop the question for five years!"

"I was trying to save up for a ring," Nash says, a petulant edge to his voice.

With a little eye roll, I turn to him. "Bless your citified heart, baby, but I told you I didn't need no diamond. All I need is you."

"Are you checking in?" the man asks.

"No, sugar. We're here because my daddy's stayin' here tonight, and we want to tell him the good news in person. But...he ain't answerin' his phone. Could you be a peach and give us his room number? Duncan Wilder."

Looking down his pinched nose at me, he shakes his head. "We take the privacy of our guests very seriously. I can't help you."

I grip the rose tight enough, one of the thorns digs into my palm. Tears prick at my eyes. With my bottom lip quivering, I look from the clerk to Nash and back again. "I don't know what I'll *do* if I can't tell my daddy the good news. He's only in town for another few hours—the oil business keeps him very busy—and this is my last chance to see him for *months!*"

When faced with a woman's tears, even the strongest man can break. This guy—the gold tag on his jacket says his name is Ron—is no different. "I can...call his room. But I'm sorry, that's the best I can do."

"Oh, thank you!" I lean both elbows on the counter, my cell phone in one hand, that damn rose in the other, and bat my eyelashes at the man. "Baby, isn't Ron just *wonderful* for helpin' us?"

"Thanks a lot. This means everything to my sweet girl." Nash lowers his voice and cups the side of his mouth with one hand. "Her father scares the shit out of me, but whatever Sierra wants, Sierra gets."

Ron picks up the receiver, and I slide my thumb over my phone's screen, activating the camera. Best case, Duncan answers and comes down to the lobby. Worst case, we get his room number.

"Tell him it's Sierra *and* Nash." One last sugary sweet smile, and Ron dials. But after a minute, he shakes his head.

"He's not answering."

No shit. "How long have you been workin' today, sugar?"

Ron straightens his shoulders. Dammit. I'm losing him. "Since ten this morning. If Mr. Wilder doesn't want to answer his phone, that's his choice. I'm afraid I've done all I can for you."

"You've been the absolute best," I say with a heavy sigh. "I'll just keep tryin' his cell phone. Come on, baby. There was a coffee shop across the street. We can hang out there for a spell."

As soon as we're back outside, I check my phone. "Duncan's in room 329."

"But we can't get into the elevator," Nash says, not moving when I try to guide him toward the corner of the building. "Even if we could, the desk clerk would stop us."

"That's why we're goin' around back to the service entrance." I give his hand a squeeze. "You did good in there."

Ryker waits for us behind the hotel. "Whiskey is keeping an eye on things out front."

"Somethin' about this whole situation is two sandwiches short of a picnic. You comin' up with us?" As much as I want to handle the former U.S. Marshal on my own, my gut tells me we're gonna need Ry.

"Yep." He pulls a small camera from his backpack and sticks it over the hotel's back door. "Base, you have a visual?"

Over comms, Rip confirms he can see the video feed.

Ry shields me while I make quick work of the lock. "Stick close," I whisper to Nash when we step inside.

I hope to all that's holy the rest of the hotel is as deserted as the lobby. Ryker ain't capable of blending in. Not when he has to duck just to make it through the door.

The scent of bleach burns my nose outside the service elevator, but in less than thirty seconds, we're on our way up to the third floor.

We don't encounter a soul on the way to Room 329. If it weren't for the television blaring across the hall, I'd wonder if even a single room were occupied.

Nash's knock goes unanswered. "Get behind me," I whisper. Ryker takes up position on the other side of the door, his Glock 19 pointed at the ground, and I slide the first pick into the lock.

When the last tumbler falls, I shove the door with my foot, and Ry sweeps into the room. "Clear," he calls ten seconds later. "Get in here. We've got a situation."

I pull Nash with me, but stop only two steps into the room. Duncan Wilder lies on the bed, fully clothed, his eyes open and staring at the ceiling.

"Is he...?" Nash reaches a hand toward Duncan, but lets it drop a second later.

"Yes." Ry holsters his gun and reaches into his pocket for his phone. "He's dead."

CHAPTER EIGHTEEN

Nash

He looks so peaceful. Like he laid down to take a nap and simply didn't wake up again.

West, who came upstairs moments ago, unbuttons Duncan's light blue dress shirt as I gape at him. "No bruises." Tugging at the man's sleeves, he runs a gloved finger over his wrists. "No obvious signs of foul play. Could have been a heart attack. Or a stroke. His muscle tone is shit, but he *is* almost eighty."

I want to tell him to leave the man alone. To have some respect. But he's not unkind, even if his eyes *are* cold as ice.

"Got his phone. I'll clone it, and Rip can check his call log." West digs a cable and a small, black box out of his bag and starts fiddling with Duncan's cell.

Ryker unpacks the small suitcase methodically, removing each item and setting it on the the small desk. "Three changes of clothes, his passport, a pair of slippers, and a blank notebook." Rifling through the pages, he whistles when a tiny scrap of paper falls to the floor. "With at least one page torn out."

I turn back to Duncan. West finishes righting the man's clothes and steps back, his gaze sweeping around the space. "It's a shitty room, but there's nothing obviously out of place."

"The chain wasn't on the door," Raelynn says. "He was worried about Nash comin' here. Stands to reckon he wouldn't be careless with his own security."

"Do you really think someone...killed him?" I'd just started to believe Hidden Agenda could protect me. That I'd be able to stay in Seattle—with Raelynn. But if Duncan was murdered...I'm not safe here. And neither is she.

Ryker rubs his palm over the back of his head. "I'd lay odds at 50-50. But we're not going to get any answers standing around here."

"What's the plan, boss?" Raelynn brushes her hand against mine, and I link our fingers. The strength of her grip is the reassurance I need to tamp down the panic threatening to pull me under.

Ryker and West exchange a look. One that says they've had this conversation—or one just like it—before. "We call it in. Pretend to be on the housekeeping staff and report a dead body. I'll find someone in the Medical Examiner's office to pay off so they expedite the autopsy and notify next of kin."

A bribe? Fuck. I don't want to owe this man—or Raelynn—anything. But I have all of a thousand dollars to my name, and I'm pretty sure Ryker's going to need a lot more than that. "I'll pay you back."

He's repacking the suitcase, and though I wasn't paying attention earlier, he clearly was as he puts everything back exactly as it was. "No."

"What do you mean, 'no'?" Dropping Raelynn's hand, I

straighten my shoulders and try to look even a tenth as threatening as the man in front of me.

"I mean 'no.'" He doesn't elaborate.

Raelynn touches my back. "Let's get out of here. Ry and West will have an easier time wipin' the room if we're not takin' up space."

"No. Not until he tells me—"

West steps between me and Ryker, and the intensity in his gaze has the protest dying in my throat. "This is what we do, Nash. Ry's not going to go bankrupt for helping you. Or even notice the dent in his bank account. K&R isn't...cheap. We do okay."

"And Rip is a genius with investments," Raelynn adds. "Helpful, since my house is a goddamn money pit."

Pulling a thick, white cloth from his backpack, West starts to swipe it over the bedside table. "If someone did this, we'll find them. You two head back to Raelynn's. Stay inside and check in every few hours. We'll know more soon."

It's an hour before we make it back to her place. Raelynn's careful, winding through half a dozen neighborhoods, back-tracking more than once to make sure no one can follow us.

We don't say a word on the drive, though she steals glances at me from time to time. I'm numb. Shocked at Duncan's death. Overwhelmed by how easily this group of people I just met accepted me, and how quickly they jumped into action to help. Terrified I'll have to say goodbye to this woman I'm falling for.

Kiki comes running as soon as we walk into the house, meowing the whole way. Raelynn drops to her knees and scratches the cat behind the ears. "You're a needy little thing.

But you sure are cute. I'll get you some food in a few minutes."

Her smile lights up her entire face. When Kiki turns his attention to me, circling my ankles and butting his head against my shins, I set my backpack on the floor and join them.

"How'd you know?" Raelynn asks. With the cat flopped on his side between us, and the look in her eyes as she stares at him, I don't need to ask what she means.

"Five or six years ago, I did a stint in Rio Vista, California. Small town, maybe ten thousand people."

Her eyes light up. "I was stationed at Travis for six months. Way before your time. There was a burger place in Rio Vista with bottomless fries. Until my squadron discovered them." She laughs, the sound almost wistful. "They stopped offerin' refills after a couple of weeks. Probably for the best. We would've put them out of business."

"One of the guys working at the hostel told me about them. He'd grown up there. Said he and his friends wanted to cry when they changed the menu." Shaking my head, I wonder if there were other times our paths *almost* crossed over the years. "Some places, it's easy to find work. Others... not so much. I needed something to do while I put up my flyers, and I started volunteering at the animal shelter. They'll take almost anyone, and they don't require a background check." I shrug, unable to meet her gaze. There's still so much of my life I haven't shared with her. Kiki rolls over and starts licking my hand. "You can tell which dogs and cats have been there the longest. They look at every potential adopter with such hope in their eyes. I wanted to take them all home with me. But...when you don't have a home to go to..."

"And Kiki had that same look?" she asks.

I nod, unsure how to tell her that the cat wasn't the only

one who needed love. Raelynn leans in and brushes her lips to mine.

She knows.

We all needed each other.

Raelynn

Pushing my empty breakfast plate away, I watch Nash work on his second helping of migas. "I'm gonna need to go shoppin' this afternoon. Not used to cookin' for two."

"This," he scoops up a forkful of eggs, "is amazing."

"Ain't nothin' special."

The way this man looks at me, it's like I've given him the world. Not a haphazard skillet of eggs, salsa, cheese, and crushed tortilla chips.

"Raelynn." He reaches across the corner of the table to take my hand. "Everything I own fits in one duffel bag. I've never had a bank account. Or a credit card. When I cook, it's ramen, mac and cheese, and whatever fruits and vegetables I can scavenge out of the grocery store dumpster."

I don't know what to say. In all of our conversations, everything we've shared over the past two weeks, he's never been this raw. This honest.

"Believe it or not, I like cookin'. I'll run through all my mama's recipes for you. As long as you do the dishes."

"Deal," he says quietly and scoops up the last bite of eggs.

"Tell me about your life, darlin'. Not the polished version you've been feedin' me. The real one."

He stares at the empty plate for a full minute before taking a long drag on his coffee.

"When Frank was alive, things were...more normal. We'd move to a new town, rent an old house or a halfway decent apartment for a year, and...live. My clothes came from Goodwill, but I had a cell phone. A second-hand computer. Basic cable. At least until I turned twenty-three."

"What happened then?"

From the look in his eyes, I'm not sure I want to know. But I need to.

"I left." He runs a hand through his thick hair. A few wisps of gray catch the light amid the brown. "Frank moved us to Reno. It was hot and dry and I was so fucking sick of not being in control of my own destiny. I thought..." Squeezing his eyes shut, he sighs. "Pretty sure everyone's an idiot at twenty-three."

Nash picks up our plates and carries them into the kitchen. I follow, leaning against the counter when he turns on the faucet.

"Even after...I did okay for a while. We had a joint bank account. Frank saved every penny, so if I needed money, I had somewhere to go. Until he got sick. Cancer's fucking expensive when you don't have insurance."

His shoulders slump, and I reach over and turn off the water. "Nash, look at me."

In his gaze, I find a mirror to my own sorrow. But his goes deeper.

Reaching into his pocket, he pulls out a flattened penny. "Frank used to call me the luckiest kid on the planet. I never believed him. It's not *lucky* to lose everyone you love. Everyone who loves you." The penny tumbles from one finger to another, the move so practiced, he can probably do it in his sleep. "I've been running so long, I don't know how to do anything else."

"You ain't alone anymore, darlin'." He wraps his arms around me, burying his face in the crook of my neck. "You can find a home here."

"Not if Duncan—"

Drawing back, I grip his shoulders. "Even if Duncan's death *wasn't* an accident. Ryker don't give up, and neither do I."

He blows out a heavy breath. "So, what happens now?"

"We wait." The answer doesn't sit well—with either of us—but there ain't much else we can do. "Tank and Graham are takin' turns sittin' on Broadcast in case Diego comes back. Ry has a contact at the M.E.'s office, but they still need to complete the autopsy."

Nash flinches. Shit. He might not have known Duncan well, but the man was the last connection to his family.

"We'll know more this afternoon, darlin'. Until then..."

A hint of a spark flashes in his eyes. "Again? I'm game if you are, but, we're going to need to hydrate first."

We both laugh. I'm about to reach for him when Kiki bounds into the kitchen and leaps onto the counter. With laser focus, he starts cleaning the last bits of egg and cheese off one of the plates.

"Nope. That shit ain't gonna fly here, you little monster. Off." Scooping him up, I give him a firm "no" and set him on the floor. Kiki meows once, expressing his displeasure, and flounces back into the living room.

"Dishes first," Nash says. "Fun later."

Nash

Raelynn carries a piece of plywood into the living room. "This big enough for you?"

I nudge the sawhorses closer together. "Perfect. Since I can't do this outside..."

"It ain't safe. We talked about this..."

We position the wood to form a makeshift table before

covering it with a drop cloth. "I know. I'm going to open the windows, though. Otherwise, the fumes could do us in."

"It's gonna be that bad?" She pushes up her sleeves, staring at the brushes and can of primer sitting against the wall.

"Depends. Your cabinet doors have so many layers of paint on them, it might take me a week to strip them first."

Laying the first one on the plywood, I pass Raelynn a screwdriver. "You can start on the hinges."

We work side-by-side for hours, talking about everything and nothing, regularly chasing Kiki from the room so he doesn't eat the long strips of paint covering the floor, and planning…a future.

Nothing long term. Restaurants we'd like to try. Line dances to learn. How Nash Grace can get a legal social security number.

"Leave that to Wren and Ripper," Raelynn says, picking up the broom and sweeping up the mess. "They gave Hope—Wyatt's girl—a new identity just last month. She started workin' as a freelance financial planner a couple of weeks ago."

"Shit. Why did she need a new identity?"

"Her ex—her *dead* ex—ran one of the largest human trafficking rings on the west coast. Hope was his punchin' bag for three years. He made her launder his money. We took down the organization—all the major players—but some of the low-level grunts could still be searchin' for her."

"Is she in danger?" I've never met the woman, and Wyatt scares the shit out of me, but I have to know.

Raelynn scoops up the paint scraps and dumps them into a garbage bag. "It ain't likely. But Ry owns the building Wyatt and Hope live in. Ripper and Cara have the unit on one side of them, with Graham and Q on the other. Hope's safer there than anywhere else on earth."

I lose my grip on the paint scraper, and the tool skips across the plywood. "Shit. This would be so much easier with my other blade. I don't suppose I could get my car any time soon? My toolbox is in the trunk."

Raelynn glances at her phone. "Still no update from Ry or the coroner's office. But I can swing by your place before I hit up the grocery store."

"You have to go today?" The idea of her out there alone shouldn't bother me. She can clearly take care of herself. But it does.

"If we want to eat, I do." She slaps my ass, brushes her hands on her thighs, and pulls her hair into a low ponytail. "Chicken caesar salad tonight, but tomorrow, I'm makin' brisket and cornbread."

Sliding an arm around Raelynn's waist, I pull her close. "It's a good thing we're getting so much *exercise* at night. I haven't eaten this well in years."

"Oh, just you wait, darlin'. Once we know you're safe, I'm startin' up my mornin' runs again. Five miles, three days a week. And you're comin' with me."

"Should I be scared? Or excited?"

"With the way you're holdin' me, the answer should be obvious." Her fingers card through my hair, and she claims my lips with hers.

The scent of orange blossoms fills my nose. I could kiss Raelynn every day for the rest of my life and it wouldn't be enough. Whenever we touch, I want more.

Backing her up against the plywood, I'm about to pull up her shirt when she wriggles free from my grasp. "We do this, ain't neither of us eatin' tonight. I'll be back in two hours. Stay inside, and keep your phone on. Call me if you need anythin'."

One last, swift kiss, and she's gone.

KIKI MEOWS loudly at the front window. Raelynn texted a few minutes ago. The winds started before she left, and they're causing a mess on the interstate. Traffic has slowed to a crawl, and it took her almost ninety minutes to make it to Broadcast.

I scratch the cat behind the ears. "She'll be back...eventually. Don't worry. I know where your food is."

He stands up on his hind legs and paws at the glass for a full minute. Outside, leaves tumble down the street, but the rain hasn't started yet. The lights flicker, then with a quiet pop, go out completely. Shit.

The electrical in this house is held together by bubble gum and a prayer.

After I find my flashlight, I check the breaker box in the basement, but everything looks good. The wind must have taken down a power line somewhere.

I'm stacking wood in the hearth when someone pounds on the front door. My gut clenches until a man's voice carries from outside. "Raelynn? It's your neighbor, Chip. I need help...my son. He...he fell. I can't get to him."

Through the small windows at the top of the door, I catch a glimpse of a tall man wearing a damp white t-shirt and jeans. He wrings his hands, then knocks again. "Raelynn? Please answer!"

I flip the lock and throw the door open. "She's not here. What happ—"

The punch snaps my head back. There's a small crack in the ceiling. Why is that suddenly all I can think about? My arms windmill, finding nothing but air.

Pain explodes across the back of my skull. The edge of the plywood looms over me. Along with a shadow. *Two* shadows.

Muffled voices. Dark hair. The man in the white t-shirt.

"Get him to the plane. We'll find out what the woman knows."

I roll onto my side. Can't let them hurt Raelynn. The couch is so far away. Where are the lights? It's getting darker. Quieter.

Stay awake!

I can smell blood. Mine, I think. Someone kicks my shoulder. I'm on my back again. Staring up at a face that's not a face. Just two dark eyes and white teeth.

I take a swing at the hazy shape, but come up empty. A shoe slams down on my wrist, pinning it to the floor. "No..." The word sounds like I'm under water.

"Shut him up."

A heavy weight straddles me. I should know what to do. But I can't think.

The next punch splits my lip. Blood fills my mouth. I can't hear anything but my own heartbeat roaring in my ears. Something tightens around my wrists, biting into my skin.

There's a pinch to my neck. Then I'm on my feet. Stumbling. A man on either side of me.

Rain pelts my face, clearing the haze over my eyes. A black SUV idles at the curb. No. I can't let them put me in the car. My arms and legs start to feel heavy. Cold.

Thrashing, I'm almost free when the one on the left jams something small and hard against my ribs. "Keep fighting, and we'll torture that pretty thing for *days* before we let her die."

My thoughts are almost clear. Enough to know they'll hurt Raelynn anyway—if she doesn't kill them first. I kick at him, but whatever's wrong with my legs...it's getting worse. I'm off balance. I crash into the other man, and he shoves me, hard. Laurel branches slice my cheek and neck. The large bush stops me from hitting the ground, but the two men grab me again. A third rounds the SUV. "Fucking idiots," he mutters as they shove me face down into the back seat. "Someone's going to see us."

I try to push myself up, but my muscles won't listen. I'm so tired. Why can't I move? The door in front of me swings open. "He's almost out," a voice says. It sounds strange. Like my ears are filled with cotton.

My lower lip is swollen and still bleeding. I spit blood onto the floor mat. "Wh-what...do you...want...?" Each word is harder than the last. My eyelids are too heavy. Can't keep them open.

I shouldn't sleep. A tiny voice in my head tells me to stay awake, but I don't listen. Raelynn. I need...Raelynn. Where...is...

CHAPTER NINETEEN

Raelynn

BY THE TIME I make it home, it's after six. I should have ordered a pizza and skipped the grocery store. The wind and rain turned the highway into a parking lot, and I've been in the car for over an hour.

The house is dark, along with half the others on my side of the street. Shit. The power goes out every time there's a storm.

Warmth pools in my core. This is the perfect excuse to build a fire and spend the night curled up on the couch in Nash's arms. Dinner by candlelight, maybe a glass of wine... I'm grinning like a fool before I get out of the car.

With a full bag of groceries balanced on my hip, I unlock the door and toe it open.

"Nash?"

The house is utterly silent. The trees cast flickering shadows across the room. The air feels *wrong*, but as I turn to shut the door, a solid weight slams into me from the side.

Groceries scatter everywhere. I hit the plywood, losing my breath and knocking the sawhorses across the floor.

The air returns to my lungs in a strained *whoosh.* Kicking out with my right leg, I catch my attacker in the gut.

Footsteps pound toward me. I scramble up, but my foot lands on a fat tomato, and I skid. My knee hits the edge of the plywood. Stars burst in front of my eyes. A loud *crack* echoes through the room seconds before my head feels like it's about to split in two.

I can't put weight on my left leg. It buckles when I try to stand. Another blow catches me across the shoulders. Thick bristles drag over my neck.

That's my fucking broom!

Grabbing the end, I yank as hard as I can. Ain't goin' down like this. The asshole who swung at me loses his balance, but I can't get out of the way in time. His skull slams into my temple.

The blow stuns us both, but the first man wraps his arm around my neck. I can't breathe.

I claw at him, but find only thick fabric. Darkness creeps in along the edges of my vision. Straining, I try to reach his eyes, his face, any exposed skin.

A hint of copper tickles my nose.

Harder. Fight. Harder.

My lungs burn. This is it. I'm dead, and I can't muster the energy I need to care.

Stinging pain spreads across my cheek. Someone's playin' my skull like a drum. But it's my shoulders that hurt the most. My arms are stretched wide, and when I flex my fingers, ropes cut into my wrists. Lifting my head takes all the strength I have, and when I open my eyes, I instantly regret it.

Diego Ruiz leans against one of the sawhorses, staring down at me. The other man...shit. He's behind me. The assholes lashed my arms to the top beam of the other sawhorse, leaving me sitting on the floor with my legs stretched out in front of me, ankles bound tight. My ass is numb, and my left knee is so swollen, I can feel my heartbeat through the blood-stained denim of my jeans.

"Where's...Nash?" My voice is scratchy, and when I swallow, I remember how I got in this mess. Diego's arm around my throat, cutting off my air.

"None of your concern." He advances on me, and I have to crane my neck to look up at him. The punch isn't a surprise, but my head slams into the metal beam, dazing me. Until white-hot pain lances through my shoulders. The sawhorse rattles, nearly tipping forward and taking me with it.

My whimper escapes before I can choke it down. It takes me too long to realize what's goin' on. The second fucker kicked me from behind.

"You're...gonna...regret that," I grit out. "Tell me where... Nash is...and I *might* let y'all live."

Diego chuckles. "You might let *us* live? Look at where you are, Ms. Harrison." He opens his jacket and withdraws a silenced Nighthawk Custom GRP from under his left arm. "I could kill you right now."

"So do it." Gritting my teeth, I bend my knees, desperate to relieve some of the pressure on my arms. Twisting my wrists, searching for the smallest bit of slack in the ropes, I groan. They're too tight. And this asshole knows my name. How?

"Soon." Diego holsters his weapon. "But first, you're going to tell us what you know about Nathan Rossi."

"Who the hell is that?"

The snap of a switchblade sends ice flooding my veins. The asshole behind me grabs my ear. The pressure lasts for only a second before blood gushes down my neck. I swallow my scream. Fiery pain licks along the wound. The blade-happy pig fucker tosses the small nub of flesh to the floor in front of me. My tiny gold stud catches the light.

"Lie to me again, and you'll lose the rest of it," Diego says with a sadistic smile. "What did Nathan tell you?"

Sweat dots my forehead. Pinpricks of light burst in my periphery. That ain't good. How much blood can you lose from the bottom of your ear? It's getting harder to focus.

The longer I stare at the floor, the more confused I am. A stain the size of my palm looks like dried blood. Nash's blood. They took him. But he put up a fight.

"I don't know no *Nathan*. But if you killed Nash, you're gonna die chokin' on your own balls."

Diego slams his booted foot down on my toes. The crunch of more than one bone is like a hot poker. Bile burns the back of my throat. If I don't find a way out of this soon, I'll be up shit creek with the waters risin'.

"Nathan is alive. For now." The hitman glances at his very expensive watch. "Mr. DeLuca has been planning his death for many years. It will not be quick or painless."

Jerking against the restraints, I spit on Diego's shoes. "So all y'all get off on torturin' innocent folk, then."

"Nathan is not innocent!" The man's backhand snaps my head to the side. Blood drips down my cheek, and Diego pulls a handkerchief from his pocket. He dabs at the large ring on his index finger. "You are trying my patience, Ms. Harrison. Kellan? Remove the rest of it."

The other man pinches the top of my ear between two meaty fingers. I scream as loud as I can, hoping someone might hear me and call 911. Thrashing my head, I loosen his grip, but that won't save me for long. Not unless I can get my arms free.

The ropes dig into my skin. Is there a tiny bit of slack around my right wrist? Agony races all the way up my left leg, but I plant my feet and twist, sending the sawhorse slamming into him.

"You fucking bitch!" Kellan roars. The switchblade clatters to the floor, and he stumbles. I don't have enough leverage to stand. But I scoot back until the sawhorse hits the front door.

Diego advances on me, his gun pointed at my head. "Scream again, and I will tell Mr. DeLuca to cut out Nathan's tongue before he kills him."

"Your boss...is a sick fuck who probably gets off on that shit."

My phone dings, then buzzes twice from somewhere to my left. Ryker. If I don't answer, he'll know something's wrong. But Hidden Agenda is at least twenty minutes away. Longer if traffic is still fucked.

Diego nods at Kellan, and he strides over to the couch to pick up the device. "What the hell does this mean?" he asks, turning the screen toward me. "Secure message?"

The phone won't unlock without my fingerprint, passcode, *and* a facial scan, but I can't take the chance they'll break me. "Voice Assist: Security Breach!" I shout. The phone bricks in an instant, and the screen goes dark.

"Big mistake." Diego presses his foot down on my knee. My hoarse cry sounds like a tortured animal.

Kiki.

"Hey, asshole," I manage through the pain. "Where's...my goddamn...cat?"

Nash

My mouth tastes like the inside of a garbage can. Nausea crawls up my throat and a headache splits my skull. Where the hell am I?

A white zip tie digs into my wrists. I'm sitting up—mostly—in a plush leather seat. Pressure fills my ears, along with a dull hum.

Turning my head, I find a small, dark window with tiny, white lights dotting the ground far below. Fuck. I'm on a plane.

Across from me, a man in an expensive suit lifts a glass of amber liquid to his lips. "Would you like a drink, Mr. Rossi?"

"Fuck you. Where are we going?"

"Somewhere you will *not* be offered eighteen-year-old Irish whiskey that costs more than your car." He reaches for a heavy glass decanter, pours a double, and sets it on a small table next to me.

It's awkward as hell to take a sip with my hands bound, but the smooth liquid helps chase the sour taste from my mouth. "Where are the guys who attacked me?" I ask, hating the desperation in my voice.

"Having some fun with your girlfriend."

I lunge for the man, but he's up in a flash and slams his fist into my gut. I sink to my knees, coughing hard enough, the liquor threatens to come back up. Two mountains of muscle step through a part in the drapes at the front of the cabin.

"Everything okay, Mr. DeLuca?" one of them asks.

"Our guest fell, Rocco. Nothing to worry about." The man takes me by the arm and shoves me back into my seat. "Tell my father he's awake."

His father? This is DeLuca's son?

Rocco disappears back behind the curtain, but the other

guy doesn't move. "Why does your father give a shit about me? It's been twenty years!"

"Do you think that matters?" Mr. Expensive Suit DeLuca takes his seat and crosses his legs at the ankles. "In two hours, we'll be in Chicago. Until then, drink up."

"Let Raelynn go. She doesn't have anything to do with this. I won't fight you. Not now, not when we land. But—"

Expensive Suit laughs. "Did you hear that, Benny? He 'won't fight' me."

"Good one, Mr. DeLuca."

I stare down at my bound hands. I could snap the zip tie, but with Expensive Suit and two of his goons in the cabin, even if I do get free, there's nowhere to go. We're thirty-thousand feet in the air on a private plane owned by one of the biggest crime families in the country.

I'm dead. It doesn't matter if they make me suffer or end me with two bullets to the head—what they tried twenty years ago—I'm still dead.

"I should introduce myself, Nathan. My name is Lincoln DeLuca. Enzo DeLuca is my father."

Well, that explains the thousand-dollar suit.

"Am I supposed to care? I shouldn't finish the whiskey, but the assholes who beat me up and drugged me are torturing Raelynn right now, and I can't do a damn thing about it.

Lincoln offers me a placid smile. "Twenty-two years ago, your grandfather ordered a hit on two of my father's enforcers."

"I haven't seen my grandfather since I was ten!"

"Those two enforcers weren't alone that day," Lincoln says in that same, mild tone. But his hand shakes when he pours himself more whiskey. "They were driving my mother and four-year-old sister to a doctor's appointment."

Lincoln's trapped in his memories now, staring into his

glass like it holds the answers to life itself. "They died that day, Mr. Rossi. But it was not a quick or easy death. The driver, Ray, was killed on impact. Lou's legs were crushed by the dashboard. He bled out, after a time. My mother broke her collarbone. It was only a minor injury, but the car landed on its side in a ravine and caught fire. She called my father when she knew she couldn't escape the flames—or save my sister. We had to listen to them scream as they burned to death."

I never knew the details. Never asked my father *why* the DeLucas wanted to kill him.

"What happened to them was terrible," I say, the words thick with the lump in my throat. "But what about *my* sister? And *my* mother? My dad was never a part of the Rossi family business. He sold real estate. Mom was a second grade teacher!"

Lincoln shrugs. "Retribution is a part of business, Nathan. My family lost everything. So yours will too. There's no breaking the cycle, even if I wanted to. Your death will close a chapter that has been open for far too long."

"And what about Raelynn? She's not a part of this."

"She is now. Her suffering is on you. It's a shame, really. She's a beautiful woman. But she won't die that way."

"You son of a bitch, I'll kill you—"

It's Benny who punches me this time. My lip splits open again, and blood drips onto my t-shirt. "I'd like to see you try, Rossi."

"It's Grace, asshole." Lincoln looks at me like I'm a complete idiot, until I add, "My *name* is Nash Grace."

Raelynn

Twenty-three minutes since Ry called and I bricked my phone. I think. It's getting harder to keep count. Ten minutes passed with Diego and Kellan arguing over whether they needed to find Kiki. Whether hurting him would get me to talk. But the cat's too smart to let himself be caught. After twelve, Kellan tried again to take more of my ear, but I threw myself back against the sawhorse and he almost cut off his own nose.

That earned me a goddamn *lecture*. From two men who plan on carving me up into little pieces. Priceless.

At sixteen minutes, they brought in one of my dining room chairs and cut me free from the fucking sawhorse. But my arms were nothing but two dead weights. I only managed to kick Kellan in the nuts before Diego punched me so hard, the world went soft and dark long enough for them to tie me to the chair.

Kellan crosses his hands over his family jewels when Diego tells him to pick up the knife again. "She's not going to talk, boss. Why can't we kill her and get the fuck out of here?"

"Because I said so," he snaps. "If she told *anyone* who Rossi really is—"

"I keep tellin' you, sugar," I say, infusing every word with as much Texas charm as I can muster, "I have no idea who you're talkin' about."

Diego pulls out his pistol and presses the silencer just above the swelling in my knee. "Last chance, bitch. I don't care if you die *with* your kneecaps or without."

It doesn't matter what I say. The truth won't save me—or Nash. My only hope is to live long enough for Ryker to send in the cavalry.

"I *might* be rememberin' somethin'. Put the gun away and maybe I'll tell you."

Diego gives me the side eye. "Without, then."

"If you shoot me, fuck-stick, you're gonna go back to Daddy DeLuca in a tiny box. With a bow on it for good measure."

That gives him pause. My ear is still bleeding like a stuck pig, and I'm so dizzy, the room spins faster than a tornado. Where the hell is Ryker? Desperate for a way to keep myself alive, I scramble for some lie or half-truth I can offer him. And then a red light flashes once in my periphery.

Diego's finger twitches on the trigger, and I throw myself to the side. The chair tips over. My head slams into the floor. Glass shatters. Kellan goes down, but Diego sends two shots toward the stairs before pressing himself against the wall and turning the gun on me.

I try to roll the chair. A quiet *pop* sounds, and fire licks across my right arm. A dark blur moves in my dining room seconds before Diego's gun crashes to the floor.

Eyes wide, he grasps for the tactical knife piercing his throat. He's already dead. He just doesn't know it yet.

No sound escapes his lips as he stumbles until he hits the wall. West stalks over to him, the black greasepaint covering his face turning his eyes deadly cold. "Well, that was fun." The SEAL retrieves his blade and swipes it over his thigh, smearing the blood into the fabric. "Indigo, get in here. I need an assist."

He cuts me loose, eases me upright with an arm around my shoulders, and gently turns my head so he can look at my ear. "Shit, probie."

"I thought we'd agreed," I manage, so fucking happy to see him tears spring to my eyes, "I ain't anyone's goddamn probie."

CHAPTER TWENTY

Raelynn

INARA HOLDS a thick wad of gauze to my ear while West drags the two bodies onto a tarp he retrieved from his truck.

"Nash..." I start to shake, and fresh tears prick at my eyes. "He's—"

"On a plane," Inara says. "The tracker we slipped into his backpack pinged a couple of times over Idaho and South Dakota. We lost the signal after that."

It takes a minute for her words to register, but when they do, I slap her hand away. "You *knew?* And you left me here for an hour? Those fucks cut off part of my ear!"

"We *didn't* know until your phone went dead." Ryker's deep, raspy voice startles me. The man ambles in from the dining room and surveys the bloody mess in front of him. "I missed the party."

"You can tape up Raelynn's window," West says as he secures the tarp around the bodies with bungee cords. "And call the doc. She needs medical."

"I *need* to know what we're doin' to save Nash from the

DeLucas." I get my right leg under me, but the room starts to spin. "Shee-it."

Ry catches me before I hit the ground. "You aren't doing a damn thing until Doc Reynolds checks you out. Sit down and try not to lose any more blood."

"Like I can control that, asshole."

He glares at me, the streaks of hazel in his eyes almost golden with his frustration. "Stay still and let Inara tend to that ear."

Pulling a roll of duct tape from West's bag, Ryker heads for the window next to the stairs. Inara's shot left a tidy hole in the glass, but a large crack spreads out on either side.

Stars burst in front of my eyes when Inara tightens the compression bandage around my head. The adrenaline has worn off, and every bruise, cut, and broken bone scream at me.

I'd care how much blood I'm getting all over my couch if I thought I could move. But since I can't, I sink back against the cushions, staring at the complete destruction of my living room. West and Ry haul the bodies out to the SEAL's truck while Inara stows Diego and Kellan's wallets, phones, and keys in her bag.

A gust of wind is quickly followed by a loud, petulant meow. "Raelynn, does *this* belong to you?" Ry asks.

Kiki stands just inside the door, back arched like he's ready to do battle if the big man breathes too loudly. His tail is twice its normal size, and he hisses once before Ryker crouches down to glare at him.

"Kiki!" Nothing is more important to me in this moment than knowing my cat isn't hurt. I shove myself off the couch, whimpering when my ribs, knee, and foot all protest the movement. But as soon as I hit the floor, I'm rewarded with a rough tongue licking my hand and little paws kneading my thigh.

"I'll take that as a yes." Ry taps his earbud once. "Whiskey, bring another tarp. Sierra has a cat she probably doesn't want rolling around in all this blood."

I scoop Kiki into my arms and bury my face in his soft fur. "You ran when they came, didn't you? Good boy. Very good boy."

THE RIDE back to Hidden Agenda passes in a haze of shock and pain. Even in Ryker's massive SUV, I feel every bump in the road. I'd let myself pass out if I weren't so worried about Nash.

My house is as secure as it can be. The cameras are back up, and West added two more battery-operated units since the wind isn't supposed to die down until morning.

Had the power not gone out, the motion sensors would have alerted me when they took Nash. "I need a generator," I say absently.

"You'll have one tomorrow. Electricians by Thursday."

"Huh?" With some effort, I turn my head to stare at the man behind the wheel. "Why do I need electricians?"

"Because Cam's people need your shitty wiring upgraded before they can install your new security system."

"I don't—"

"Bullshit." Ryker hits the brakes hard enough, my ribs protest the snap of the seatbelt. "You need a fucking transfusion, Raelynn. If West and Inara had been five minutes later..."

The raw edge to his voice shocks me, but it's the fear in his eyes that has the comeback dying in my throat. He's always been granite. An unfeeling, unmoving, uncaring mountain who barks orders and makes things happen. Except with Wren.

But now, the man who isn't scared of a damn thing looks stricken. He runs a hand over his scarred head, then turns to stare at the warehouse. I didn't even realize we were in Hidden Agenda's parking lot.

"I had to listen over comms. I was still two miles away when Inara took her shot. And if West's throw had been half an inch off center, Ruiz would have shot you."

"He did," I whisper. At Ry's swear, I add, "Only a graze."

"Only. For fuck's sake." He slams the driver's door and rounds the vehicle, giving me a frosty glare when I scoot to the edge of the seat. "If you think I'm going to let you walk, you're worse off than I thought."

I stifle my whimper when he lifts me in his arms. The world starts to spin. "Gonna be sick..."

Ryker tightens his hold and breaks into a run. "Doc!" he shouts, throwing open the door to the warehouse with a bang. "She's in trouble!"

"Put her on the table." Doc Reynolds wraps a cuff around my arm. The beep rouses me, and I blink hard to clear the cobwebs from my vision. "You're the only one here with O-Neg, McCabe. Pull up a chair."

Nash

Benny and Rocco muscle me down a set of stairs. I haven't set foot in Chicago for more than twenty years, and I have no idea where we are. It's dark, and I couldn't see shit lying on the floor of the SUV. Rocco shoves me through a door, and I stumble.

"Careful, Nathan," Lincoln says from behind the two enforcers. "My father would prefer you not be...*too* damaged before tomorrow."

"Your father can go to hell."

Benny advances on me, and I back up until I hit the wall. The basement is mostly empty. The only distinctive feature is a large, reddish stain in the middle of the floor.

The enforcer pulls a multi-tool from his pocket and snaps the zip tie around my wrists.

"The windows are barred," Lincoln says. "And security patrols the grounds at night. So don't get any ideas about escaping."

"Whatever you're going to do, just get it over with." I shove Benny, but he only takes a single step before punching me in the face.

My ass hits the floor. How many more blows until I lose my faculties completely?

"What was that about being damaged?" I ask, spitting blood onto the concrete.

"Benny, stick to soft tissue for now. My father needs his rest," Lincoln says. "Have a good night, Nathan. In the morning, you'll pay for your family's mistakes."

The door slams, leaving me alone. I spend five minutes—I think, as there's no way for me to tell time down here—exploring the room. Concrete walls. Two barred windows close to the ceiling. A toilet and sink in a tiny bathroom. No furniture. No bed or blankets. Guess I'm sleeping on the floor.

My body aches. It's impossible to find a position that doesn't aggravate one or more bruises. Dried blood mats my hair.

God, I'd give anything to see Raelynn. To know she's still alive. Still safe. Ryker and his team will protect her. If they know she's in danger. Why didn't I ask Lincoln for proof they had her?

What good would that have done? You can't do a damn thing about it. You're going to die in the morning.

I think...I might have loved her. If we'd had the chance, she could have been my forever.

Raelynn

With a full pint of Ry's blood flowing through my veins, the dizziness has subsided, but now that the adrenaline has worn off, even the smallest movement makes me want to cry.

"Does this hurt?" Doc Reynolds asks, palpating my neck gently.

"That fucker put me in a headlock until I passed out. Yes. It hurts."

"Raelynn, this is serious. Tears to the blood vessels in your neck can cause a pseudoaneurysm."

I don't know what that is, but it sounds bad, so I hold my hair back and let him examine me.

"Only a small bit of petechial hemorrhaging," he says, more to himself than me. "Let's take a look at that ear."

I almost pass out from the pain. Lying on the big dining table with my head turned to give him full access to my mangled lobe, I watch the other members of Hidden Agenda —everyone but Wren—huddle in front of the monitors. They're talking in low, hushed tones, and the screens are still dark, but I see at least one or two tablets. Rip and West, I think.

"How much longer, Doc? I need—"

"A hospital," he mutters. "A chest x-ray. An orthopedist to examine that knee. But since that's not possible, you'll rest. For at least two weeks."

"Hell no." I push up on an elbow. Big mistake as he'd pressed a wad of gauze to my ear and the motion tears the wound open. "Shee-it!"

Ryker's head snaps up, and he stalks over to us. "She's bleeding again."

"She wouldn't be if she'd stay down. Don't give me that look, McCabe. You called, I came. Like I always do. Only this time, I'm here. In the one place we agreed I'd never be."

The doctor pinches what's left of the bottom of my ear so hard, I have to stifle my whimper.

"You can't afford to lose any more blood," Reynolds says, gentling his tone. "Breathe through the pain. In. Out."

My eyes water, but the tears don't stop me from seeing the look that passes between the two men hovering over me. There's more history there than I realized.

"I didn't have a choice." Ry rubs the back of his neck, the motion highlighting the bright pink compression bandage around his elbow. The man sat by my side for half an hour giving me his blood while Reynolds taped up my knee and three broken toes, cleaned the gash on my cheek, and asked me question after question to make sure I didn't have a severe concussion. "We need her here."

"F-for what?" Reynolds sputters. "She needs rest. Two weeks of it. At least. Maybe more for that knee. You can't seriously expect her to be field ready after all this!"

"I'm not a fucking idiot." Ryker's frustration bleeds through his tone. "She's benched until you—"

"Hell no." This time, I'm careful not to move my head. But I reach up and grasp Ry's forearm with all the strength I can muster. "You can't. Nash..."

"You almost died!" he shouts. "On my watch. So you're staying here with Rip and Wyatt while the rest of us go—"

"Enough!" Reynolds glares at Ryker. "You say another goddamned word and I'm taking my patient out of here. You broke our deal, and if I didn't owe you..." He shakes his head. "Step away, McCabe. Or we're through."

The chair Ry used earlier sails fifteen feet, landing with a clatter next to the boxing ring. I've rarely seen our fearless leader this angry. "Patch her up and get the fuck out of here."

With a sigh, the doctor goes to work cleaning and bandaging my ear, while Ry stalks back over to West and the team. "I'm sure you want to shower. But try not to get the wound wet. You can take the compression wrap off to wash your hair if you're careful—or have help. But that's it."

Help.

The lump in my throat makes it hard to swallow. "I need to be field ready, doc. Please."

"No." He pulls off his gloves and tosses them into his bag.

"You don't understand. Nash...he's..."

The man's eyes flash with such intensity, I snap my mouth shut. "No, *you* don't understand, Raelynn. I'm a doctor. Maybe not a respected one, but I swore an oath. I broke it once. I won't do it again."

For a full minute, I'm too shocked to reply. But I can't let him leave me like this. Unable to fight. To help save the man I'm falling for.

"Have you ever been in love?" I ask when he slides an arm under my shoulders and helps me sit up.

He gets a faraway look in his eyes and nods. "Once. You remind me of her."

Across the room, West has a hand on Ry's shoulder. Rip stands on his other side, his gaze pinging between me and Reynolds.

"My husband died in my arms," I say quietly. "Four years ago." The look of sympathy on the doc's face is too much, so I drop my eyes to my hands. To the bright red welts from the ropes those assholes used to tie me up. "I didn't think I'd have another chance to find love. Hell, I didn't want one. Until I met Nash."

"And now he's in trouble." Reynolds's voice carries a lifetime of pain.

I fiddle with the hem of my flannel shirt. It's stiff with dried blood. My blood. "They'll kill him if we can't get to him in time. That's why we're here. Why you're not at my place right now. Why I ain't lettin' Ryker bench me, no matter what."

With a heavy sigh, Reynolds rummages in his bag and comes away with a syringe and a small vial of clear liquid. "Nausea, vomiting, confusion, memory loss, or blackouts could be signs of a serious concussion. The tape job on your knee should last for a few days, even after a shower. Keep your leg elevated as much as possible. Ice it, and absolutely *no* running." He fills the syringe, then waits for me to meet his gaze. "This is cortisone. It should start to work within twelve to eighteen hours. But it's not a cure-all, and it won't do a damn thing for the pain tonight."

"I can handle pain."

Sorrow etches deep lines on the doctor's face. "Then breathe deep. This is going to hurt." Dark spots creep into my vision as he slides the needle under my kneecap. "Almost done."

I'm sweating by the time he pats my thigh.

He drops the syringe into a red plastic container and zips his bag. "If you feel sick, lightheaded, *anything* out of the ordinary, call me immediately. Even if you're not...in Seattle."

"Thanks, Doc," I manage. "For everythin'."

CHAPTER TWENTY-ONE

Raelynn

SLIDING OFF THE TABLE, I test the wrap job on my knee. My leg doesn't buckle, but it feels like someone's driving an ice pick through my patella. The first step is pure agony.

Inara jogs over and tries to wrap her arm around my waist, but I shake my head. "I can do this."

"I'm sure you can," she says, lowering her voice so the guys can't hear. "That doesn't mean you *should*."

"I have to show Ryker I'm field ready." We face off, the only two women operators on the team. If anyone knows what I'm up against, it's her.

"You're so far from field ready, it's laughable." She touches my hair and comes away with a smear of blood.

"If it were Royce...?"

Her gray eyes darken, and she drops her hands. "It *was* Royce once. Go slow, okay?"

It takes all my concentration to reach the couches without toppling over. I'm dizzier than I expected. It's a damn good thing Reynolds is gone. He'd see right through me.

Ryker narrows his gaze. Shit. He and West are two of the most observant men on the planet. If I'm not careful, he's gonna know I'm barely holdin' it together.

"Sit down before you fall down," he orders. "Or I'll have Wyatt take you home right now—and make sure you stay there."

I do as I'm told, choosing the plush recliner so I can elevate my legs. West retrieves an ice pack from the freezer and lays it gently over my swollen knee.

The monitors on the wall flicker to life as Ry picks up his tablet. "The medical examiner called two hours ago. Duncan's body showed extensive post-mortem bruising. He was restrained, probably in a stress position, for at least thirty minutes before he died. Cause of death *was* heart failure, but given his age, it was likely brought on by the torture."

"We should have insisted on goin' straight there," I say.

"It's possible he was already compromised when we talked to him. No way to know now. Diego and his asshole partner were likely watching us the whole time. Which brings us to how they found you." Another few taps to his tablet, and a slew of text messages appear on the center monitor between Diego Ruiz and someone named Lincoln. "Next time you need a car, don't use an ID with your home address on it. They broke into the rental company offices last night."

Oh my God. Nash was taken because of me. Because I lost focus. Because I didn't think how easy it would be to identify a rental car.

"It...it was my fault. All of this—"

"Raelynn," West says sharply. "What's done is done. When this is all over, you're getting a fresh cover packet. New last name, new ID, updated property tax records...all of it."

Ryker levels me with a hard stare. "This isn't on you,

Raelynn, it's on me. After we get Nash back, I'm doing a full audit on *everyone's* cover stories and identities."

Not if. After. Ryker doesn't say a single word he doesn't mean. He believes there's a chance Nash is still alive. That we can save him.

He taps his tablet again. "We put a tracker in Nash's backpack the other day, but we weren't actively monitoring his location because he was with you."

A map of the United States appears on the center screen with a blip over northern Idaho and a second one over South Dakota.

"When you wiped your phone, West and Inara were closest," Ry says. "I was home with Wren. She confirmed your location, then checked Nash's tracker. That's when we figured out he was in the air. We lost the signal after the second ping."

"Why?" I glance at the clock in the corner of the screen. "If they took him to Chicago...shouldn't it be transmittin' all the way there?"

"An airplane is a giant Faraday cage." Ripper stands apart from the rest of the group, looking vaguely uncomfortable, despite Charlie pressed to his side. "But the tracker hasn't come back online. Either they tossed the backpack or found the device."

Nash's entire life was in that backpack.

Oh, God. Bandit!

Is the little stuffed sloth still on my dresser? Why didn't I ask Ry to check?

Because you were delirious. Focus.

"Rip was able to confirm that a private jet left Boeing Field at 3:46 p.m. bound for Chicago. It landed forty-five minutes ago," Ryker says.

"Why are we sittin' here, then?" I snatch the ice pack off my knee, but Ry holds up his hand.

"Because our pilot was in Portland for his biennial flight review. He's still an hour out. We'll be wheels up by midnight."

West taps his tablet screen, and in unison, all the phones in the room vibrate. "Packing lists. If it looks like a lot, it is. We've got no idea what we're walking into, so we need to be ready for anything."

With no phone—and no idea if Ryker will even let me on the plane—I don't move when the rest of the team scatters. Until Inara kneels next to the recliner. "I'll help you clean up. If you want."

I touch my hair. It's sticky. Doc Reynolds split my jeans all the way up to my thigh, and my flannel looks like I was an extra in the *Texas Chainsaw Massacre.*

"That bad, huh?"

She chuckles. "Yes. And Ry hates it when we get blood on the plane seats."

"You're assumin' he's gonna let me go." I lean on her heavily as we limp toward the showers.

"He will. But don't expect to leave the van once we get there. I can only work one miracle a day."

GRAHAM SETS a cup of coffee in front of me. The plane is stocked with fresh beans every time, thanks to West, and the rich scent is a small sliver of normalcy in this awful night. It's after 2:00 a.m. We only left Seattle forty minutes ago—some hassle filing our flight plan—and I'm dragging.

I should try to sleep. West, Tank, and Inara are all stretched out in the fully reclining seats, but it's only a four-hour flight. If I tried, I'd end up worse off than I am now.

"Base to Alpha Team." Wren's voice fills the cabin from the speaker in the center of the plane's conference table. "I broke the encryption on Duncan's cell phone. He's got some *very* interesting messages. Sending to your screens now."

Ryker flips the switch on the wall monitor. "Base, you should be asleep."

"Tell that to your daughter. She's been dancing on my bladder for the past two hours. I'm *fine*, Romeo. Look at what I sent you."

Duncan: I'm in Seattle. When can you get here?

AR: Tomorrow night. He's going to hate me, you know.

Duncan: He's your son. He'll forgive you. Eventually.

AR: I hope you're right. Call me when you've made contact.

"Holy fuckin' shit. AR?" I sit up straighter, wincing as my various bruises protest the movement. "Angelo Rossi is alive?"

West whistles. "And Duncan knew—probably the whole damn time. I think we need to make some calls. Base, you and Charlie get everything you can on the DeLucas and the Rossis. Any players you can identify, base of operations, rumors...anything. We'll reach out to Stars and Bars. Romeo can call AR. Someone should tell him his son has been taken. If we're lucky, he'll help us get him back."

"Brent was madder than a hornet," Connor says, stifling a yawn. The former FBI agent—and Graham's boyfriend's brother—holds the phone in a mostly dark room, a single light to his left casting shadows over his face. It's still early as fuck in Texas. "Said he *thought* puttin' me out to pasture would let him sleep through the night more often. But he confirmed that Angelo Rossi is not only alive, he's been the head of the Rossi crime family for the past *thirteen years*."

"You've got to be fucking kidding me." Ryker cracks the seal on a bottle of water and offers it to me. "Drink. You're about to pass out."

"He ain't wrong." Connor moves the phone closer. "You look like five miles of bad road in the middle of nowhere. Why'd you let her on the plane, McCabe?"

"Didn't have much of a choice." Ryker lowers himself into one of the plush, leather seats. "She's as stubborn as you are."

Connor's chuckle riles my anger.

"Ain't you the one who took down a drug ring *and* saved your kid with a severe head injury?" I ask.

"It was aphasia and major concussive syndrome. I was damn lucky." Pride infuses his tone. "And my kid is a badass."

"Can we get back to business?" Ry asks. "We land in ninety minutes. I still need to call Angelo and convince him to stay the fuck out of our way. And let Nash return to his life when this is all over."

Connor runs a hand through his hair, the dark brown strands sticking up in all directions. "The FBI has extensive files on both the DeLucas and the Rossis, but Brent's exact words were, 'You ain't gettin' your hands on shit.' There are at least five active investigations goin' on, so watch out for surveillance."

I cringe. Knowing Diego and Kellan were outside the Pinnacle Hotel when Nash and I showed up was a blow. West threatened all of us with weeks of training when we get back.

"You'll keep working him?" Ryker cracks his neck. "Anything you can get us will help."

"I ain't got an ounce of quit in me," Connor says with a weary smile. "But if Brent has me arrested for interfering in a federal investigation, you're payin' for my lawyer."

"Deal."

The call ends, the video screen going dark, and Ry takes a healthy swig of coffee. "West? Wake up. We're calling Angelo."

The SEAL's out of his seat almost immediately. "Not without caffeine, we're not. Raelynn? You want some?"

"Any more, and I'll be in a world of hurt." I shift my foot on my rucksack, and a flare of pure agony races up my leg.

Ryker shakes his head. "You're already there. I knew this was a mistake."

"Nash is in this mess because of me." I push to my feet, clenching my jaw when the cabin threatens to spin around me. "You ain't sidelinin' me for this one."

"You can barely stand on that knee. No fucking way you're leaving the van."

"I'm a part of this team—"

West ambles up to us, coffee in hand. "If we have to fight our way in—or out—of anywhere, you're a liability, Raelynn. You have to see that. I can give you a shot of lidocaine for your knee, but it's not going to fix the broken toes, the damage to your shoulder, or the fact that those assholes used you as a punching bag for over an hour."

Before I can protest, he stares up at Ryker, a single brow arched. "But you can't expect her to sit quietly and let us handle shit either, Ry."

"Yes, I can," he growls.

"Russia."

With that single word, West shuts him down. Ryker grabs the seat back next to him, his fingers digging into the leather so hard, I can hear it over the hum of the engines.

"You gonna hit me again?" he asks the former SEAL. "Because I'm ready for it this time."

"Nope. Don't need to. Because now you remember how it felt knowing Wren was in danger. She was never going to stay in the van."

I'm shocked West is on my side. Even more shocked when Ryker shakes his head and mutters, "Fine."

Five minutes later, we huddle around the conference

table, our earbuds connected to a burner phone Wren spoofed with the dead U.S. Marshal's number.

"Duncan?" Angelo's voice is scratchy, a little dazed with sleep. It's only 7:00 a.m. in Chicago, and we won't land for almost an hour. "Where have you been? What's going on?"

"Duncan Wilder was killed by Diego Ruiz," West says, "on orders from Lincoln DeLuca. Mr. Rossi, the DeLucas have your son. We're going to get him back."

Nash

The cold, concrete floor leaches all the warmth from my body. I shivered half the night, tossing and turning in the dimly lit basement, replaying the moment I knew I was going to die.

If I'd ignored the man at the door—or hidden in Raelynn's crawlspace—I'd still be in Seattle. I could have warned her. Maybe even saved her. Instead, I'm watching the sky outside the windows get brighter and brighter, wondering how much longer I have before Lincoln or one of his goons puts a bullet in my brain. An hour? Less?

A single, weak ray of sunlight breaks through the clouds, and I stand on my tiptoes, desperate to see something—anything—outside.

The heavy lock *thunks* and I press my back against the wall.

Please, make it quick.

Rocco enters first, with Benny on his heels. The second enforcer aims a gun at my chest.

"Get it over with," I manage.

From the doorway, a man who can only be the patriarch

of the DeLuca family chuckles. "You are the spitting image of your father, Nathan."

"Didn't these idiots tell you? My name is Nash."

Rocco rushes me, grabs my shoulders, and slams me against the wall hard enough to rattle my teeth in my head. I'm too dazed to block the punch to my gut that follows. Retching, I sink to my knees. If there were anything in my stomach, it'd be all over his polished wingtips.

Enzo DeLuca stands over me, his son at his side. "You can be buried under whatever name you'd like, *Nathan*. That does not change who you are. Or why you're here."

"I never did a damn thing to you or your family, DeLuca. Neither did my father. You're the one who kept up this ridiculous vendetta." I stagger to my feet, still wheezing, and point to the thick scar at my temple. "So go ahead. Shoot me. Finish the job you started twenty years ago."

"Oh, I will. But I didn't bring you all the way to Chicago to simply put two bullets in your brain." He nods to Lincoln, who pulls a cell phone from his pocket. "And you are wrong about one thing. Twenty years ago, your father might have been an innocent bystander. Collateral damage, if you will. But today...he's anything but."

I'm still dazed. I have to be. His words don't make any sense. "My father died with my mother and sister."

Enzo smiles, showing off blinding white teeth. "Angelo Rossi has been the head of his family for the past thirteen years. And now that I have you, he'll give up everything he's built before he watches you die."

Lincoln taps his phone, and holds it up so I can see the photo on screen.

My father stands on an outdoor patio, leaning heavily on a cane, but very much alive. His light brown hair has turned snow white, but his blue eyes are as intense as ever.

"Oh my God. Dad."

CHAPTER TWENTY-TWO

Raelynn

"PUT THIS ON," West says, tossing me a black knit cap. "That bandage is bright enough to be seen from the Space Station."

I flip open the vanity mirror and carefully ease the hat over my head. The only compression wraps Doc Reynolds had in his bag were neon pink and electric green. Though there ain't a color on this earth that would blend in. Not wound around my skull like a 1980s headband.

"You really think it's the bandage he's gonna notice? You've seen my face, right?"

Two black eyes—one of them swollen half shut—a busted lip, and an inch-long gash on my cheek. At least my sweater hides the bruising around my neck.

"I have. And you'd be in the van with Inara, Graham, and Tank if Angelo weren't suspicious as fuck."

I check the side mirror. The black Econoline is six cars back. They'll wait half a mile from the Rossi family compound, ready to breach should West, Ryker or I drop off comms or press our panic buttons.

Fingering the tiny GPS transmitter hidden in the cuff of my black sweater, I close my eyes and picture Nash as I last saw him. Covered in dust, his white t-shirt straining over his biceps, chasing Kiki away from the pile of paint shavings. God, I hope we're not too late. That there's a chance we'll get him back. That he'll still be...the man I'm falling in love with.

Ryker pulls up to the heavy, iron gates, lowers the window, and jabs the intercom button. "Rossi is expecting us."

"Your name?" the crackling male voice says over the speaker.

"I'm the goddamn Tooth Fairy."

"Ry," West warns. "We need him."

"He needs us a hell of a lot more."

By some miracle, the gates open, and Ryker guides the sedan up a long driveway with tall, perfectly manicured hedges cutting us off from the outside world.

West tucks his comms unit into his ear. "Indigo, you copy? We're approaching the house."

"Copy," Inara says. "There's no perch that'll give me a shot inside the compound. If things go south, all we can do is ram the gates and hope for the best."

"We're gonna lose our deposit on the van again, aren't we?" West runs a hand through his dark hair. "Stay focused. We're approaching the house."

The mansion sits amid an acre of lush, green grass. Sun reflects off the white limestone facade, and wrought iron graces every one of the dozen windows across three stories.

A massive fountain feeds into a reflecting pool with an honest-to-God *bridge* leading to the house. "Well, he don't ride two to a mule."

"The fuck?" Ry asks.

I glare at him—as much as I can with two black eyes. "All this time, and you still need a Texas translator?"

West leans forward from the back seat. "Cut the chatter. We've got a welcoming committee."

Two men in dark gray suits stand on either side of the front door. From the bulges under their jackets, they're armed. I shudder. They've got the same look as Diego and Kellan. The same training. The same attitude.

West opens my door and helps me to my feet. I'd refuse, but I'm holding off on the lidocaine shot until we know where Nash is, and my knee is screaming.

"Lean on me," he says quietly. "It won't hurt for Angelo to see what the DeLucas did to you."

"Unless he's blind..." Despite my words, I'm grateful for the SEAL's strong arm around my waist as we follow Ryker up the steps.

"Name," the guy on the left demands.

"The Tooth Fairy." Gesturing to West, he adds, "And he's the Easter Bunny."

"We got a comedian here, Joey."

The second man chuckles and takes a step toward West and me. "Assume the position."

"If you think you're checking us for weapons, you're a fucking idiot." Ryker gets right in the first enforcer's face while West takes Joey to the ground in two moves. "He's a Navy SEAL, and I'm Special Forces. We don't *need* weapons but we're sure as shit not giving them up. If we wanted to end you, we'd have done it already."

The man scowls, but touches his earbud. "Sir. They're refusing to relinquish their weapons or give their names." After a beat, he shoots Ryker a look of complete disdain. "The library is through the foyer to the left. Mr. Rossi is waiting for you."

"Amateurs," West mutters and helps me step over the still prone Joey.

The inside of the house is a sea of polished marble. The

floor bears an intricate design of a compass with the letter R marking due north. Through the foyer, a giant spiral staircase winds its way to the second floor, the railing an ornate mix of black and gold.

Past a set of French doors to the left, the mood and design change completely. Floor-to-ceiling shelves are filled with books quite obviously not for show. A fire roars in the hearth, casting light on the gleaming hardwood. One corner of the room is taken up by a fully stocked bar, complete with a fancy espresso machine. In the other, leaning against a massive desk, is a glimpse of what Nash might look like in twenty-five years.

He has the same eyes, the same chin, the same build—if Nash lost a good thirty pounds. But that's where the similarities end. Angelo Rossi wraps his fingers around the handle of his cane, straightens, and walks right up to Ryker. "Give me one reason why my men shouldn't make you disappear."

"They'd be fools to try," Ryker says. "And if you want to save your son, you'll let us do our jobs."

"Your jobs? You've refused to tell me your names, how you got Duncan Wilder's phone, or how you know Nathan. Your 'job,' from what I can tell, is intimidation and subterfuge."

Ryker glances at West and shrugs. "Close enough. We're K&R."

Angelo's ruddy cheeks pale slightly. "You picked the wrong man for a shakedown."

"We don't need your money, Rossi. And no amount of cash is going to save your son from the DeLucas."

Angelo snaps his fingers. Four men—including Joey—block the French doors. "You have exactly thirty seconds to tell me what you know about Nathan."

West slams his fist into the closest enforcer's throat. Sweeping his leg in an arc, he catches a second behind the ankles. I grit my teeth, spin on my good leg, and ram my injured knee into Joey's balls. He doubles over, which lets me grab his shoulders and repeat the move, this time breaking his nose. Blood splatters the polished wood floor.

The *oof* behind me from the biggest and meanest of the bunch is Ryker's doing. My leg buckles, but West catches me before I fall.

"We can do this all day," Ryker snaps. "But that won't get your son back. Are you ready to listen?"

Nash's father gapes at the unconscious, bleeding, and moaning men behind us. "I don't know where Nathan is," he says, his face showing every one of his sixty-seven years. "I sent two men to Seattle after Duncan went dark, but Kellan hasn't checked in since yesterday afternoon."

"Kellan?" My voice ain't steady, but I manage to extricate myself from West's supportive arm and step out from behind Ryker. "You've been had, Angelo. Kellan is working for the DeLucas."

"He *was* working for the DeLucas," West adds.

"Impossible! You have no proof—"

I remove my hat, not bothering to stifle my wince at the motion. "*I'm* the proof. Kellan is the one who cut off part of my ear when I wouldn't tell him and another of DeLuca's idjits what I knew about Nash."

Shock and confusion war in his expression. "Nash? Who the hell is Nash?"

"Your son. His name is Nash Grace now, and we're..." My throat feels it's full of a whole mess of cotton, and I swallow hard. "I went and fell in love with him, Angelo. But the DeLucas took him before they worked me over, and he ain't got much time left."

Joey grabs me and presses the barrel of a gun to my temple. "You're dead. All of you."

I roll my eyes at Angelo. "This one ain't too bright." Slamming my foot down on Joey's instep, I duck while West relieves him of his weapon, ejects the clip and tosses both pieces onto Angelo's desk.

"We can do this with you, or without you, Rossi," the former SEAL says. "But I'd wager DeLuca's endgame involves you. If you want to save Nash's life, you'll come with us. Right now."

Nash

On my hands and knees, I spit blood onto Rocco's shoes. The Neanderthal kicks me in the gut. "How much more, boss?"

Lincoln, who's spent the past hour leaning against the wall, glances over at me. "Keep going until my father comes back. Just don't kill him. Yet."

Rocco bends down to peer at me. "He doesn't look too good."

"Fuck...you...asshole," I wheeze. Grabbing his ankle, I jerk it toward me with all the strength and speed I can muster. He lands on his ass, and Benny strides over and slams the butt of his gun against my temple.

Dazed, I curl into a ball. In my periphery, the high windows show off clear blue sky. What time is it? Does it matter? I'm going to die today, but not before Enzo finds some way to kill my father too.

Shadows move above me. Someone—Rocco?—grabs my left wrist and wrenches my index finger hard enough something pops.

My scream echoes off the concrete walls. Pulling my hand to my chest, I fight the darkness racing for me. I'm alone. Raelynn is probably dead. Tortured until Enzo got what he wanted out of her, then tossed away like yesterday's trash. My father is alive, but for how long?

A second pop. This time, I can only moan. Blinking hard through my tears, I start shaking. Nausea crawls up my raw throat. Fingers aren't supposed to bend that way.

"Sit him up," Lincoln says sharply. "Against the wall."

Rocco drags me by my throbbing hand. The motion snaps one of my fingers back into place. My whimper sounds far away. Like someone's wrapped my head in cotton.

The cement wall is blessedly cool through my t-shirt. I lift my head, needing to know what's coming next. They were careful. Kept the punches to my ribs, my back, my jaw. I can still see, and I wonder why they care.

Enzo saunters into the room, a cell phone in his hand. "The men I left in Seattle just reported in, Nathan. Your girlfriend died screaming."

No.

I try to stand, desperate to make Enzo pay for what he did to Raelynn, but I don't rise more than a couple of inches before collapsing again.

Enzo nods to Rocco, who pulls a zip tie out of his pocket and tightens it around my wrists. The plastic digs into my skin, burning more with each beat of my heart.

My ankles are next. Idiots. Didn't they see me fall only seconds ago?

Benny moves next to me, his gun aimed at my head as Enzo dials.

"Angelo."

"Where is my son?" The voice pulls a choked sob from my swollen lips.

"Dad..." I whisper.

"See for yourself," Enzo says and turns the phone around.

I start to cry. It's been twenty years, but the memories come rushing back in a tidal wave. Dad cheering me on at the state championships. Laughing over *Monopoly*. Hugging me before bed.

"Nathan. Oh, God. You piece of shit. What have you done to him?" The video shakes. I have to talk to him. Keep him calm. Warn him what Enzo is planning.

"Dad...don't listen—" Benny fists a clump of my hair and slams my head against the wall.

"Keep quiet, *Nathan*," the enforcer snarls.

Enzo chuckles. "Imagine my surprise when one of my men called me from Seattle and said he was certain he'd found your son.. Ran right into him on the street. He looks so much like you did at his age. Or...he used to."

"I'll kill you for this, Enzo," my father snarls.

"No. You won't. If you want Nathan to survive, you'll listen carefully and do exactly what I tell you."

I want to wipe that gleeful smile off Enzo's wrinkled face. With a battering ram. Or a chainsaw. Or a nail gun.

"Anything. Just let him go!" My dad's anguish bleeds over the call. God, I wish I could talk to him. Hug him. Tell him I love him.

"At 8:00 p.m., I will text you an address. You will have thirty minutes to show up. Alone. If you're late, Nathan dies. If my men see a single one of your enforcers, Nathan dies. If you call the police or the FBI, Nathan—"

"Dies. I get the picture. What do you want, DeLuca? Are you going to try to kill me? Again?"

"Hardly. When you arrive, you'll record a video confessing to the murder of my wife and daughter, as well as all the other crimes you've committed over the years. Do that, send it to the authorities—along with your location—and when they come to arrest you, I will release Nathan."

My heart cracks into pieces. Enzo won't let me live. My father has to know that.

"Why should I believe you? You've spent twenty years

trying to finish what you started. I didn't order the hit. My father did. Yet you came after my family. Killed *my* wife and daughter. Shot my son. And me. Isn't that enough?"

"It will *never* be enough! Laura and Iris died screaming. Burning. You're lucky I'm still the head of this family. Because if my son were in charge, he'd carve Nathan into pieces and mail them to you. One a week. For years."

Enzo nods at Benny, who wedges the gun under my chin hard enough to force my head back. Flipping the phone so my father can see me—and the gun—he smiles.

"Enjoy your last few hours of freedom, Rossi. Because tonight, your control of this city ends. For good."

I don't care if he shoots me. I have to warn him. But before I can say a word, the screen goes black.

CHAPTER TWENTY-THREE

Raelynn

ANGELO SLUMPS back in the chair, and I snatch his phone before it hits the floor. "DeLuca's going to kill him."

"No shit. That's why we're here."

I'm so angry with the man in front of me. How could he send his son away, let him think he'd lost everything, and *never* contact him? If Angelo had kept Nash with him, maybe...

Then he wouldn't be...Nash. But he might be...safe.

Living in the world of "what ifs" won't help me save him. Or do anything but leave me two sandwiches short of a picnic.

Nash knows he's going to die. It was in his eyes. His body language. His desperate attempt to warn his father. The man I'm falling in love with—who am I kidding? I've fallen, hard—could barely move. Bloody, bound, beaten...

"We're in position," Ryker says over comms.

Angelo grabs my wrist. I don't think. Sweeping my arm

across my body in an arc, my free hand holding his in place, I twist and send him to his knees. "Not. Another. Word."

On my laptop screen, five green blips move toward the target. Before Ryker and West deposited us in this hotel suite, Angelo gave them the location of the DeLuca compound, and they're about to breach, hoping to find Nash long before 8:00 p.m.

"Body cam on," West adds. "Sierra, check the feed."

Scrambling for the computer, I pull it with me and take a seat on the bed. I made Ryker promise he wouldn't keep me in the dark, but I never expected this. When did we get body cams?

The GPS signals move closer to the house, each with one letter inside the little dot letting me know who's who.

From Hidden Agenda's warehouse, Ripper pilots one of the new drones over the grounds. "Two heat signatures," he says.

Only two? That can't be right. Five minutes ago, there were at least three people in that basement. Nash, Enzo, and the guy holding the gun. Even if they shot Nash the second the call ended, his body heat would still register. And there's no way in hell the place isn't crawling with muscle.

"Say again, Base?" West asks.

"Two heat signatures. And yes, the drone is working. I see the five of you outside the perimeter, and another dozen folks on the street within a two mile radius. Sending the data to your wrist units now."

Something's very wrong. The two red dots on screen move from one room to another, but casually. Slowly. Like they don't have a care in the world.

"What's going on?" Angelo asks. "You're worried."

"You're goddamn right, I'm worried. DeLuca's so crooked, if he swallowed a nail, he'd spit out a corkscrew. Now hush up. They're about to go in." I tap a few keys, and link our comms system to the laptop's speaker.

West's body cam shows him scaling a twelve-foot-tall stone wall. He's up and over so quick, he's not even winded.

Lush grounds, covered with dogwood and redbud trees in full bloom, provide cover, and the green dots creep closer and closer to the house.

"Indigo, any movement?" Ry asks.

"Negative. It's a ghost town."

"Tango and Golf, prepare to breach." West finds the junction box, places a small det charge around the conduit, and backs away. "On my mark. Three. Two. One. Mark."

With a loud *crack* and a hiss, the explosion takes out the power. The two red dots stop moving. Less than a minute later, Graham shouts, "On your knees, hands in the air!" But it's his next words that make my heart sink. "Both hostiles surrendered. Looks like the chef and a housekeeper. Securing them now."

"Dammit!" All my pent-up fear and frustration spill over. "Check the basement," I say. "The target has to be..."

"I'm there now. This isn't the same room." West turns in a circle, shining his flashlight to give me a better look. Enzo had Nash against a concrete wall. Sitting on cement. Natural light came from above his head. This room is completely underground, with wood-paneled walls and white, shiny tile covering the floor.

He's not there. He was *never* there. Any chance we had of finding him before tonight slips away.

"Fall back. Bring the two hostiles. We'll stash them away until this is over so they can't tell Enzo anything about us," the SEAL orders, and I cut the comms feed from the laptop.

Angelo paces, his cane making soft *thumping* noises on the thick carpeting. "Stash them away? What does that mean? Their bodies? How would they tell DeLuca anything?"

I tap my comms unit to mute it. "They're still alive. My guess? Enzo left those two in case you sent anyone to his compound. There might have been a panic button somewhere, or he was countin' on you lettin' them go when you didn't find Nash."

"Nathan," Angelo snaps.

I push to my feet, ignoring the stab of pain through my knee so I can get in the man's face. "His *name* is Nash. You lost the right to call him Nathan when you abandoned him and let him think you were dead."

"I did that to protect him!"

"Well, bless your heart, sugar. Ain't you just the sweetest, most dotin' father on the planet. Did he look safe to you?"

Angelo's shoulders slump. He leans heavily on his cane, all the fight leaching out of him in a single, heavy sigh. "No."

I ain't done with the man. Not yet. "Did you know he still has one of Mae's stuffed animals? He's kept Bandit safe for twenty years. Through more moves than he can count. The first thing he told me about his family? How he always let her win at hopscotch."

Tears glisten in the older man's eyes. Where Nash's are the blue of a summer sky and just as warm, Angelo's are frosty. A winter's morning, pale and cold and clear as ice. "Bandit saved his life. Nathan tripped and the shots went wide. He was barely breathing when the ambulance arrived."

"And where were *you*?"

Angelo pulls a handkerchief from his pocket and swipes at his cheek. "In the hall. The bullet grazed my spine. I couldn't feel my legs for weeks. Lincoln—Enzo's son—wanted me to watch my family die. But a neighbor heard my wife scream and called the police. He ran before he could finish me off."

With nothing to distract me from the horrors of Nash's

childhood, I lower myself onto the edge of the bed and rub my knee gently. "Whose idea was it to send Nash away?"

"Mine." Angelo moves to the window and stares at the park across the street. Children play on swings. Mothers stand at the fringes with strollers, coffee cups in hand. "When Stella found out she was pregnant with Nathan—*Nash*—I told my father I was out. He tried to convince me to stay, but when that failed, he called Duncan."

"Shut the front door. Your *father* got you into Witness Protection?"

With a soft smile, Angelo nods. "He let the FBI raid one of his clubs—on a night some of Enzo's generals were there for a meeting—in exchange for our entrance into the program. The first time I met Duncan was in my father's office a week before we left Chicago."

"Ten minutes out," Ryker says in my ear. "Base, are you there?"

I shoot Angelo a look. "Hold up. I need to listen."

"Base here," Wren says. "What do you need?"

"Property records. Anything owned by the DeLuca family that might have a basement. We searched the pool house and the garage. But a guy like this...he's got a mistress stashed somewhere. Maybe two. Same with the son."

"On it."

I tap my earbud, activating the mic. "Romeo, what's goin' on with the two...not-hostiles?"

"Whiskey will interrogate them. If they know anything, he'll get it out of them."

"You're bringin' them *here?*" I don't know why this surprises me. We're in a new city, no resources beyond what we brought with us, and very little intel.

My phone—an exact copy of the one I bricked—vibrates, and I unlock the screen.

Ryker: Is Angelo listening?

"Negative," I say quietly.

The bone-conduction mics are so sensitive, I think I hear Ryker sigh. "I don't trust that asshole. But he'll have insights into Enzo's behavior we don't. I'd stash these two somewhere much less *comfortable* than the Five Points, but Base would have a harder time monitoring the camera feeds."

He's right. All of the Five Points hotels worldwide run Oversight, the business security software West's wife designed. Cam wasn't thrilled we asked for backdoor access to the system, but even her strong moral code won't stop her from doing anything to keep West safe.

"Ignore me. I'm near about past goin'."

"What the fuck does that mean?"

I snort, then wince. "Means I've been up for twenty...no, *thirty* hours, not countin' the time I spent unconscious."

"We're pulling into the garage now. As soon as we're settled, you're relieved. Take an hour—or three. If anything breaks, we'll come get you."

I want to protest. But my thoughts feel like they're moving through quicksand. If I don't sleep, I'll be worthless as teats on a bull.

Five minutes later, I stretch out in the second bedroom. As I drift away, I offer up a quick prayer that wherever Nash is, he knows we're comin' for him.

Nash

I jerk awake, Raelynn's name on my lips. For a few brief moments every hour, I fall asleep. Or pass out, I can't be sure. After Enzo and his goons left, I dragged myself across the basement to the sink. Half a dozen times, I tried to stand, until finally, I got my bound feet under me and pulled myself up.

The water tasted like sweet relief, though the bitter tang of blood still coats my tongue. Hunger claws at my stomach, warring with bouts of nausea. No one's bothered to bring me food. Why when they're going to kill me in a few hours?

Lying on my side, a few feet from the sink, I stare out the windows high on the opposite wall at a single tree in the distance. Its leaves sway gently in the breeze. The sun paints it in a dull, orange glow. It has to be past 6:00 p.m. I only have another two hours to live. At most.

I wish I could have seen Raelynn one more time. I don't know when I knew I'd loved her. On the plane? When Lincoln told me they were going to kill her? Or in the back of the SUV on the way here? Wherever *here* is.

Why did I ask her to get my tools? I could have worked with that narrow paint scraper. I would have picked the paint off one chip at a time with my fingernails—or my teeth—to save her life.

Every bad decision I've ever made plays on a loop in my head. From leaving Frank in Reno to opening Raelynn's front door, thinking her neighbor needed help.

Had I changed even one of them...she'd be safe.

The basement door creaks open.

No. I'm not ready.

Rocco and Benny don't give me a choice. They each take an arm, dragging me out of the room and up a set of stairs. My knees thud against each step.

"Please," I manage. "You don't have to do this."

Rocco laughs. "Didn't think you were that dumb, Rossi."

"Fuck you."

Benny shoots him a questioning look, and the two men drop me. My head hits the railing on the way down. The world spins when they lift me again. Why didn't I keep my mouth shut?

At the top of the stairs, in a small kitchen, Lincoln waits for us. On the counter next to him, a roll of duct tape and some black material, wadded up in a loose ball.

"Hold up." He tears a strip off the tape and nods. Rocco shifts his hold and yanks my head back.

"No, don't!" I thrash and jerk, pain pricking my scalp as a chunk of my hair pulls free. But it's no use. Lincoln slaps the tape over my lips as I scream obscenities at him.

I can only scream as he pulls a hood over my head, closing me in a dark, stuffy cocoon. Every breath is a struggle. Panic takes over. My limbs flail helplessly, the zip ties tight enough they cut into my wrists.

The scent of rubber and exhaust hit me through the hood. The enforcers shove me. My back hits a hard surface, and one of them grabs my feet and forces me to bend my knees. An engine rumbles to life, the trunk lid slams over me, and I wonder if this is where I die.

CHAPTER TWENTY-FOUR

Nash

I DRIFT IN AND OUT. The dull roar of the engine and the steady *thump, thump, thump* of the road conspire against me. Or...are they doing me a favor? The panic fades with every mile, and my mind wanders.

Will it hurt? Dying? How will it happen? A bullet to the head? Been there, done that, have the scar to prove it. An overdose? Enzo—or one of his men—could slit my throat. Does anyone still use the old "tied to a cement block and thrown off a pier" thing? Or is that just in the movies?

The car slows. Turns. Stops.

Is this it?

Voices. Enzo, I think. Rocco. I can't make out what they're saying. I wish they'd get it over with.

The trunk opens. Fuck. I don't want to die. All I can do is whimper when rough hands drag me from the car. The ground is uneven, my shoes dragging, toes catching on small divots every few steps. Fresh air replaces the stench of exhaust, even under the heavy black hood. All I can see are my bound hands, two fingers horribly swollen.

It gets brighter for all of a couple of seconds before a heavy door opens. Inside, the floor is smooth, the air stuffy.

Ten steps. Fifteen. Counting stops me from losing control and sobbing until the end. I want to see my dad one more time. Enzo will make sure he knows I'm here. That I'm alive. Maybe I can warn him. Somehow.

Someone snaps the zip tie around my wrists. But with my ankles bound, the freedom does me no good. I'm dragged until my back hits a pole, and my arms are wrenched behind me.

"No. Use the ropes," Lincoln says sharply. "Less evidence, in the end."

Balling my hands into fists, I try to make myself bigger—like West did for his self-defense class. Rough fibers drag over my skin, cinched so tight, I'm not sure my efforts will do any good.

They cut my legs free, then force me down onto my ass before they tie my ankles together, and pull off the hood.

A shadowy figure looms over me. Enzo. "Do you know where you are, Nathan?"

Gagged, I can't tell him to go fuck himself.

Of course I don't know where I am, shithead. Your goons put a hood over my head and threw me in the truck of a car.

"This is one of your father's warehouses." Enzo sweeps his hand in a wide arc, and I squint into the distance. Hundreds of boxes are stacked against concrete walls. Bourbon. Gin. Vodka. "He forced me out of the liquor business five years ago. Would you like to know how?"

I don't give a flying fuck.

"He burned my inventory to the ground." Excitement brightens his eyes as Lincoln hands him a bottle of vodka. Enzo cracks the seal and takes a swig. "I'd offer you some, but..." He shrugs, leans down, and taps the bottle to the tape over my lips.

All around the building, men rip into the boxes, open a bottle or two, and pour the contents over the cardboard. But it's not until Enzo upends the vodka all over my legs that I realize what he's planning.

"No. You can't. Just shoot me!"

My pleas dissolve into muffled grunts. Enzo grabs my chin and squeezes hard enough, tears spring to my eyes. "My wife and daughter burned to death. My liquor business burned to death. You and your father will do the same."

I jerk against the ropes, desperate for any slack, any way to get myself free. Until Benny jogs over, pulls a gun from under his jacket, and presses it to my collar bone. "We're ready boss."

"If he moves, shoot him in the kneecaps," Enzo says. "Lincoln? Start the car. I want to be on the ridge overlooking the warehouse in plenty of time to watch Angelo arrive. I'll be out in five minutes."

The younger DeLuca passes his father a cell phone. "I want to see that son of a bitch when you tell him where we are."

"No. Start the car. I am still the head of this family, and I will *not* have my son challenge me!" Enzo's hand flies, the slap echoing off the concrete walls.

Shock gives way to anger, but when Benny stands up straighter, Lincoln drops his head. "I'll be in the car."

Enzo gives him a terse nod, then unlocks the phone. "Time to call your father, Nathan. I'm sure he'll be *dying* to see you again."

Raelynn

The two blessed hours I slept were enough to take the edge off my exhaustion, but getting up again almost broke me.

I've checked my phone a dozen times in the past five minutes, and it's still only 7:45 p.m. Limping out to the main room, I find West and Ryker with a French Press pot of coffee between them. "Any chance y'all have a cup to spare? Or a lidocaine shot? Or both?"

West looks me up and down. "What did Connor say on the plane?"

"Five miles of bad road in the middle of nowhere," Ry says.

"I ain't lookin' to win a beauty pageant. You gonna help a girl out? Or not?"

Ryker lumbers to his feet and retrieves one of the collapsible mugs from a duffel bag on the floor while West snags his med kit.

"Drop your pants and sit." The SEAL hooks his foot around a chair and tugs it closer.

My left leg is a mass of blue and purple bruises—one in the distinct shape of Diego's shoe. Disapproval and concern war in West's eyes. "Promise me you'll stay in the van unless one of us calls for assistance."

If I didn't know what those words mean to the two men, I'd lie through my sore and slightly loose front teeth. But when I joined Hidden Agenda, Ry sat me down, a grave expression on his scarred face.

"We don't have many rules here, Raelynn. Always answer your phone. Show up for workouts. Don't tell civilians what we do."

"Okay, boss—"

"I'm not done," he says. "There's one more. You don't make a

promise you can't—or don't intend to—keep. If you say 'I promise,' you better make sure you mean it."

"Raelynn? I need to hear you say it," West prods.

"I love him." Those three words break me. I don't cry. I can't. But somewhere deep inside, a canyon of grief waits to swallow me whole.

"We know." Ryker drops a hand on my shoulder, giving it a gentle squeeze. "Trust us to get him back."

I let my gaze ping between the two men. They gave me a chance. A life when all I wanted was to hide away from the world—or burn it all down.

Eyes locked on West, I take a deep breath. "I promise I won't leave the van unless it's the only way to save him. That's all I can give you. *Please.* That has to be enough."

He nods and unzips his med kit. "It's enough. You ready? This is going to hurt."

"Do it."

West gently raises my leg so my foot rests on his thigh, then chuckles. "Reynolds deserves a raise."

"I pay him well enough," Ry mutters. "He's not hurting for cash."

Leaning forward, I scan the bright green tape criss-crossing the joint. Just under my kneecap, the doctor drew a small *X* in black pen.

West skims his fingers on either side of the mark. "This has to go under the patella. Ry, stabilize her leg. If she moves, I'll do more harm than good."

Ryker kneels next to me, one big hand around my calf, the other pressing down on my thigh. A thin, high-pitched whimper escapes my lips when the needle hits the nerve. It's like ten thousand volts shooting all the way up my leg.

Graham rushes into the room, gaping at the sight of me: half naked, tears streaming down my cheeks, my foot in

West's lap, and Ryker holding me down. "What the hell?" he asks as Inara joins him.

"Y'all better not...breathe a word...of this...to anyone," I hiss through the pain.

"Done." West caps the needle and shoves it into a portable sharps container. "Wait five minutes before you put any weight on it."

"With my ass hangin' out? Get me a blanket or somethin'."

Ry slides his hands under my arms and lifts me to my feet. I barely have time to grab my pants before I'm upright. "Warn a girl, next time, will ya'?"

"I think the words you're looking for are 'thank you.'"

Using the table for support, I turn so I can meet his gaze. "I ain't one for trustin' people. Can't say it'll ever come easy. But y'all are...family. Thank you."

The throbbing in my knee that's been my constant companion since the previous night fades away. "Whoa. That shit is magic."

"You only get one," West says with a grim smile. "But the cortisone the doc gave you should take over in a day or so."

"Get in here!" Tank calls from the next room. "DeLuca's calling!"

Ryker picks me up with one arm around my waist and deposits me directly in front of Angelo. "Remember, Rossi. You need proof of life before you go *anywhere*."

Nash's father nods. His hands shake. Ryker passes him the phone, a cable connecting it to West's laptop so we can all see what Angelo sees, without the camera catching sight of us.

We spent hours this afternoon drilling instructions into the man. Don't say a word about us. Work in the words Bandit, West, or cat. Anything to let Nash know he's not alone.

"DeLuca. Where is my son?" Angelo snaps.

Enzo switches the call to video. Nash sits on the ground against a thick yellow pole. A strip of duct tape covers his mouth, but it's the gun pointed at his neck I can't take my eyes from.

"As you can see, he is alive. And he will stay that way if you follow my instructions."

Nash screams something behind the gag, and the man at his side cocks the hammer on the gun.

"If your son does not calm down, he will spend the rest of his life with two shattered knees," Enzo says.

I cut my gaze to West, who tucks a comms unit into his ear. I mirror the motion. "These assholes are unoriginal as fuck," he whispers.

I'd laugh if it weren't for the desperation in Nash's eyes.

"Nathan, stay calm. I'll get you out of this. In a few hours, this will all be a painful memory. You can go back *west*—back to Seattle."

"Enough talk." Enzo turns the phone around so his face fills the screen. "I'm sending you the address now. When you arrive—alone—you will enter the building. You will find a phone on the floor. Pick it up and record your confession. When you're done, you'll receive further instructions. Good bye, Angelo."

"Wait!" Nash's father shouts. "Let me talk to my son—"

"You can talk to him when you get here. Have a nice little family reunion. Don't be late."

The call ends, and Ryker immediately taps his earbud. "Base, tell me you got *something*."

"Nothing worth spit," Wren says. "From the way Enzo's voice echoed, the walls are concrete or cement. Ceilings twenty to thirty feet tall. The camera caught a few boxes, but we can't tell what's in them. I can try to enhance the video, but—"

"Liquor," Angelo says. An hour ago, West caved and

offered the man a comms unit of his own with strict instructions to give it back the second Nash was safe. "Enzo sent the address. It's a small warehouse down by the docks. For the past few years, I've stored all my liquor shipments there."

West plugs the address into his phone. "Pack up. It's twenty minutes away. We're out of here in five."

Everyone starts to move like a well-oiled machine. But I stay still for a long moment, my eyes closed, and send out a silent plea to the man I love.

"We're comin', darlin'. Hang on for me."

CHAPTER TWENTY-FIVE

Nash

BENNY STANDS AT THE DOOR, his gaze trained on me. As soon as he left my side, I relaxed, hoping I'd done enough to create slack in the ropes around my wrists, but they're still too tight for me to escape.

For a few minutes, I tried to feel for the ends, but he snapped at me to "stop moving" and pointed the gun at my head.

My eyelids feel like coarse-grit sandpaper, and my ribs ache with each breath. The tape tugs at my split lips. But the worst part is the overwhelming stench of vodka coming from my jeans.

Benny pulls a lighter from his pocket, flicking it on and off while chuckling. Smoke inhalation will get me before the flames. At least...I hope it does. But what about my father?

Has it been half an hour? Dad has to know this is a trap. Maybe he won't come. Maybe the cops are on their way right now. Maybe they'll get to Benny before he can shoot me in the head. Or set the liquor-soaked boxes on fire. Maybe I'll live through this.

The door opens, and Rocco slips into the warehouse. "He's here. Boss says he's alone."

"Hear that, asshole?" Benny asks. "Hope you've made peace with your maker."

"Fuck you!"

I might as well be singing him a lullaby for all the good shouting through the tape does me. The two enforcers share a laugh before Rocco pulls a gun from under his jacket and Benny retrieves a length of rope from a small, black duffel bag. They take up positions behind the door.

My father enters without hesitation, making it half a dozen steps into the warehouse before Rocco comes up behind him and jabs the gun against his ribs. The cane clatters to the floor, and Dad's gaze locks onto mine.

"That's far enough," Rocco says. Benny levels a hard punch to his jaw, sending him to his knees.

"Nash..."

The anguish in his voice breaks me. Tears gather in my eyes, lending a shimmer to the room. Dad pats the ground twice before the two thugs drag him to another pole twenty feet away, and in under a minute, have his arms bound behind him. Benny retrieves a full bottle of vodka and pours it over my father's white hair.

I scream at them, begging them to stop, then cursing them and their entire families, but they ignore me.

"Enjoy your last few minutes together," Rocco says. He strides over to me and rips the tape from my mouth, tearing my wounds open so blood drips down my chin. "So you can say your goodbyes before you burn."

"Dad!"

He's shaking, unable to stop the alcohol from dripping

into his eyes. "I'm sorry...son. I thought I was keeping you safe."

Benny holds the door for Rocco, who withdraws a silver case from his pocket, opens it, and lifts a cigarette to his lips. "Arson investigators won't find shit when this is all over. Except this. Steel. Fireproof. One smoke missing."

Chuckling, he drops the case, lights up, and flicks the cigarette in an arc toward one of the boxes. The glowing tip flares bright red, and a second later, the box starts to burn.

Raelynn

"Idiot," West mutters. "We're sure his comms unit was working?"

I glance at the tablet in front of me. "It's still green. So it's transmittin'."

God, I wish we knew what was goin' on inside. The concrete walls of the building render our drone's thermal imaging capabilities useless, but twelve separate readings within a quarter mile are all likely Enzo's men.

"Angelo," West says. "What's going on? Angelo?"

"Somethin's wrong. We need to get in there. Now." I hate being this far away. We couldn't risk driving the van all the way to the waterfront, so I'm half a mile down the shore road, while Angelo took the sedan—outfitted with a small camera on the dash—and parked less than a hundred feet from the building.

"Too many unknowns." This, from Ryker. "I've got eyes on Enzo and Lincoln. Indigo?"

"In position. Two hostiles on the roof across from me in my sights."

On screen, two goons slip out the door of the warehouse,

laughing. The guy on the left, I recognize from the video calls as the one holding a gun on Nash.

So...does that mean Nash is unguarded?

"Who's on the idjits who just came out of the target's location? They ain't movin'." I check the monitor again, gripping the steering wheel so hard, my knuckles turn white. Still nothing from Angelo. "Base? If the walls are too thick, could that mess with comms?"

"We've tested through eight-inch-thick concrete with only twenty percent degradation," Wren says. "Searching for the building blueprints—"

Ryker cuts her off. "Fuck this shit. Whiskey, call it."

"Indigo, take out the hostiles on the roof, then lay down cover fire for Tango so he can hit the two at the target location. Golf, you've got the three along First Avenue. Romeo, you're on Enzo. I've got the two at the southeast corner of the fence. Sierra...don't move until we give you the all clear. Stay low, stay alive. Go, go, go."

The green blips on the left half of the screen start to move —all but mine and Inara's. On the right, the two men who were just inside with Nash and Angelo lean against the wall of the building to the west. The asshole with the gun—Wren's facial recognition program identified him as Benny Montrose —takes a puff on his vape, while the other one checks his phone.

Sharp pops pierce the night air. "Two down," Inara says quietly. "Tango, on your mark."

The hostiles—red dots from the drone's thermals—all move at once. Shots come from every direction. One M4 and at least two pistols.

"Enzo's rabbiting!" Ry shouts. "I'm going for the sedan. Base, stay on them with the drone as long as you can!"

Shit. This op is goin' to hell on a rocket, and I've got no

idea if Nash is still alive. I can't sit here and do nothin', even if I did promise West I'd stay in the van.

"Unless it's the only way to save him."

The engine rumbles to life, and the tires spin on the gravel shoulder for a split second before I take off, gunning it down the shore road toward the industrial park gate.

"Got a problem!" Inara says, fear threading her tone. "Target's location is on fire!"

Nash

Flames spread from box to box, faster than I thought possible. Across from me, my father strains against the ropes. "Can you get free?" he shouts.

"What does it matter?" The fire is a physical being now. Roaring, climbing the walls, desperate for more fuel. The first bottle of liquor explodes, the sound of glass breaking, followed by another, and another, and another.

Coughing, my father chokes out, "Your friends..."

Holy shit. "Dad? What friends? Names!" I twist my hands, feeling for the ends of the rope trapping me.

"Don't know...but your girl...she's waiting..."

Oh God. Raelynn's alive. She's *here*.

"Slow your breathing, Dad. Please!" He's closer to the fire than I am and drenched in vodka. If I don't get to him fast, he'll die. My swollen fingers send electric shocks of pain through my hands, but I find one blunt end of the rope and start working it through the knots.

Smoke burns my lungs. The first cough steals my breath. More bottles shatter. Bits of cork and plastic arc through the air. Another knot unravels. How many more? God, I need to be able to see. My eyes are watering, each cough pure agony on my ribs, and my father slumps forward.

Fuck! The flames are only a few feet away from him.

Tugging with all of my strength, I wrench my right arm free. Then my left. I strip off my shirt, tearing it in half and tying it around my mouth and nose.

It takes me precious seconds to loosen the ropes around my ankles, and when I try to stand, the room dissolves into a swirling miasma of orange, red, and gray.

"Dad," I croak. "I'm…coming!"

Twice, the dizziness takes me down. Each time, the concrete under me gets hotter. Crawling the last few feet, I attack the knots. As soon as his arms are free, I drag him to the center of the room.

It's getting harder to breathe. Harder to see. Smoke covers the ceiling, curling around the rafters, desperate for somewhere else to go. A window behind us shatters, and the *whoosh* of air fans the flames even higher.

My father coughs weakly. My t-shirt is the only article of clothing we have not soaked in vodka, so I rip it into two long strips and wind the second one around his head. "Dad, wake up," I plead, slapping his cheek gently. "We have to find a way out of here."

The smoke is so thick, I can't see the door. There has to be more than one.

"Nathan…" he wheezes. "Leave me."

"No. I lost you once. I won't do it again!" A coughing fit steals my voice. We don't have much longer.

Behind me, there's a narrow gap in the flames. Crawling, my breathing ragged and tears streaming down my cheeks as I drag my father behind me, I see a metal door.

Ten feet away, I have to let him go. The fire's too close.

I push to my feet, fighting the darkness creeping along the edges of my vision. The knob burns my palm, but I ignore the pain and twist. Nothing happens. Feeling all along the metal, barely able to see, I search for a lock. Some way to get through. But after a full minute, I collapse, my knees slamming into the hot cement.

Above me, windows shatter, and glass rains down over my head, shoulders, and back like hundreds of tiny missiles. I pound on the door with everything I have in me.

My father stirs. "Nathan...it's...no use..."

He's right. We're going to die, and Raelynn will be the one to find our bodies.

"Sorry, sweetness," I choke out. "I love...you."

Raelynn

I take the corner on two wheels, and floor it down the hill toward the warehouse. The windows—all along the roof line—glow bright orange. Half a dozen of them have already exploded from the heat, and smoke rises fifty feet in the air.

Inara races across the parking lot, and I slam on the brakes to avoid running her down. "Shee-it!"

A shot hits the side of the van as I jump out. Another whizzes close to my ear before I duck. "Indigo! Takin' fire!"

She drops to one knee, lifts her rifle, and sends half a dozen shots across the parking lot. "Get to the building. I'll cover you."

My knee threatens to buckle on my first step, but I grit my teeth and run for the door. It's too hot to touch. Yanking my sleeve down over my hand, I try the knob. "Son of a bitch!" Even through the fabric, it burns.

There has to be another entrance. Some way in that isn't the temperature of molten lava. But there's so much smoke. Why didn't I insist we take the warehouse sooner?

On the east wall, there's another door. This one's a mite cooler. But it won't budge. It's not locked—the knob turns easily—but even when I throw my shoulder against the metal, nothing happens.

"Whiskey, I can't get in. The door won't budge!"

West grunts, then I hear a single shot from his M4. "Metal expands." Another shot. "You need the battering ram. Or another way in."

I hightail it back to the van. Inara's still laying down cover fire. "Fucking asshole just won't die," she mutters as I pass her.

The portable ram weighs close to forty pounds. More than once, I stumble, off balance, as I drag my ass back across the parking lot and around the building. Adrenaline lends me strength I shouldn't have, but the pain in my shoulders almost sends me to my knees on the first hit.

The second connects solidly, but the door doesn't buckle. A third is off center.

"Nash!" I yell, swinging with everything I have in me. The metal screams, and I'm starin' at a wall of flames bigger than hell and half of Texas.

"Nash!" I lift my sweater over my nose and mouth, and step into the firestorm. There's so much smoke, I can't see shit until I trip and land on something big and bulky and...oh, God.

The man I love is face down, covered in blood. He doesn't stir. Neither does Angelo, who's lying next to him, holding Nash's hand.

For a split second, I can't move. Nash would want me to save his father first. But...

"If you die on me," I scream as I hook my arms under Angelo's and drag him back toward the door, "I'm *never* gonna forgive you!"

The inferno spits at us, and sparks hit Angelo's legs. In a

heartbeat, his pants catch fire. Dropping him on the asphalt, I strip off my sweater and start beating at the flames. Nash is still in there, but I can't let his father burn.

"Move!" West shouts. I leap out of the way, and he jumps on top of Angelo, wrapping him in a thick, wool blanket to smother the flames.

Racing back inside, I roll Nash over. He starts coughing and jerks when I grasp his arms. "Don't fight me!" I snap. "We're gettin' out of here."

His eyelids flutter and he stops flailing. Each step feels like a mile. He's got thirty, maybe forty pounds on his father, and I'm fadin' fast. But then Graham's at my side. "I've got him. Trust me. We're right behind you."

Trust me.

Last week, those two words wouldn't have meant spit. But now, I can let go. Nash is alive, and my family's got my back.

CHAPTER TWENTY-SIX

Nash

"DARLIN'? Can you open your eyes for me?" Gentle fingers caress my cheek.

My throat burns, and I start to cough. Panic has me struggling to sit up. Everything's hazy, like I'm seeing the world through a dirty window, but nothing could hide Raelynn's blond hair. Or the bright pink streak across her forehead.

Someone hands her an oxygen mask, and she presses it over my nose and mouth. "Just breathe. You're safe. We're all safe."

After a few seconds, I can't *not* hold her. The mask hits the bed, and then she's in my arms. "Thought...I'd lost...you," I wheeze.

"I'm too ornery to die." Her tears drip onto my shoulder, and I start crying too. Until a man clears his throat from behind her.

"I'll be outside." West touches her arm briefly, and Raelynn grabs his hand.

"Thanks for stayin' with me. I couldn't..."

"Had to make sure you didn't test that knee," he says, a hint of a smile curving his lips. Turning to me, he sobers. "Nash, your father's in the ICU with severe smoke inhalation. His doctors don't think he'll need to stay there more than twenty-four hours though. He also sustained second-degree burns to both legs and his hand. He'll have some scarring, but overall, he was lucky."

"Lucky you were there, you mean," Raelynn says. "West came runnin' with a blanket like a *gen-u-ine* super hero."

The former SEAL slips out the door, and I take my first good look at the woman sitting on the bed next to me. The bright pink streak is a stretchy bandage wound around her head and over her left ear. Two black eyes, a deep gash on her cheek, bruises at her throat... "Shit, Raelynn. What did they do to you?"

"I could ask you the same question, darlin'." She takes my hand, gently touching my swollen fingers and the red welts around my wrist. "But I don't want to. Can I just...hold you for a while?"

Lying back, I let her snuggle against my chest. "I never should have left you," she says softly. "If I'd stayed..."

Talking hurts, but I can't stand the guilt in her voice. "No. You saved me. Fuck. You found my father and saved him too."

She lifts her head and brushes a tender kiss to my bruised and split lips. When she pulls back, tears glisten in her eyes. "I love you, Nash."

Hearing her say the words should make me the happiest man in the world, but instead, all I can think about is how I almost gave up in that warehouse. "Enzo told me his men had killed you," I manage. Tightening my arm around her waist, I stare up at the ceiling to hide my shame. "When the fire started, I figured...that was it. We were going to die, and I...I didn't care."

"Darlin'—"

I shake my head and find the courage to look her in the eyes. "My dad said something about my 'friends.' Then my 'girl.' That's when I knew I had to stay alive. I had to see you again so I could tell you...I love you too."

Raelynn

The thick brace makes every step awkward as fuck, but all that runnin' didn't do me any favors. I'm getting a lecture from Doc Reynolds when we get back to Seattle. He said as much this mornin' when he called to check in.

West dropped off some new clothes for Nash an hour ago, and I help him on with his t-shirt. More than a dozen cuts and twice as many bruises cover his torso, but he was lucky. A couple of bruised ribs, two dislocated fingers, and a mild concussion. In a few weeks, he'll be good as new. Physically, at least.

I watched him sleep for hours before I lost the battle with my heavy eyelids and passed out with my head on his chest.

"You going to tell me what happened here?" he asks, skimming a knuckle over the soot-stained pink compression wrap.

"Discharge paperwork," Graham says, poking his head into the room. "Nash is officially sprung."

I step back, pulling my hair over my bandaged ear.

"Shit. I interrupted something. Sorry." The youngest member of Hidden Agenda slips back into the hall, his cheeks flushing a dark crimson.

"Is he always that...?"

"Adorable? Yes." At his wounded look, I take Nash's hand

and bring it to my heart. "He's gay, darlin'. And even if he weren't, you're the one I love."

I can't kiss him the way I want. Not with his bottom lip split in two places. Or all our various injuries. Still, we're alive. Together. If only the future didn't have more questions than answers.

Graham pushes off the wall when we emerge. "Your dad's awake, Nash. He's one floor up. Elevator's this way." The young man sticks close—West's orders, I'm guessin'—until we reach Angelo's room. "I'll be out here. Take as long as you need."

"Do you want to go in alone?" I ask, though I keep a firm grip on his uninjured hand.

"No." Nash glances through the small window in the door. His shoulders slump. "I don't know what to say to him. He let me believe he was dead for twenty years. And..." He cups my cheek, his thumb skating just under my eye. "I almost lost you because of it."

The raw emotion in his voice chips away at the tenuous control I've fought to maintain since he was taken. He's not wrong. But in the end, Angelo was willing to do anything to save his son.

"He made mistakes, darlin'. And he knows it. I ain't sayin' he deserves a father of the year award, but give him a chance to explain."

Nash holds my gaze for so long, I start to worry, but after a heavy sigh, he nods, and we walk through the door together.

"I NEVER SHOULD HAVE SENT you away," Angelo says, his voice weak and raspy from the smoke. "But I didn't know what else to do. Duncan was convinced there was a mole in his office, so getting you out of the system was the only option."

"But why didn't you come with me?" Nash and I sit side by side in the hard plastic visitor's chairs. I rest my hand on his thigh, squeezing gently. He listened as his father explained how he'd survived the shooting, the 911 call, and begging Duncan to keep Nash safe.

"My father forbade it." Angelo's shoulders slump, and his hand shakes as he clutches the thin hospital blanket to his chest. He's weak, and a little loopy from the amount of morphine they're giving him. "He insisted the only way he could stop Enzo DeLuca was with my help. He said he... needed me."

Tears glisten in Nash's eyes. "*I* needed you! And you sent me to live with a stranger. I couldn't take *anything* with me except Mae's little stuffed sloth, and the only reason Frank let me keep *that* was because I swore I'd run away if he didn't."

"Nathan—*Nash*—I'll regret what I did for the rest of my life. But all I can do now is try to fix my mistakes." He turns his gaze to me. "Your boss came to see me this morning. The big one with the scars."

"Ry—"

"Code names only," I say sharply, cutting Nash off. "What we do ain't legal. Go on, Angelo. What did Romeo have to say?"

The older Rossi swallows hard before he'll look his son in the eyes. "He brought a man from the FBI with him. Special Agent Moss has been investigating me, and he has enough evidence to send me to prison for twenty years."

"No..." Nash leans forward and takes his father's hand in his. "Dad, I can't lose you again."

Angelo smiles. "'Romeo' knows people, son. Moss offered me a deal. Give up the 'family business,' help him shut down my suppliers, and I'll only do a year."

Nash studies his father, clearly wary. "And after that?"

I've worked with Ryker long enough to know exactly what

he'd demand before he let the FBI anywhere near Angelo. The man has connections all the way to the White House.

"The Rossi name is a death sentence, son. But 'Romeo' offered me a new one." Angelo's exhausted. Each word is weaker than the last. But the hope in his eyes burns bright. "I lost twenty years with you. I'll give up one more for the chance to see you again. To get to know the man you've become."

"Dad..." Nash hugs his father, and both men start to cry. I slip out of the room so they can have a few minutes alone, and lean against the wall next to Graham.

"Did you know about the shit with the FBI?" I ask.

He nods. "It was Connor's idea. Moss wanted to arrest Angelo on the spot."

"When's it gonna happen?"

Graham angles a glance at the nurses' station. Two men in suits stand at the desk. "As soon as Nash leaves. Angelo won't be released from the hospital for a week, but he'll have round-the-clock protection."

"We sure that'll be enough?" While the doctors worked on Nash the previous night, Ryker went after DeLuca and his son. Their car flipped over on a sharp turn. In what would have been the textbook definition of poetic justice, the impact sparked a fire, but Hidden Agenda's leader ain't one for prolonging the inevitable. He shot them both in the head, *then* let their bodies burn.

Graham gives me an "Are you kidding?" look. "Tank's sticking around for a few days. Long enough for Ry and Dax to make some calls and get a couple of guys they trust to take over."

"I'm guessin' you think I don't know nothin' from nothin' now."

Nudging my shoulder, Graham stares down at me. "I've been where you are, Raelynn. Remember?"

"Yeah. I do." My first mission with Hidden Agenda was to rescue Graham's boyfriend, Quinton. I was a stranger to him then. Hell, we'd gotten off on the wrong foot only days before, but he still trusted me when it counted. And last night, I finally returned the favor.

I swallow the lump swelling in my throat, and give the younger man a quick, one-armed hug. "Never got a chance to say thanks. For pullin' Nash out of that building."

We share a quiet moment, neither of us quite sure what to say, until Graham smiles. "That's what we do."

Nash

West hands me a brand new smartphone. "About time you upgraded to something made in *this* century," he says. "Raelynn has your new number. Figured you'd want one local to Seattle."

"What do I owe you?" As soon as I say the words, I regret them. First, because there's no fucking way I can afford a brand new device, then, because West gives me a sideways glance and shakes his head.

"We buy them a case at a time." Raelynn eases herself down on to the couch in the Five Points hotel suite. "You don't want to know how many we go through in a year."

"Where's...everyone else?" I ask. Graham is at the window, texting, but Tank, Inara, and Ryker are nowhere to be seen.

West starts the hotel's water kettle and spoons coffee grounds into a collapsible French press. "Ry's on his way back to Seattle with Inara. Tank's watching over your dad."

I have so many questions, but the first one I have to ask is, "You brought a coffee press *with you*?"

Raelynn's laugh soothes me like nothing else. "West is damn serious about his coffee, darlin'."

"Tactical genius doesn't happen without caffeine," the former SEAL deadpans. "You two probably want to shower and sleep, but give me ten minutes first."

"Only if you're makin' enough to share. I've been chewed up, spit out, and stepped on."

"Means she's tired," Graham calls from the next room. "I speak Texan."

"His boyfriend grew up there." Pouring the water in a slow circle, West inhales deeply. "Nectar of the gods, according to Cam. None of us have slept much in the past thirty-six hours."

"I got at least two hours overnight." Raelynn settles back on the sofa, her hand finding its way to my thigh. "Despite Nash's snorin'."

"I don't snore!"

"You did last night, darlin'. Smoke inhalation." Leaning in, she brushes a kiss to my cheek and drops her voice to a whisper. "You can saw wood every night for the rest of our lives and I won't care, because it'll mean you're safe. With me."

"I'd tell you to get a room," West says, retrieving three mugs from the little kitchenette and setting them on the coffee table, "but there's a perfectly good one through that door. *After* we talk about a few things."

The coffee helps me focus as West, Graham, and Raelynn tell me what happened after they got to Chicago. Meeting my father, discovering one of his men was loyal to Enzo, invading the DeLuca compound. And more.

"The chef and the housekeeper are being debriefed by the FBI. They turned on Enzo in a heartbeat. Apparently, he didn't believe in paying them very well." West shakes his head. "Asshole."

"We tried to send you a message through your father," Raelynn says. "When the call came in with your location, Angelo said you could go back 'west.' Did you catch that?"

"I don't remember anything from that call except how badly I wanted to warn my dad not to come. I didn't know you were here—that you were alive—until the fire started."

I'm suddenly so tired, not even one of Adam's double espressos would help. "What happens now?" I ask.

West drains his mug. "You and Raelynn rest. The plane will be ready whenever you are. If you need more than another day in Chicago, Graham and I will go back to Seattle, but a couple of the Boston crew can come take our place."

The SEAL pushes to his feet, but I reach for his arm. "You don't think we're safe here?" Truthfully, I'd return to Seattle right now if I thought I could do much more than stumble into the next room and collapse onto the bed. But I have to know.

"I think some of the most dangerous and unpredictable assholes go into organized crime. The Five Points is the safest hotel chain in the world, but we don't take chances. Not where family's concerned."

THE SUN SETS outside the large picture window in our bedroom. I slept for six hours with Raelynn in my arms, and room service delivered steaks, buttery potatoes, asparagus, and two slices of chocolate cake when we woke up.

But now, Raelynn strips off her tank top, and I get a good look at the deep purple bruises covering her stomach, back, and arms. I know I don't look much better—not with all the cuts from falling shards of glass—but she hasn't said a word about what Enzo's men did to her, and I need to know.

"Tell me about this?" I ask, fingering the pink compression wrap around her head.

She leads me into the bathroom and sheds her knee brace before leaning against the counter. "Enzo wanted to know what you'd told me. Whether they had to worry about anyone else knowin' they were after you." Her eyes pinned to the floor, she unwinds the stretchy bandage to reveal a blood-stained piece of gauze covering her left ear. "They were spittin' mad when I wouldn't talk."

Her fingers tremble as she loosens the single strip of tape holding the white fabric in place.

"Oh, God." A bright red, angry nub is all that's left of the lower lobe of her ear. "I...fuck."

"Nash? It don't matter." She stops me before I can flee back to the bedroom, her grip on my forearm almost desperate. "I'm alive. So are you. And we're together." A sob wells up in her throat, and a single tear tumbles down her cheek. "There ain't nothin' they could have done to me that would stop me lovin' you. Please, darlin'. Tell me you understand."

I gather her against me and tip her head back so I can stare into her bright blue eyes. "You're the strongest person I've ever known, Raelynn. I understand. And I love you."

EPILOGUE

SIX MONTHS later

Raelynn

"I'm home!"

Kiki thunders down the stairs from his favorite perch in our bedroom window, leaping over Ripley, the Staffordshire Bull Terrier puppy flopped on the landing.

Wiping my hands on the dish towel, I turn and lean against the kitchen counter, watching the man I love rub the cat's belly for a full minute before he rises and saunters toward me, a hungry look in his eyes.

The kiss rocks me down to my boots, and if the fryer weren't hot as a stolen tamale, I'd drag him upstairs right now. Instead, I drape my arms around his neck. "How'd it go?"

"Dad looks good. Awkward as hell to have a decent conversation in that place, though."

"He'll be out soon." With good behavior, Angelo's sentence won't last more than another six weeks, and Connor is already working with the FBI to stage the man's "death" so he can assume a new identity.

Nash's shoulders heave with a heavy breath, and he pulls me tighter against him. "He doesn't have to live in Seattle, does he? Maybe...Portland? Or San Francisco?"

Every month, Nash drives two hours south to the federal prison in Olympia to see his father, but despite a hell of a lot of therapy, he still hasn't made peace with what Angelo did twenty years ago.

"We can set him up wherever you feel comfortable, darlin'. He'll be a free man. If you decide after a spell you want him closer, we'll make it happen."

"You're sure? Y'all have given me so much already—"

The laugh escapes before he can finish his thought. "Y'all? And here I thought you didn't know a bit from a butt. I'm rubbin' off on you."

All his stress melts away as he kisses me again, long and hard, like it's the very first time and he can't get enough of me. Even after six months of makin' a home together, fightin' over paint colors and teachin' the world's most stubborn puppy that the rug is for nappin', not pissin', we haven't cooled one bit.

"You can rub—"

"Stop right there, Nash Grace. Dinner's fixin' to be ready in twenty minutes, and Ripley needs her walk first." I slap his ass, and he pinches mine before he lets me go. "Now git outta my way. This chicken ain't gonna cook itself."

As the credits roll on screen, Nash brushes his lips to my neck, just below my scarred ear. "You're right. The original *Halloween* was pretty awesome."

Most nights, if I'm not on mission, we end up here. On the

couch, the cat and dog curled up in Ripley's bed at our feet, watchin' TV or workin' on some project—like the new banister that went in last week. I worried, for a time, that Nash would get tired of stayin' in one place. That he'd want someone who was always up for an adventure. But after moving around for more than half his life, I think he craves this—home—as much as I do.

He slides his hand along my hip, setting my core on fire. "Ready to turn in?"

"If by 'turn in' you mean 'ready for you to strip off all my clothes and have your way with me,' then yes. I am."

"That's exactly what I mean."

Upstairs, he backs me against the wall, his rough palm skimming over my throat to my jaw. Raw need flashes in his eyes, but behind it, there's so much more. "You're everything I never knew I wanted, Raelynn. My home. My heart. I love you."

"Then kiss me, darlin'. Because I love you too."

THANK you for reading *Trusting His Instincts.* I hope you enjoyed Nash and Raelynn's story. They have their happy ever after, and I think the whole team at Hidden Agenda got a little closer in this one.

I love to write bonus scenes for my books, and those are always available for my newsletter subscribers. Head on over to my website and sign up now!

You can also check out my reader group on Facebook, Patricia's Unstoppable Forces They were instrumental in naming Nash and Raelynn's puppy, as well as being a constant source of joy in my life. It's a great place, and we'd love to have you.

If you're curious about everyone else's stories (and haven't read the rest of the Away From Keyboard series yet, here's where you can find each couple.

- **West** & Cam - Breaking His Code
- **Inara** & Royce - In Her Sights
- **Ryker** & Wren - On His Six
- **Dax** & Evianna - Second Sight
- **Ford** & Joey - By Lethal Force
- **Ripper** & Cara - Fighting For Valor
- **Trevor** & Dani - Call Sign: Redemption
- **Graham** & Quinton - Braving His Past
- **Ronan** & Zephyr - Protecting His Target
- **Wyatt** & Hope - Defending His Hope
- **Connor** and Isabel - Rogue Survivor

And that brings us to *Trusting His Instincts.*

The next book in the series is one I never intended to write. But who's ready for Doc Reynolds' story? Coming in early 2024!

And don't forget Nomar and Lisette's story, Rogue Operator, releasing in October!

ABOUT THE AUTHOR

Patricia D. Eddy writes romance for the beautifully broken. Fueled by coffee, wine, and Doctor Who episodes on repeat, she brings damaged heroes and heroines together to find their happy ever afters in many different worlds. From military to paranormal to BDSM, her characters are unstoppable forces colliding with such heat, sparks always fly.

Patricia makes her home in Seattle with her husband and very spoiled cats, and when she's not writing, she loves working on home improvement projects, especially if they involve power tools.

Her award-winning *Away From Keyboard* series will always be her first love, because that's where she realized the characters in her head were telling their own stories—and she was just writing them down.

You can reach Patricia all over the web...

patriciadeddy.com

patricia@patriciadeddy.com

facebook.com/patriciadeddyauthor

twitter.com/patriciadeddy

instagram.com/patriciadeddy

bookbub.com/profile/patricia-d-eddy

tiktok.com/@patriciadeddyauthor

ALSO BY PATRICIA D. EDDY

Away From Keyboard

Dive into a steamy mix of geekery and military prowess with the men and women of Hidden Agenda and Second Sight.

Breaking His Code

In Her Sights

On His Six

Second Sight

By Lethal Force

Fighting For Valor

Finding Their Forevers (a holiday short story)

Call Sign: Redemption

Braving His Past

Protecting His Target

Defending His Hope

Trusting His Instincts

Gone Rogue (an Away From Keyboard spinoff series)

Rogue Protector

Rogue Officer

Rogue Survivor

Rogue Defender

Rogue Operator

Dark PNR

These novellas will take you into the darker side of the paranormal with vampires, witches, angels, demons, and more.

Forever Kept

Immortal Hunter

Wicked Omens

Storm of Sin

By the Fates

Check out the COMPLETE By the Fates series if you love dark and steamy tales of witches, devils, and an epic battle between good and evil.

By the Fates, Freed

Destined: A By the Fates Story

By the Fates, Fought

By the Fates, Fulfilled

In Blood

If you love hot Italian vampires and and a human who can hold her own against beings far stronger, then the In Blood series is for you.

Secrets in Blood

Revelations in Blood

Holidays and Heroes

Beauty isn't only skin deep and not all scars heal. Come swoon over sexy vets and the men and women who love them.

Mistletoe and Mochas

Love and Libations

Restrained

Do you like to be tied up? Or read about characters who do? Enjoy a fresh COMPLETE BDSM series that will leave you begging for more.

In His Silks

Christmas Silks

All Tied Up For New Year's

In His Collar

Made in the USA
Monee, IL
27 June 2023